SKELETON CREW

SKELETON CREW

psycop 14

Jordan Castillo Price

jcpbooks.com

First published in the United States in 2024 by JCP Books
www.JCPBooks.com

ISBN 978-1-944779-40-5
First Edition
Also available in audiobook

I am an invisible man.

I am a man of substance, of flesh and bone, fiber and liquids—and I might even be said to possess a mind.

I am invisible, understand, simply because people refuse to see me.

-Ralph Ellison

CHAPTER 1

The ceramic cherub stared at me with unsettling white eyes. Its wings were folded, its head was canted slightly to one side, and its pudgy hands were clasped together in a gesture that was no doubt meant to be adorable.

I shuddered and threw a newspaper over it. Obviously, though, I was still well aware of its presence. Probably staring at me right through the newsprint. With its blank...white...eyes.

I sighed, picked up the paper, and turned the statuette around to face away from me.

Better.

Until I spotted the reflection of its empty eyes on the screen of our dark TV.

My discomfort with clutter—even clutter incapable of *looking* at me—is well-known. In fact, my predilections might even have risen to the level of an inside joke. Or maybe not-so-inside, given that pretty much everyone in my phone contacts knew better than to saddle me with any tchotchkes or knickknacks for our anniversary.

Everyone, apparently, but Jacob's sister.

"Is that today's?" Jacob asked, then plucked the newspaper from my grasp before I even answered. He settled into his side of the sofa—the side next to the too-bright reading lamp, where he can pretend it doesn't bother him when a handy pair of cheaters is nowhere to be found—and curled up to fill himself in on the day's corruption, mayhem and murder.

Completely ignoring the thing on the coffee table. Staring at our reflection.

Or maybe just at mine.

Objects can't be haunted. I knew that for a fact. If they could, we'd be able to come up with a *way* better screening test for mediums. Still. That cherub gave me the creeps.

Would Jacob notice if he woke up tomorrow morning and it just happened to be gone?

Probably. That husband of mine will be totally oblivious to the leftovers he stows in the back of the fridge until they grow legs and walk away, but heaven forbid something of "his" ends up in the trash bin...especially if there's enough time for him to haul it back out before the garbagemen show up.

"So," I ventured, hoping Jacob would magically take up the thread and observe that the figurine clearly had no place in our decor and suggest getting rid of it. When he didn't, I tried a pointed sigh. That didn't work either. Finally, I had no choice but to come right out and say, "You really wanna keep that thing?"

Jacob looked up from the paper with a *What thing?* expression that made me wonder if maybe I could have gotten away with slipping the thing into the trash after all...but now, clearly, I'd blown my chance by calling attention to my discomfort.

"The gift." I somehow managed to say it without air quotes.

"I mean.... It doesn't really go with, uh...anything."

Jacob glanced at the back of the cherub's head and shrugged. "You know I don't know much about art." He looked back down at the paper. "Barb said it was valuable."

The discussion of whether or not it even qualified as *art* could be shelved for another day. "Valuable, how?"

"Collectible, I guess."

Was that an opportunity I spied? Jacob might be able to overlook a single creepy cherub. A whole slew of them, however.... "People collect all kinds of things," I said casually. "No accounting for taste, I suppose. But the thing about collections is, once word gets out that you collect something, before you know it, you'll be inundated. There was a community liaison officer back at the Fifth who got a little stuffed pig from God-knows-where, and before you knew it, suddenly her desk was covered in 'em. Pig coasters. Pig office supplies. Pig salt-and-pepper shakers."

Jacob glanced up from the paper and crooked an eyebrow. "That's what happens when you're a cop. Pig jokes come with the territory."

"But it's not like all of us were buried in stupid pig clutter. Just her. Because people had pegged her as a collector, so they were never at a loss for what to give her for every random occasion. And you know what she told me? She didn't even *like* pigs. Saw a swine farm once on a grade school field trip and it took a week to get the stink out of her nose."

It looked like the threat of umpteen cherubs showing up on our doorstep every year was enough to make Jacob part with the gift, but then he second-guessed himself with, "It seems like a shame to just toss a valuable collectible."

"Who said anything about tossing?" Yes, that *had* been the solution I was angling for. But I've learned that sometimes, in order to get what you want, you need to course-correct. "Plenty of New Agey types love angels—just the type of person who'd shop at Crash's store. We can give it to him."

Offloading the angel on Crash would be a serious win-win. Not only would it get the statue out of our house, but if it truly was as valuable as Barb seemed to think, he might make a profit. Everything was more expensive these days, but the last time I tried to pay extra for our house-smudging, Crash read me the riot act. So, whenever there was an opportunity to share the wealth with him in a way that let everyone save face, we jumped on it.

But I didn't let him know we were coming. Just in case he asked for a photo, determined the thing was worthless, and told us not to waste our time.

If there's any profession with even worse hours than law enforcement, it's retail. The summer sun hung low and it was going on eight by the time we got to Still Goods, but the lights were on and a few customers were still milling through the antique mall. The first thing that struck me as we stepped inside was not how dusty it all was–the dust was normal–but how humid.

"AC's on the fritz," Crash called out by way of greeting as we made our way into his shop. He and his stupidly attractive boyfriend Red seemed unfazed by the heat. Then again, they were both young and hot enough to wear the tattered remains of punk rock T-shirts that flashed all kinds of skin, whereas I'd be worried about a random stranger getting a glimpse of something they shouldn't. Not because I'm a prude, mind you. Certain angles are just less than flattering.

Pointedly looking anywhere but the sculpted, tattooed shoulders and inadvertent flashes of nipple, I set my sights on the counter with the objective of divesting myself of the creepy angel, ASAP, when I nearly tripped over a scampering, skittering ball of fur.

"The dog is Snickerdoodle," Crash said. "And here I thought *Curtis* was an unfortunate name."

Red answered him with a resigned head-shake that was much more expressive than my sigh that Jacob had ignored.

The creature flopped onto his haunches and began to scratch. Vigorously. Red said, "He has a skin condition. Allergies. Or maybe mites." I found myself absently scratching my own forearm. "We're waiting on tests."

Crash said, "If you think owning a house is a money pit, try getting a used dog."

"We'll be reimbursed," Red said.

"Yeah, but we still gotta front the cash."

"He's a foster," Red explained in his infinite patience. *At least you don't have to deal with it forever.* The words were on the tip of my tongue, but I had enough tact to leave them unsaid. "One of our friends from Rainbow Dharma was set to take him in, then she was put on bed rest for her last trimester, so...."

I glanced down at the displaced animal only to find Jacob down on one knee making kissy-faces.

Just when you think you know a guy.

"He likes you," Crash said. Empathic? Or just being nice? Scratch that, Crash is plenty of things. *Nice* isn't one of them. "Take him for a walk and he'll love you forever. Plus, we'll finally get to count out our drawer in peace and blow this pop stand before midnight."

Jacob perked up visibly, and Red handed him a boho macrame leash. "There's a park just up the next side street. Can't miss it. His bladder thanks you—and so do we."

Good thing Snickerdoodle was smaller than a breadbox. He obviously knew what the leash meant—and he would've hauled off Jacob's arm in his eagerness to get outside...where he proceeded to lift his leg and pee on the door frame. And the light post. And anything else that wasn't currently moving.

As we waited for him to anoint a nearby bike rack, Jacob said, "My parents never let me have a dog."

"Really?" I couldn't imagine either Jerry or Shirley putting their foot down.

"As a kid, Dad was bitten by a neighbor's Doberman—nasty thing—so he didn't trust dogs around small children. He kept putting it off 'until you're older' and 'until your sister is older'...until finally I was looking at colleges and dorms and...." He shrugged.

Yeah. That sneaky approach was way more his parents' style.

We found the park Red had mentioned easily enough—the sound of screaming children really carries—and Snickerdoodle started huffing and puffing in his excitement to have more things to pee on.

Jacob, by contrast, seemed uncharacteristically quiet. I gave him the side-eye and saw he had that sappy, faraway look he gets whenever something hits him directly in the feels.

Now he wanted a dog.

Well, shit.

And given that Snickerdoodle was a foster, we could very well end up with this specific dog. This very itchy, very pee-filled dog.

Since I'm always riding Jacob about his age, I could hardly make the excuse that we should wait 'till he was older, could I? Although maybe I could suggest we wait for retirement. After all, we spent ridiculous amounts of time at work, and we both knew it.

We were both lost in dog-thoughts when someone from the park called our names, startling us both. "Jacob? Vic!"

"Exactly how many of your exes were we gonna run into tonight?" I muttered to Jacob as I gave Keith and Manny an obligatory wave.

The guys were seated on a park bench overlooking a sand-box where a few kids were barraging each other with hand-fuls of sand. Our friends were both gym rats. Both rocking skimpy tank tops. And both middle-aged. But the similarity was superficial, at best. Smiling, Manny stood up from the bench, motioning us over. He was the sweet one, always up for a bit of gossip.

Keith was the bitter one. He didn't bother getting up—or smiling, for that matter. I took solace in the fact that he hated everybody—not just me.

"Oh my *god*," Manny gushed. "You guys got a *dog*."

"We're just borrowing him," Jacob said.

"Isn't he precious?" Manny knelt and let the dog scurry over and sniff his hand. Thankfully, Snickerdoodle knew better than to pee on him.

Cripes, if that was the most positive thing I could come up with, I'd need a better game plan to quash Jacob's dreams.

Manny started scratching the dog behind the ears before either of us could mention the skin condition, and

Snickerdoodle's hind leg thumped the ground in time with the scratches. But aside from the jimmy-leg, the way he looked at Manny with his liquid, dark eyes was pretty darned cute.

Though that didn't mean I wanted those eyes staring at me when I got out of the shower.

"Are you on a stakeout?" I asked the guys, hoping to remind Jacob exactly how much we all worked.

Manny glanced back at Keith, grinning. Keith crossed his arms and looked especially resigned. Manny said, "We just came here to...think."

"Adoption," Keith blurted out. "It can take years. So if we want to get the ball rolling—"

"You want a *kid*?" Yeah, that sounded just as bad coming out of my mouth as you'd imagine.

But Manny didn't take offense—and Keith would have been offended no matter how I'd reacted. "I've always wanted a big family," Manny said. "For the longest time, I never really thought I could have one."

"One kid at a time," Keith said.

Manny shrugged. "You never know—we might find some siblings that need to stay together."

The mere thought of waking up to an instant family was enough to make me break out in hives. Or maybe it was a sympathetic dog mange I'd developed. Either way, I'd bet my last tube of cortisone cream that Jacob hadn't pictured himself with a gaggle of kids either, growing up in the era we had. We'd never even seen ourselves as marriage material, for crying out loud. Let alone parents.

Now, look at us. Not just out—even at work—but an official

married couple.

My face was normal, I think, as Manny chitchatted about what it might be like to have a daughter or a son. A baby or a teenager. And whether race really mattered when he was Latino and Keith was white—that maybe the family could just be one big rainbow. (Keith winced a little at that remark. Can't say I blamed him.)

"Of course, I'll get to be the fun parent—and Keith will be the responsible one. But what matters most is that we give them lots of love and understanding. Right, boo?"

Keith grunted.

Mosquitoes were now whining in our ears, so we wrapped up the conversation and got out of there before the bugs could eat us alive. We hurried back toward the shop, though the dog felt the urgent need to re-pee on everything he'd hit the first time around.

Neither Jacob nor I spoke. No doubt his thoughts had turned to "family"—people from stable homes tend to feel nostalgic about these things—while I wondered if it was too late to suggest getting a dog. But, no. Jacob wasn't even looking at the damn dog anymore. Just staring moodily off into the distance.

Careening into damage-control mode, I said, "Foster kids."

Jacob paused, and Snickerdoodle snapped to the end of his silly leash, plunked down on the sidewalk, and began to scratch.

"Plenty of kids need a foster family," I told Jacob. He did a double-take. "Not necessarily for the long haul." Like eighteen-plus years. "Just until their permanent situation gets all worked out."

Never mind that I'd *been* one of those foster kids, and my "permanent situation" had involved moving around until I finally aged out of the system. It sounded way better than, *Don't you dare even think about saddling me with a freaking kid for the next twenty years!*

Jacob narrowed his shrewd eyes. "*You* want to be a foster parent?"

"Just making an observation."

"Huh."

Backpedal. Quick. "Although it might be better to start with a dog. A *foster* dog. Like Crash and Red. See how it goes."

"But we're never home."

Wait, now he *didn't* want a dog? You think you know a guy. "Actually, Jacob, you're right. We can barely handle Veronica's cats—and they keep each other entertained."

Jacob nodded thoughtfully. "Besides, I'm not ready to be the responsible parent."

"Hold on, mister...you're saying I'd be the *fun* parent?"

"Well, obviously."

"In what world? Who's the one always picking up around the house? Me. Who's the one who lets in that mind-numbingly chatty meter reader? Also me. And who's the one holding down the fort so you can go play the FPMP Hunger Games this weekend—?"

Jacob interrupted. "Are you saying you *don't* want to be the fun parent?" He had me so turned around by now, I didn't know *what* the hell I even wanted. "If you wanted in on Operation Finder, you should have said so."

Frankly, I'd rather watch a dog mark every streetlight in the city than subject myself to dozens of federal agents trying to prove who had the biggest dick. I'd had more than enough of that competitive machismo on the force, thank you very much. The fact that the Federal Psychic Monitoring Program was dressing it up as a "friendly" scavenger hunt made it all the worse.

Navigating a strange city. Working as a team. Talking to strangers. That might be Jacob's idea of a good time, but it sure as hell wasn't mine.

But it might help me prove a point. "I've got zero desire to go to make a fool of myself at some institutional team-building exercise...but it's nice to have the option. Which I wouldn't, if we had a dog."

I'm not sure if Snickerdoodle could sense the tension between us, or if he just understood the word "dog." He turned to look at me as if to say, *Maybe you would be giving up some freedom...but wouldn't the love of another living creature be worth it?*

Connection. Such a tenuous thing. And yet, with those limpid brown eyes boring into mine, I couldn't deny that it was tempting....

And just as my *hell no* shifted into a conditional *maybe*, Snickerdoodle gazed deep into my soul, squatted...and took a massive dump.

CHAPTER 2

"You gonna clean that up?" Jacob asked dryly. "Since you *are* the responsible one."

Lucky for me I'd been carting around the ridiculous cherub statue this whole time in a flimsy plastic grocery bag. Locking my eyes with Jacob's as intently as the dog had been staring into mine, I dumped out the knickknack, slipped the bag over my other hand, and grabbed.

Squishy, I'd expected. But did it have to be so warm?

Suppressing a shudder, I pitched everything into a nearby trash can, cherub and all. Jacob had the good sense to keep a straight face while he refrained from comment.

Though I strongly suspected he was grinning on the inside.

Thankfully, there was a restroom in the antique mall where I could scrub off the top few layers of skin while Jacob returned Snickerdoodle to his foster parents. The soap was a dried-up sliver that reeked of fake sandalwood...but at least it wasn't soft and moist.

On the way home, Barb called, but Jacob let it go to voicemail.

"Aren't you gonna get that?" I asked.

Jacob navigated a traffic snarl caused by a guy trying to parallel park in a spot he'd be lucky to fit into with a shoehorn and a crane. "I'll call her back. She's probably just making sure we got the gift."

He spotted a gap, tried to go around, and was quickly cut off by someone in a rusty pickup with nothing to lose. His phone rang again.

"She seems awfully invested in that thing," I said. "What if she asks you to send her a photo?"

"Like we're holding it ransom?" Jacob muttered a few choice curses at the guy ahead of us. "Why would she do that?"

Because I threw it out, obviously. And even if we were to turn around and go back for the damn cherub, no doubt some opportune weirdo had already fished it out of the trash by now and was using it to store their weed.

The phone rang *again*.

"We'll tell her I broke it," I said. "I'll take all the blame."

Jacob cut his eyes to me. "Why wouldn't you? You're the one who threw it out."

We both knew damn well that he didn't want the dumb figurine in our house any more than I did, but before I could get into it, *my* phone rang. I glanced down at the caller.

Barbara.

I flashed the incoming number at Jacob. He sighed. "You don't have to field this—she's my sister. I'll call her back as soon as we get home."

"Hopefully she won't keep you on the line *too* long." This would be our last night together before Jacob—and most of our co-workers—flew off to Nantucket Island to take home some ridiculous trophy and score bragging rights for the entirety of the Midwest. Seriously, the last thing I'd care to do. But right up Jacob's alley.

I didn't pretend to be interested in the actual mechanics of the game, but I could emphasize the fact that the parting sex would be good—and the reunion sex even better. I snaked a hand awkwardly across the console and gave Jacob's thigh a squeeze. "Speaking of home—I'll need to give you something to remember me by while you're gone."

Jacob had been clutching the steering wheel in a death grip, but the color returned to his knuckles and the tension around his eyes eased as he slid my hand a quick look. "Is that so?" he said playfully. "What if I need to conserve my energy for the competition?"

I inched my hand up his inseam. "You can always sleep on the plane."

The corner of his mouth twitched up. I'd gotten his attention.

"I have it on good authority that the coffee table makes for some interesting angles," I said. "Especially now that it's free from extraneous tchotchkes."

Jacob's nostrils flared.

Call me selfish, but I didn't want to share him with a dog, let alone some random kid. Our time alone together was precious. And if it meant me carrying around the coffee table texture imprinted on my bare ass all weekend to remind him of how precious that time was—so be it.

By the time we finally pulled up in front of the cannery, we were both more than ready to be home. As I was unbuckling my seatbelt, Jacob slipped a hand behind my head, carding his fingers through my hair, and pulled me into a kiss.

Not a middle-aged, married-guy kiss, either.

A forceful, eager, scorching kiss that promised all the dirty things he wanted to do to me. On the coffee table. And the dining room table. And maybe even the stairs, if I was lucky.

Fingers tightened in my hair and anticipation zinged down to my groin as Jacob nuzzled me, skimming my jaw with his beard. In his smokiest bedroom voice, he said, "Let's get inside before we scandalize the whole neighborhood."

He didn't need to tell me twice.

I was halfway up the walk with my keys in my hand when a car pulled up behind the Crown Vic. I didn't think much of it—all the neighbors have cars, after all, and parking's always at a premium—though the slam of the driver-side door was, in retrospect, pretty darned aggressive.

And then there was the annoyed shout that followed.

With the heavy Wisconsin accent.

"What the heck, now neither of you answer your phone?"

Barbara.

I gave an inward wince and turned to face the music.

Literally...given the big black instrument case Barbara yanked out of the car.

My guilty mind went into overdrive trying to find the connection between the cherub, the fact that Jacob's sister was storming up the sidewalk, and the case in her hands. And then the passenger side door swung open and Clayton sulked out. (*Sulk* being an apt description of pretty much every action he'd performed since puberty took root.)

"Barb?" Jacob said with great eloquence.

She paused at the foot of the walkway, glared at her brother, and jerked her chin in Clayton's direction. "Maybe *you* can talk some sense into him!"

Clayton sighed.

"We were just in Galena," Barb said. "Picking up a new trumpet."

They don't have freaking trumpets in Wisconsin? I thought. But the part that baffled Jacob was, "You drove here from *Galena*?"

Barb ignored him. "And then *this* genius had to go and announce that he'd signed up for some band trip for school and he'd be gone for ten whole days! In New Orleans. With 24-7 liquor and girls going around flashing their—" she huffed. "He's not ready for something like that!"

"You never let me do anything," Clayton muttered.

"He claims I'm being overprotective. Wanna know where he learned that word?" Uh oh. "So here we are. *Uncle Jacob* needs to do something about this kid before I have a heart attack."

"Back up," Jacob said. "The school's not gonna haul a minor across state lines without parental permission."

Barbara gave him a look that made me glad she hadn't inherited the telekinetic gene...at least as far as we knew. Then something occurred to me that I don't normally think much about: Clayton did have two parents. And I'm guessing he was well aware which one was the "fun" one.

"He's thirteen," Barb said. "He's never been gone longer than overnight, and no farther than a bike ride away. I told him to prove he's ready by spending the weekend in Chicago with his uncle—just something simple to start out with. Give him a real taste of what it's like to be away from home."

Jacob's eyes narrowed.

Barbara crossed her arms. "I told him if he wants me to

sign off, he needs to show that he can handle it."

"I can't just call off work at a moment's notice, Barb. I've got plans."

What came over me at that particular moment, who's to say? Was it sympathy for the fact that Clayton had been dealt a shitty absentee dad thanks to some psychic breeding program he didn't even know about? Or was it just the need to prove I was plenty responsible?

I may never know.

"I've got this," I said. Barb and Jacob both looked at me like I was nuts...which only made me lean into the idea harder. "Jacob will be back Sunday afternoon. I'm sure we can survive without him. I'll need to go in to work for a couple of hours on Saturday and make the rounds, but I'm guessing the Cannery would be pretty hard to burn down."

Barbara was suddenly none too keen on leaving her kid behind. "Y'know what? Never mind—"

Jacob chimed in, "We'll do it some other time."

And now I felt like I had something to prove to him. "You're saying Clayton would be fine for an entire week in New Orleans, but he can't be trusted unsupervised for a couple of hours in the living room?"

If Jacob had a problem with that, he should've considered what he was getting himself into when he claimed I'd be the "fun" parent.

"Fine. Then, it's settled." Barb shoved the trumpet case into Clayton's hands. "I'll be back Sunday night, and then we'll see who's so eager to go on this ridiculous trip."

"Wait," Jacob said. "You're leaving your kid for three days with nothing but a trumpet and the clothes on his back?"

Barb narrowed her eyes. "You have a washing machine. Don't you?"

"Not even a toothbrush?"

"There's a twenty-four-hour Walgreens at the end of the block. I'm pretty sure he'll survive. Especially since he's so capable and mature."

Thunder rumbled in the distance as Barb stormed away, climbed into her car, and headed back to Wisconsin.

And then the enormity of what I'd gotten us into sank in.

We weren't expecting company, after all. Our spare bedroom was set up as an office. I'd eaten the last of the cereal this morning. And though our porn these days was mostly streaming, there was a handful of DVDs we kept around for old-time sake, so some kind of warning would've been appreciated.

That'll teach us to save a phone call for "later."

Jacob and I watched her tail lights disappear. Then I charged into the house with him close on my heels, hoping against hope that there was nothing embarrassing lying around. Thankfully not. But that didn't make the situation any less awkward.

"We got this," I told Jacob.

"If you say so." He looked entirely unconvinced as he ushered Clayton into the cannery. "I'll get out the air mattress."

Clayton strolled past me like I was part of the woodwork, flopped onto the leather couch, whipped out his phone, and proceeded to do something that involved a lot of thumbwork. Texting a friend, I presumed...until I craned my neck and saw he was engrossed in some mindless game.

The air mattress hadn't seen any use since the time Agent

Garcia's apartment was getting fumigated, so Jacob seemed eager to put it through its paces. Everything is automated these days—including air mattresses—and all you had to do was plug it in and wait for the thing to inflate.

In theory.

In practice, the motor filled the mattress about a quarter of the way, made a weird, high-pitched sound, emitted a smell like burning plastic, and promptly died.

"Not a problem," Jacob said with just a smidge too much confidence. "There's a valve on the side we can fill with a bike pump."

Easier said than done. I don't know if the emergency stop-gap was actually meant to be used. With the first plunge of the bike pump, the hose shot out, and half the air went with it.

"You have to fill it really full," Clayton said, without lifting a finger to help. "Or else I'll just sink down the middle."

It was a two-man job, with one of us keeping the hose shoved into the hole while the other one pumped. We took turns, initially. Until we realized that handing over the reins just let out as much air as we'd put in. Every time he heard the hiss of air escaping, Clayton was sure to let us know he'd never be able to sleep on a saggy bed.

To expedite things, I ended up taking care of the valve while Jacob worked the pump. Not at all how I'd seen the evening panning out...a thought I came back to again and again as I watched him pumping away with all the determination and focus you'd expect.

Finally, though, the mattress was full enough to bounce a quarter off, and we did manage to shut the valve without losing much air. Even Clayton seemed to think we'd done a good job, if his lack of complaining was anything to go by. But when I turned to glory in my obvious and undeniable responsibility, I discovered the kid wasn't admiring our hard work—he was splayed on the massive leather couch, out like a light.

CHAPTER 3

Clayton might've slept easy, but the same could definitely not be said for Jacob and me. It was pretty late by the time we turned in. But neither of us made a move to turn out the lights.

"It's not like you'll be gone forever." I was whispering, I realized, even though there was slim likelihood of the kid hearing me from all the way downstairs. "A day and a half. Thirty-six hours. And eight of those, he'll be asleep. Are you saying I can't handle him for twenty-four hours?"

"Thirty-six minus eight isn't—"

"Look, all I'm saying is, give me some credit. Your nephew, too."

"He's thirteen."

"He's in junior high." I'd been held back a couple of grades—thanks a lot, math—so junior-high-me had been older than Clayton. But my friends at the time were all his age, so I had a pretty clear idea of what being a brand new teenager entailed. "And don't tell her I said this, but maybe Barb is right. If the kid can't handle being away from home, it's better to find out now, where I can have him back on his own doorstep in three hours flat."

My husband looked entirely unconvinced.

"Listen to me, mister." I jostled Jacob under the covers. "All I need to do tomorrow morning is make a quick circuit of HQ to be sure the resident repeaters stay put, and then I'll come right back home. The cannery is pretty solid. I'm sure it'll still be standing by the time I get back."

Of course, there was plenty more that could go wrong, and we both knew it. After all, we *had* been thirteen-year-old boys once ourselves—even if that was back in the Stone Age. I suspected I was a lot more street-smart than Clayton was. But he was a lot less rebellious than me, so I hoped it would all even out. And if he did end up getting into some porn...well, I'm sure that on the internet he'd already seen all that and worse.

Lights were out and I'd curled into my customary gangly fetal position. I was starting to nod off when Jacob said, "We should set some ground rules before we go."

The thing about explicit rules is that they're just begging to be circumvented. Whereas a grim warning, like *Don't do anything stupid,* is a lot harder to weasel out of. But I was the responsible one, so I'd need to come up with something. "Fine. We'll tell him to mind his Ps and Qs before we leave the house. Satisfied?"

"Maybe. I don't know. What does that mean, exactly?"

Don't do anything stupid.

I groaned and flipped onto my back. "Don't use the weight bench without a spotter. Don't start a fire. And for god's sake, don't open the door to a stranger. Remember, Jacob, I'll be home again in just a couple of hours, probably less with Saturday traffic. Then I can sit here and twiddle my thumbs while he ignores me 'till you get back Sunday night. Does that about cover it?"

"It's just...he's so young. Younger than we were."

While it was tempting to challenge Jacob's math...I knew what he meant. At Clayton's age, I'd spent my spare time dicking around on the train tracks and pretending to be interested in my friends' titty mags. I was a city kid, born and bred. I'd been through three foster families and had already developed a decent sense of self-preservation. In comparison, Clayton was a sheltered, small-town kid. And nowadays, the world somehow felt a lot more risky.

Still.... "It's only a couple of hours."

Jacob slung an arm around me, ground his face into the pillow, and sighed. "I just hope he doesn't do anything stupid."

Yeah. You and me both.

CHAPTER 4

To say Clayton was underwhelmed by our rule-setting the next morning would be putting it mildly. He didn't go so far as to say "duh" when we told him not to let anyone in—no matter what kind of sob story they might have. But we stopped emphasizing how convincing con artists can be when he asked if he was allowed to go to the bathroom without a lifejacket and a helmet.

Not for the first time, I was glad for the cannery's haunted reputation. Any grifter going around with an unlikely story about being stranded (and an empty gas can just to prove their point) would hopefully think better of knocking on that battered old door.

We headed downtown together, since the plan was for Jacob—and all the other over-competitive federal agent types—to shuttle to the airport from the FPMP. The drive to HQ was pensive, but we'd made our inflatable bed, and there was nothing to do now but lie in it.

We don't go in for the mushy stuff in front of our fellow agents, but I did let my hand linger on his when I manhandled his roller bag out of the back seat. "Have fun at your thing," I said sincerely. "Clayton and I will manage just fine."

Jacob's gaze lingered on mine, and the corner of his mouth quirked. "A couple of years ago, I don't think either of you would've even considered the arrangement."

Just goes to show how *responsible* I've become. "Yeah, well, let's hope Barb doesn't make a habit of foisting the kid off on us. At least not with zero advance notice."

I don't think I looked too sappy as I watched the shuttle pull out of the garage, though I'd be lying if I said I wasn't touched by the fact that Jacob trusted me not to emotionally scar his favorite kid.

Speaking of whom...I sent a quick text to Clayton to make sure everything was okay. Three dots appeared in the reply. They pulsed a while. Pulsed some more. And just when I'd convinced myself that the cannery had fallen down around his ears, a thumbs-up appeared.

Well...it was proof of life, at least.

I proceeded to do my sweep of the building. It felt weird emptied out, with most of the agents either off for the weekend or on their way to the "friendly" competition that, for some unknown reason, people like Jacob enjoy. The techs who monitor the monitors were around, but they were quiet sorts who kept to themselves. Aside from the three repeaters in Con's old office and a maintenance guy refilling the water coolers, I was pretty much alone.

It was peaceful. Dare I say, even nice.

And while it might seem like a perfect time to try and dredge up my permanent record and sneak a peek, I was under no illusions that I was truly flying solo. There were cameras everywhere—and probably cameras trained on the cameras, too. Continual surveillance was a given. And I suppose my acceptance just goes to show what you can get used to, if you're exposed often enough.

A quick check of the lab, and I'd be back to the cannery in no time. Maybe I could even pick up a pizza—kids nowadays still liked pizza, didn't they? Not that I thought I'd score any brownie points, mind you. I was just looking for an excuse to try the new pizza/burger/taco joint I'd passed on my way to work.

The FPMP labs were in a sub-sub (sub?) basement of the old industrial building, buried way down deep—all the way down below the parking garage, and the busy city streets, skimming the neighboring railyard. Not only was it the most isolated spot in the building, but I'd wager it could withstand a nuclear blast.

No dank walls, cobwebs or weird mildew smell here. The halls were well-lit, for a basement, and the atmosphere was controlled to the nth degree. Temperature, humidity, everything within a very rigid set of parameters. The elevator opened into a lobby that was pleasantly bland and modern, like most of the agency decor—though the overt security presence was unique to this floor alone.

Upstairs, you could get where you wanted to go with a swipe of your badge. But down here, there was an actual security checkpoint with a level of surveillance somewhere between an airport and a prison. First, a set of keycard doors lets you through a wall of thick, reinforced glass. Then a radio wave scanner takes a stunningly unflattering snapshot—one that renders you digitally naked. Finally, said picture is scrutinized by a human pair of eyeballs. Typically, one belonging to a guy that's heard the "naked machine" joke way too many times and responds with a forced smile that's more of a wince.

It takes a certain kind of person to do security work. Plenty of ex-cops go into private security once they've had enough of the force. But, me? I'd rather chew pennies. The vigilance-boredom combo would drive me to drink within a week. And I don't even like booze.

I didn't personally know the Saturday guy, if this even was the regular Saturday guy, but this one checked all the usual boxes. Tall. Broad. Phenomenally stoic. There were no guns allowed in the lab, which was fine by me. As I submitted my exorcism kit to his inspection and surrendered my service weapon, I scanned the guy's name badge and realized he sounded familiar. Not because I'd met him in the lunchroom, either...but sometime in my own murky past.

Darnell Thompson, NP, was an African American man around my age with a shaved head, a neat goatee, and the typical coiled earpiece tucked behind his ear. His black suit was as impeccable as his posture, and while he might be a handful of inches shorter than I was, I had no doubt he could not only deadlift me, but toss me across the tasteful lobby without breaking a sweat.

A typical FPMP security type. But the cant of his eyebrows... the shape of his ears....

"Third grade," I blurted out as I stood inside the Naked Machine with my arms raised above my head.

Darnell's eyes flicked up from his monitor. Zero recognition.

"Mrs. Smith," I helpfully supplied.

Darnell ignored me and continued working through

whatever checklist the guards were supposed to perform. The weekday guys aren't quite as thorough—they see me once a week—but I couldn't say the same for Darnell. So I patiently waited until he gave me the all-clear.

"McKay School?" I added.

Darnell gave his head a single shake. "Sorry, Agent. I don't really remember."

A chill fingered its way down my spine as I wondered if he'd been left with gaps in his memory as one of Dr. Kleinman's patients. But before I could suggest hypnosis, he said, "We moved around a lot when I was a kid. Single parent, you know how it is. I been to five different grade schools, so...."

Right. And I'd been held back the next year, so it was likely we hadn't known each other long enough for me to make much of an impression. I resorted to naming some neighborhoods, hoping to ring a bell. "Brighton Park? Archer Heights?"

"Yeah, we lived around there for a couple of years when I was a kid but...." Darnell shrugged. "It was a long time ago."

Electromagnetic locks clicked as he granted me passage to the inner sanctum. Once I was on the other side of the safety glass, I remembered an incident that would surely jog his memory. One morning, a weaselly kid named Jason Gorecki begged the teacher for a hall pass and was told in no uncertain terms it would need to wait until after the Pledge of Allegiance. I dunno how many boxes of Sunny D Jason had sucked down that morning--more than an eight-year-old's bladder could hope to contain. Soon it was everywhere. Running down the kid's pants. Creeping across the floor. And pooling in the rounded depression of the molded fiberglass seat.

Surely, Darnell would remember that.

But when I turned back to the glass, he was busy dutifully stowing my sidearm in a safe, and I felt weird about insisting he remember me. Or maybe the pee story just seemed a bit too intimate to holler through several inches of double-paned safety glass—whether or not the facility was pretty much deserted.

Still, as I started my usual sweep of the underground laboratory, my mind kept wandering back to how strange it was for someone not to remember me. Even if they're not entirely creeped out by the knowledge that I talk to dead people, the height never fails to make a lasting impression. Frankly, it's a wonder the FPMP has managed to keep me off the radar all these years. But I supposed that before my growth spurt, I was just another random kid with scraped elbows and a shitty head for math.

The lab seemed even emptier than the rest of the building, with banks of computers running in a dimmed room to a low electronic hum, and the various offices darkened for the weekend. The only living things being experimented on were of the plant variety, and apparently they did just fine with the occasional mist from an automated irrigation system.

As basement psychic research labs went, it was all fairly innocuous. Or it would have been—except for the cold storage room where, back in our early days at the Agency, Jacob and I had wrangled Jennifer Chance's flailing corpse.

Whenever I swept the lab, that was where I'd start—and once I got it out of the way, I was free to meander up and down the hallways without worrying that her ghost was creeping around behind me. Since National made off with Chance's body, thankfully, my encounters with cold storage had been blessedly uneventful.

Even so, when I pushed open the thick metal door and found something moving inside, I may have suffered a mild heart attack—at least until I registered that the guy in the lab coat on the stepladder was very much alive.

"Who are you?" he demanded. "Don't you know this area is restricted? People can't just traipse in and out of here, y'know."

"I'm Agent Bayne," I flapped the ID on my lapel in his general direction, "and I'll be out of your hair just as soon as I do my job." I don't generally take a tone with people right off the bat—but accusations of traipsing were serious business. Especially when I'd rather be anywhere *but* the FPMP morgue. I eyed the vault he was standing by and said, "What is it you're doing in here, anyhow?"

"Double-checking the temperature gauges. Though why they're mounted so high is anyone's guess." He climbed down from the step and gave me an appraising once-over. He was maybe 5'7" on a good day, Caucasian, forty-something, with a shock of messy dark hair and glasses that didn't quite sit right on his face. "So, you're the infamous fifth-level medium. Howard Jibben." He gave me a cursory handshake...then wiped his hand on his lab coat the moment we disengaged.

Ah. *That* Howard Jibben.

No, I'd never met the guy, but if anyone was infamous here, it was him—and to say his reputation preceded him would be putting it mildly. Howard Jibben, the night manager of the FPMP lab, was notorious among my fellow agents, who referred to him as Heebie Jeebie. As someone who heard "Spook Squad" every time I darkened the doorway of a murder scene, I could commiserate. But I couldn't help being a medium, while he could've avoided the nickname by simply being less abrasive. It wasn't just his tics and twitches and his tendency toward OCD that made the name stick, it was his tendency to talk down to everyone.

He scowled at my badge and said, "We haven't been formally introduced, but I'm familiar with your work."

He said the word *work* like he was being generous.

I didn't take it too personally. Not only did I have it on good authority he spoke to everyone that way, but the thought of me penning the scientific literature on mediumship continued to amaze me, too. Hoping to get off on the right foot, I gestured toward the step stool and said, "I can grab that reading for you."

He looked as if I'd just offered him a dead lab rat. "Don't be ridiculous. That's far too risky."

I cut my eyes to the two-foot safety hazard. "I think I can manage to avoid an accident."

Jibben's eye ticced. "Accidents are simply a manifestation of one's lack of perceptiveness—the individual's lack of ability to assess and react to their surroundings. Maybe you've heard of the Risk Compensation Theory? It suggests that people adjust their behavior based on the perceived level of risk. The safer one feels, the more risks they're likely to take, often leading to harm. I always maintain a balanced perception of my environment, neither too safe nor too dangerous, ensuring I act optimally."

An awfully long-winded way of calling me careless, if you ask me. "Fine, suit yourself. I'll just make my rounds and be out of your hair."

"Rounds? What rounds?"

"The rounds I make every week," I said. He twitched. "To make sure we're clear of nonphysical entities."

I'd used the technical term for "ghosts" in an attempt to make myself sound official. Jibben was clearly unimpressed. "You can't be intending to walk around the lab by yourself— entirely unescorted."

Sure I could. Who knows? I might even traipse. "Look, I've gone through the lab every week for the past couple of years now, so I think I can handle myself. I'll even be sure not to take any undue risks while I'm at it."

"That's not it. There's nothing we're working on at the moment that should present a hazard. I'm more concerned about you contaminating our studies."

It was tempting to say, *How do you like this for contamination?* and fling a handful of salt on the floor just to be petty, but I had to get back home to Clayton, so I didn't have time to pick a fight. "I'll be in and out before you know it, and I won't touch a thing."

"Physically, maybe not. But it's your electromagnetic field I'm worried about."

So—it was gonna be one of *those* days. The kind that made me wish I was still with the Chicago PD. "I promise, I'll keep my field to myself."

"You may think it's all a big joke, but I guarantee, it's quite real. Every individual carries a unique electromagnetic signature—like a fingerprint, but for one's bio-field. Over time, as individuals work within a specific environment, particularly one as sensitive as this lab, a mutual adaptation occurs. The person becomes attuned to the lab's particular electromagnetic landscape, and the lab, in a sense, gets acclimated to that individual's bioelectromagnetic emissions."

"Then it's a good thing I do this *every week*. Now, if you don't mind...." I turned on my heel.

"Wait!" he said. I paused. "I'll come with you. Just let me make sure our new arrival is at temperature, and we'll be on our way."

His tone was entirely matter-of-fact. But the words *new arrival* sent a chill straight down my spine. "What new arrival would that be?"

"I'm surprised you hadn't heard. FPMP National finally released the body of Jennifer Chance."

CHAPTER 5

I see ghosts. It's what I do. And now that I've given up on Auracel, I see them all the time.

All. The. Time.

And so, my "traipse" through the lab should've been a walk in the park. But having the uptight lab manager tagging along—not to mention my history with one of the cadavers—I suddenly found myself second-guessing my every last impression.

That weird draft on the back of my neck—HVAC, or the cold spot of Jennifer Chance?

The distant whooshing—lab machinery, or a disembodied whisper from Jennifer Chance?

That odd shadow...well, you get the drift.

It didn't help that Jibben kept *talking* to me.

"Once a week really isn't enough to form a proper attunement—"

"Look," I said, "the better I can focus, the sooner I'll be done."

Jibben narrowed his eyes, then resettled his lab coat with a twitch.

The experiment rooms were all clear, and the hallways were empty. We headed through an open plan office section where the atmosphere was more relaxed. It was nowhere near as private as the office I shared with Carl, but it was a lot less generic than the research areas that had to be held to such exacting standards. There was paperwork. There was clutter. There was a stupid pun on the whiteboard: *Our ideas are sharper than our pencils!*

Normally, this area housed a half-dozen sciencey folks doing stuff that was incredibly normal, considering the fact that they were conducting top-secret psychic research in an underground bunker. Typing. Chatting. Betting on the football pool. Today, it seemed weirdly quiet.

I paused beside a desk with an impressive dual monitor setup. There was a scratch pad nearby with an equation on it that nearly made my eyeballs bleed...and candid photos of smiling kids taped around the monitors. There was a husband in one of the shots, a good-looking Hispanic guy with a bit of a paunch and a laughing toddler on his hip. I tried to recall if the scientist whose butt usually warmed this seat was a man or a woman, but I came up blank. Either way, the husband, the kids....

Was *that* what Jacob actually wanted?

I didn't think so. At least, not until Keith and Manny went and brought the whole kid thing up.

Boy, Jacob was gonna be thrilled to hear you-know-who was back. Maybe I could use that information to derail any potential conversations about adoption. Sure, I was spooked about her reappearance. She'd offed my doctor, and kidnapped me, and drugged me. And she definitely wouldn't have hesitated to "terminate" our experiment—meaning, me—in a heart-beat. But that was all normal. Normal...ish, anyhow, at least in terms of what we think is physically possible.

But Jacob was the one who'd been forced to hold her flailing cadaver down in a tank of antiseptic fluid while her venge-ful spirit struggled to escape. True, in the end, we'd shoved her through the veil—but if Bob Zigler was scarred for life by seeing a few bodies twitch in a zombie basement, Jacob's intimate encounter with the animated corpse would definitely be expected to leave a mark.

I was about to head back for one final check to make sure Chance's ghost had not somehow slipped back through the veil when a text dinged my phone.

Clayton.

There's nothing to eat.

I knew for a fact this was untrue. Not only was there oatmeal in the cupboard, but at least half a dozen eggs.

But did I really want an unsupervised thirteen-year-old monkeying around with the stove?

Toast, I texted back. Then I decided that didn't sound par-ticularly *responsible*, and added, *I'll grab us lunch in a few.*

I paused in the cold storage doorway—no doubt letting all the cold out—and scanned the wall of hermetically sealed vaults. A bank of innocuous square cubbies, not unlike the metal lockers back at McKay School. But there were no scrib-bled-on textbooks and abandoned lunches behind these plain metal doors. Each door was marked with a simple engraved number. I knew which cubby Chance's cadaver used to reside in—I couldn't help but double-check—but for all I knew, now that I'd banished the ghost, they could have moved her. Or incinerated her. Or chopped her up in tiny little pieces.

I'd meant to get in, get out, and get on with my life. Unfortunately, the memory of that haunting encounter was pretty hard to push through. Even for me.

So, of course, Jibben noticed my pause—and felt the need to comment.

"It's perfectly normal to have a negative reaction to cadavers, Agent. Our society regards the dead in such a taboo and superstitious light—"

"I did twelve years in homicide," I snapped. "You don't need to tell me about death."

Jibben wisely shut his mouth.

I eased into the room, carefully skirting the vaults, and visually scanned for ghosts. Nothing. Listened hard. Also nothing. And while the breath leaving my parted lips in a slight curl of frost would normally be a sign to break out the exorcism gear, with the temperature in the room at a constant zero, it was no cause for alarm.

"Welp," I said as I turned to leave, "no one's got up and walked away."

"What?" Jibben's startled tone made me realize I'd been talking to him like he was Carl—like he'd done the perimeter check with me so often it was just a routine. "Were you expecting something else?"

"Let's take this discussion out into the hall," I said, since one of us wasn't wearing a nice big lab coat.

Even as I shouldered past him out the door, he kept on talking. "You can't blame me for being curious—and, I'll admit, skeptical. I *am* a man of science. And the only recorded evidence of motion in a cadaver comes from an oddball case involving jimson weed and precogs that was never definitively proven."

"Yeah. That was me."

"Oh." Jibben plucked at his sleeve a few times. "Well, your documentation was shoddy."

I wanted to throw him into a dark basement full of twitching corpses and see just how eager *he* was to freaking document.

Jibben said, "There's a pervasive cultural belief that the etheric body holds an attachment to the physical after death, but this notion is not supported by any scientific evidence. In fact, once the etheric connection is severed, there's no reason to believe that the body itself retains any kind of special connection to the spirit world. It's simply a lifeless vessel. No more likely to be haunted than a table or a chair."

It irked me that I agreed with him. The newly departed might follow their dead body in confusion, at least until they found the veil. But lingering ghosts had a tendency to stick to the spot where they'd croaked. Not wherever they were eventually planted.

With Jennifer Chance, though, it was a double-whammy. Not only was her corpse back in the cooler, but she'd smothered herself in a holding cell just one floor above us. Which, I reminded myself, I'd already checked. And no one was there, living or dead.

"At any rate," Jibben went on, "even if a spirit were able to reanimate one of these bodies, their tissues are frozen. They're in sealed vaults. And the lab is on its own shielded power grid with a 48-hour generator backup. So clearly, there's nothing to worry about."

Peachy.

I was eager to get away from the bodies, popsicled or not. Though my relief turned out to be short-lived, once another text from Clayton pinged my phone.

How do you turn off the smoke alarm???

"Sonofabitch." I jabbed the call button, went to voicemail, then hung up and repeated it three more times, until the kid finally picked up.

"Go outside and call 911," I said.

"Everything's fine," he said testily—I could practically hear him rolling his eyes—as the smoke alarm bleated away in the background.

If I took off now I could be home in fifteen minutes flat—

"There was just some bread stuck in the toaster. That's all."

My adrenaline spike was insisting I hurry back before the whole city went up in flames, but since I'd accidentally smoked plenty of bread myself, I turned my panic down a few notches.

"So, nothing is currently on fire?"

"No," said his voice...while his tone said *duh.* Even over the shrilling of the smoke detector.

"You're sure?"

"I'm *sure.*"

Thankgodthankgodthankgod. "Okay. Fine. But put on some oven mitts and go put the toaster outside. Just to be safe."

"It's raining out."

Was it? In the swaddling of the underground science bunker, everything was as calm and quiet as the grave.

I shuddered. Heebie Jeebie did the same.

"There's a button in the middle of the smoke alarm," I told Clayton, "and there's a broom behind the kitchen door. Grab it by the bristles and use the handle to push the button."

Several long seconds of jostling sounds, and then the shrilling on the other end of the line went quiet enough for me to hear Clayton's mouth-breathing where he held the phone too close to his face. "When're you coming back?"

"Soon." I was acutely aware of Jibben staring at me again, and knew I wouldn't get away with cutting any corners in the lab. But if I had the pizza delivered instead of stopping to pick it up.... "Half hour. Forty-five minutes tops."

"Whatever." Clayton hung up without any sort of actual "goodbye."

And then Jibben piped right in. "Smoke alarms are extremely important in any environment. Sensor technology is critical in the lab, for instance, where one preventable fluctuation could end up costing us months of work."

His voice trailed off as I tuned him out. My thoughts were consumed with the image of Clayton standing in my kitchen, unsupervised, with nothing to entertain himself but a broom and a smoking toaster.

I strode off to finish my rounds so I could get the hell out of there before Clayton brought the cannery down around his ears. I was heading for the final quadrant when a text from Jacob pinged my phone.

Everything okay?

Why would he think otherwise? Hopefully I could air out the burn smell by the time he got home tomorrow night. A few waves of a smudge stick should cover up any lingering char.

Go enjoy your weekend, I texted back responsibly. *I got this.*

Before I could even pocket my phone, Jacob's text turned into a call.

I quelled a sigh and picked up. "Listen," I said, "you don't need to check on me—"

"Where are you?" Jacob's voice was laced with concern.

While it was tempting to claim I was home, lying felt like more trouble than it was worth. Or maybe I just wasn't up for getting caught, since I couldn't trust Clayton would corroborate my story, and for all I knew, he'd just ratted me out not two minutes ago. "I'll be home soon—I'm just finishing up at the office."

"I know. I'm in the car."

But I'd watched him board the shuttle. "What car?"

"Our car. Here. In the parking garage, waiting for you."

Good thing I hadn't gone with the lie. "Your thing got canceled?"

"I didn't like the look of the sky, so I stayed on the shuttle and came back."

Didn't like the look of the sky. Says the guy who went for a *jog* in a torrential downpour just last week.

"Are you serious? You've been salivating over that stupid scavenger hunt for weeks, and you blow it off because of a little rain?"

"Vic—"

"So, that's how it is. You didn't think I could manage without you."

"I never said that."

"You didn't have to."

"Where are you?" Jacob asked. "Specifically."

"In the lab. Specifically." I knew full well how snippy I sounded, but frankly, I was pissed.

And it wasn't lost on Jacob, because now he was clearly in

damage control mode. "I'll be right down."

I was a grown-ass man—perfectly capable of handling Clayton's sleepover. Maybe it said something more about Jacob than me, that he was willing to cancel all his plans at the drop of a hat instead of doing something he's been looking forward to for ages.

Lack of trust in his partner?

Or an overdeveloped sense of responsibility?

I pinched the bridge of my nose, then remembered I had an audience and cast a sideways glance at Jibben.

He plucked at his collar.

It would've been easy to give the remaining lab space a quick glance, call it good, and go resume my argument with Jacob somewhere more private. Instead, I stuffed down my self-righteous annoyance, put my feet on the grid, and resumed my scan. Anger doesn't seem to affect my talent one way or the other, but my time on the force has taught me that when a situation escalates, if you don't keep a cool head, you're way more likely to make a dumb mistake. I hadn't found anything new lately. But with all the experimental shit that went on down there, I wasn't about to take any chances.

Because I was plenty responsible, too.

There's no hiding from Jacob within the walls of the FPMP. He's in the Oversight Division, so his clearance is just as high as mine. I was halfway through the "research bays" (basically bland rooms with bland furniture where the effects of various gizmos on psychic abilities were tested) by the time Jacob surrendered his sidearm to Darnell and came and found me. "I'm sure you and Clayton would normally be fine without me," he said, and only then registered I wasn't alone. "Excuse me," he said to Jibben in an attempt to get rid of the guy so we weren't airing our dirty laundry in front of a coworker.

"No problem." The lab manager stayed right where he was.

Since Jacob needed to look all conciliatory for me, he settled for ignoring Jibben instead of telling him off. "I'm serious," he said to me. "The clouds are black and the sky's got this yellow-green tinge to it. Who knows if the flight will even get out? They might end up sitting at O'Hare all day, then heading right back home."

"As if the flights from Terminal 4 are ever grounded."

And then, as if to prove me wrong, the lights chose that particular moment to flicker.

CHAPTER 6

Jibben looked up at the light fixtures. "That's unusual."

"It's Chicago," I said. We had brownouts and blips all the time, and periodically found our various clocks and timers flashing 12:00.

"Unusual for the lab, I mean. The power surge technology should prevent something like that from happening."

We all went quiet and looked up at the lights as if daring them to flicker again.

They glowed steadily.

"Maybe it's a one-time thing," I said.

Jibben wasn't mollified. "Even so, not good. I'll need to make a sweep of the computers and make sure nothing's rebooted. Don't move. Don't touch anything. And whatever you do, stay away from any active experiments."

Uh oh. The lab was practically made of computers. I said, "How long is this gonna take?"

"That depends on what I find."

"Ballpark."

"An hour? Maybe two?"

In which time Clayton would no doubt topple the cannery without us. I made an executive decision to give the rest of the lab a cursory glance on my way out and head back home. I strode out into the hall, ignoring the grumbling it prompted from Jibben, with Jacob hot on my heels.

"Don't touch anything," Jibben called after me.

I had no intention of it. Once I verified that all was quiet on the nonphysical front, I'd be out of there.

While anger doesn't do much for my talent, adrenaline does seem to make it burn just a little bit brighter. I pulled hard at the white light and gave the remaining few rooms a visual power sweep. Everything was clear. It always was— unless you counted the flailing corpse incident, which was definitely the only reason I wasn't already halfway home.

The place was as clean etherically as it was physically—and believe me when I say, you could eat off the floor. So without further ado, I headed back toward the lobby to retrieve my gun, resume my argument with Jacob, and head back to the cannery before things got any worse....

Only to find Darnell wasn't in his usual spot to buzz us out. Across the bay, the elevator stood open and a delivery guy in coveralls—extremely wet coveralls—was struggling to force something very large out of the elevator while Darnell hovered beside him. I couldn't hear what they were saying, so it stood to reason they couldn't hear me. But I have very hard knuckles. I rapped on the safety glass in a cop-knock that was impossible to ignore.

Darnell glanced over and held up a just-a-minute finger.

Damn it.

I planted my hands on my hips, and Jacob stood beside

me and mirrored my pose. He said, "I can see you're upset." Ya think? "But I just didn't feel right about leaving. Granted, I'm no precog. But I like to think I'm observant, that I made decent choices. If I was off goofing around when it turned out you needed me, how could I ever live with that?"

"So, it's raining. I'd wager the kid and I have each experienced the phenomenon and lived to tell the tale."

"Look—clearly, I hit a nerve. I'm sorry." Wow, for Jacob to actually apologize, I must've really sounded peeved. "But the damage is done and I'm here now, so why don't we just—"

I'm not sure what he was about to suggest, because out in the lobby, a potential altercation was brewing—a lot more serious than the one currently taking place between my husband and me. Jacob and I both dropped our conversation and zeroed in on the drama unfolding on the other side of the glass.

An apparatus piled high with crates—something between a hotel luggage cart and a pallet jack—was parked in the middle of the lobby. There were two deliverymen in navy uniforms—or delivery *people*, to be more accurate, since only one of them was actually male. The Caucasian guy was easily as tall as me, and damn near as wide as he was tall. He dwarfed his partner, a fairly substantial African American woman who looked downright petite next to his bulk.

The massive guy stood by sheepishly, looking like he wished he was anywhere but there. And the woman was busy giving Darnell a piece of her mind. I couldn't hear it—not through the glass—but with all the finger-wagging on her part, it didn't look good.

When it became clear the Darnell situation might drag

on—I pulled out my phone and gave Clayton's number a jab to tell him I was running late. He picked up right away this time. But there was all kinds of racket on the other end.

"What the hell is that?" I demanded.

Clayton answered with a concerning lack of surly teenage ennui. "Thunder. It's, like, really loud." As if to prove him right, the sky on the other side of the line boomed like a rifle going off in my ear. "Car alarms are going nuts all up and down the street."

"You're okay. You'll be fine. Jacob's not flying out after all, and the two of us will be home just as soon as—"

Another boom blotted out my words.

"So, uh, what would happen if the cannery got hit by lightning?" Clayton asked with the slightest quaver in his voice.

Hell if I knew. But Jacob had been leaning in, listening. I angled the phone so we could both speak, and he said, "Nothing will happen," with all his usual maddening confidence. Except this time it was more reassuring than annoying. "It's a sturdy building. All brick. Just don't touch anything conductive."

More booming. Followed by, "What does that mean?"

"Anything metal," Jacob said. "Or water. And, while you're at it, don't touch any light switches, either."

Knowing this wasn't exactly the best time for an impromptu science lesson, I told Clayton, "Just hunker down on the couch 'till we get home and you'll be fine. We're leaving any minute."

When we hung up, I turned back to the glass and showed it the business side of my fist.

Bam-bam-bam.

Ow.

It smarted. But it made the finger-wagger shut up long enough for Darnell to lean into his podium and buzz us back into the elevator bay. Between the crates, the big guy looking awkward, and the woman throwing attitude, a space that was more than ample before suddenly felt crowded and close.

I paused beside the station where my sidearm was stowed. Jacob did the same. But when Darnell turned to retrieve our service weapons, the angry deliverywoman sidestepped and planted herself right in his path. "Don't you turn your back on me, Darnell—I'm not through."

She knew his name. And not in a just-learned-it kind of way, either.

He said, "You really gonna do this right now, Alisha? I'm at work."

"Oh, and you think I just go around dressed in coveralls 'cause they make my butt look good?"

"Listen," I said, "If we could just grab our—"

"Excuse me." Now Alisha's finger-wagging was directed at me. "We were having a conversation."

Bzzt. Bzzt.

We all turned to find Jibben standing at the safety glass door, pushing a buzzer (one I hadn't noticed before) with great urgency.

Bzzzzt.

Not quite as emphatic as my cop-knock, but it got the job done. Darnell reached over and hit something on his control panel that caused a magnetic lock to disengage, allowing Jibben to crowd out into the bay with the rest of us.

"How long has this delivery just been sitting here?" he demanded. "It needs to go in containment, immediately."

Alisha gave him a look that could wither a plastic fern. "I'd be happy to oblige, *sir*, but ain't no way I'm going through no damn *naked machine*."

"It's called a millimeter wave scanner," Darnell said.

Behind me, Jacob gritted out, "We do *not* have time for this."

I said, "It sounds like you've all got your work cut out for you. Once Darnell gives us our sidearms, we'll be out of your hair."

Darnell turned back to his guard station—or, at least, he tried. But a pissed-off Alisha was in his way. "First things first. This man was just about to explain exactly why he blocked my phone number."

Oh, I could wager a guess.

"Ma'am," Jacob said stiffly, "we'll need you to step aside—"

Alisha did an affronted double-take at him—noting his golf shirt, khaki shorts and gym shoes—tossed her hair over her shoulder, and proceeded to ignore him. "Not until I got my answer."

Meanwhile, Jibben squeezed around her and went for the pallet jack, grabbing onto the handle.

"Whoa," said Big Boy, "hold on, that's a two-person rig."

"Then help me," Jibben snapped.

"Stop," Darnell commanded. The word rang out deliberate and clear, and everyone quit their squabbling and fell silent. "No one goes into that lab without a security check, period. I don't care if we went to grade school together, I don't care if we been talking on Datechat—hell, I don't care if you're my own mother. Rules are rules. And if that's a problem, then you need to clear the premises."

Alisha arched an eyebrow, looked Darnell square in the

eye, and said, "Then I guess we'll unload right here...and be on. Our. Way."

Beside her, Big Boy winced—though he didn't dare contradict her.

"But the shipment needs to go in containment," Jibben said helplessly—and everyone ignored him.

Other people's drama doesn't interest me at the best of times. By all accounts, though, Mother Nature was having a way bigger conniption fit than Alisha, and suddenly thirteen didn't seem anywhere near old enough to be left all alone. But abandoning my sidearm was out of the question. Especially when it was literally three feet away.

Since I currently looked more official than Jacob, I'd need to be the one to insist. I pulled out my federal ID and held it up coolly for Alisha's inspection. "Federal Agent. I'll need you to stand down, ma'am."

"But the delivery—" Jibben said.

"Is your problem, not ours. We're leaving." I cut my eyes to Darnell, then indicated the lockbox. "Agent Thompson?"

The tone worked, or maybe it was the ID. Either way, hallelujah. While Alisha smoldered, Darnell unhooked a key from his utility belt and knelt down to retrieve our service weapons. But just as his back was turned, Jibben reached across the security podium and smacked a button, buzzing open the lab door.

"Hey," Darnell said, startled. Now Jibben had one foot wedging open the safety door while he hauled on the handle of the delivery cart. The cart moved, though not at the best angle. Just enough to roll through the naked machine and wedge itself in the doorway—the doorway that was *supposed* to be secure.

Big Boy heaved a sigh of resignation, as though he hadn't

quite expected the day to turn out any better, but was none-theless disappointed to see it go to shit so spectacularly.

"Our sidearms," I said.

But Darnell was no longer paying me any attention. "Dr. Jibben! Those cases need to go through the scanner—there could be explosives."

Wide-eyed, both Alisha and Big Boy took a hasty step back.

Jibben, meanwhile, hauled on the handle with a grunt. "This isn't some random paper bag I found at the bus stop. The delivery firm is vetted—we've been using them for years—and we were expecting this shipment. Which needs to go into containment *right now*."

Whatever was inside those boxes was perfectly safe. Not only were the cases clearly sturdy, but the whole shipment was wrapped up tight in several layers of protective plastic film—which made it even more awkward for Jibben to work it through the lab door, since it wasn't shifting so much as an inch. But he wasn't about to take "no" for an answer. Planting his feet, he gave the cart handle a good yank....

And nothing happened.

At least, not until the whole thing teetered and toppled through the door and landed right on top of him, wheels spinning in the air. "Call 911," Darnell barked out as he and Jacob immediately mobilized to pull the massive crate off.

I made the call. Or, at least, I keyed it in. But I found a big fat nothing on the other end, and a NO SIGNAL where my bars usually were.

"My phone's not working," Alisha said nervously.

Big Boy shook his head. "We're too far underground to get a signal."

That didn't make any sense. I'd just been talking to Clayton not two minutes ago.

"There's a repeater," Darnell said as he strained against the weight of the cart.

I pulled down white light as I spun on my heel in search of some telltale flicker of movement, wondering how the hell a repeater had managed to slip past all my weekly checkups.

"A cell tower repeater," Big Boy told Alisha. "It extends the range."

Oh. Well, that made a lot more sense than a random guy from second grade knowing my personal terminology for ghost residue. It was likely just a power surge that made the cell phone repeater reset. Luckily, no one else had noticed me acting squirrelly. Or if they did, they just chalked it up to the chaos of the moment.

The cart was wedged in too tightly for Jacob and Darnell to pry it upright, but they were at least able to lift it off well enough for Jibben to drag himself out from under its weight. Through the safety glass, I had a front-row view. There was no blood—that was a plus—but judging by the sheen of sweat on Jibben's brow, he was in some serious pain.

Big Boy jabbed at the elevator until the doors opened. "I'll go up to the surface and make the call," he said as he stepped inside. The doors closed, and the numbers on the display ticked steadily up to the parking garage, then stopped. At least something had gone right.

Alisha nodded toward Jibben, then told me, "That man's gonna pass out." Given his pallor, it was a good possibility. "Saw a guy in the warehouse crush his leg once. Never walked right again." She strode over and elbowed Darnell aside, brandishing a keychain with a nail file on the end. Tiny, but very pointy. "Get out the way. We gotta cut these boxes loose."

I half expected Jibben to groan about contamination. But instead, he just groaned in general. I hoped for his sake the ambulance would show up soon. And for our sake too. Because now I was busy imagining everything in the cannery that could fall over and squash a thirteen-year-old boy.

Jesus. I hoped he didn't decide to start dicking around in the basement by all the heavy canning equipment. Because, let's face it...that's probably exactly what I would have done.

Alisha slashed the cling wrap with her little nail file so that Jacob and Darnell could extricate the cases one by one. Finally, they shifted enough crates off the cart that we could step over it and get into the lab entry. If you're gonna hurt yourself in a stupid and unnecessary way, you might as well do it in front of a woman with some common sense and a couple of ex-cops trained in first aid. Darnell seemed to know what he was doing, too. I kept Jibben conscious by elevating his uninjured leg to help his blood circulate to his head while Jacob set off in search of an ice pack to minimize swelling.

Darnell, meanwhile, slashed the leg of Jibben's pants open with the nail file keyring. I steeled myself for a compound fracture, but the skin was intact. Though he did have one hell of a bruise.

Jacob came back with a single-serve frozen lasagna—the sort that advertises itself as healthy. He normally won't touch the things, and claims they're all starch and water bathed in chemicals and sodium. Nice to see he finally found a use for one.

"What in the hell does Leonard think he's doing?" Alisha

demanded, glaring at the elevator. "How long does it take to make a single phone call?"

As if Big Boy—*Leonard*—could hear her complaining, the number on the elevator display changed as he came back down. It went from the parking garage to the level below. And the level below that. And then....

Went totally dark.

CHAPTER 7

"The elevator," I said, and my voice came out raspy and dry. I cleared my throat and repeated, "The elevator."

Jacob was busy trying to strap the frozen lasagna to Jibben's leg with scotch tape, while on the other side of the glass wall in the elevator bay, Alisha jabbed at the dead button and said, "What's wrong with this thing?"

"Stay calm," Jacob told me. "The generator will kick in."

"And if it doesn't?" I wondered.

"We take the stairs."

Alisha was apparently willing to let bygones be bygones with Darnell—at least for the moment—when she hauled at his arm and said, "You can't leave Leonard in the elevator. He'll have a panic attack! And what if it's the paramedics in there? What then?"

"Take a breath," Darnell told her—and she actually did. It wasn't the words, but the way he'd said them. Calm, matter-of-fact, competent. "We'll get those doors open. I've got a drop key."

I personally wouldn't have named anything related to a

malfunctioning elevator a "drop" key. But since Leonard was stuck just above the lowest level, I supposed at least he wouldn't have very far to fall.

Darnell unhitched a heavy keyring from his belt and quickly found what he was looking for. It wasn't a traditional key. More like a tool—one of those specialized screwdrivers that we've always got in every size and configuration except the one we need. He fit the end into a little round hole on the elevator door—one that I'd never taken much notice of before—and gave it a wiggle.

"It's stuck, ain't it?" Alisha said, hovering.

"Just gimme a sec." Darnell felt around with the key. "Gotta catch the release mechanism is all." Everyone held their breath as he dug around, then gave the key a solid turn. "Right...there."

A click.

Unfortunately, not the kind of click we'd been hoping for.

Darnell held up the drop key and the end had snapped clean off in the hole.

"Oh my God!" Alisha wailed. Tears threatened. "You *broke* it!"

"Take a breath," Darnell repeated, but even his uber-calm tone was no help now that the key was busted. A rap sounded from behind the elevator doors, followed by Leonard's muffled voice. "Alisha? Can you hear me?"

"We hear you—we're gonna get you out of there, don't you worry."

"It's dark—Alisha, help!"

I cut my eyes to Jacob as if to say, *Can you believe this crap?*

He met my gaze and gave his head a subtle shake. "Go get the crowbar," he told me.

But the second I eased Jibben's good leg off my lap, his eyelids fluttered. I grabbed the keys from my pocket, got Alisha's attention with a wave, and lobbed them through the door. They landed by the naked machine with a jingle. "Black Crown Vic at the top of the stairs. Crowbar in the trunk."

She grabbed up the keys and hustled through the stairwell door, which clunked heavily shut behind her.

"Hey," I said softly, and Jacob met my eyes again. Worry etched a stark line across his brow, and the muscles in his jaw worked as he ground his teeth in frustration. "Clayton might be a little sheltered, but he's not stupid. He'll be okay 'till we get home."

"Your boy might be okay," Jibben said woozily, "but I can't say the same for the artifacts."

Our boy. Right. If this didn't convince Jacob we weren't even capable of caring for a gerbil, nothing would. But we could I-told-you-so later.

I said to Jibben, "Your precious artifacts are sealed up tight. Nothing's gonna happen—" I'd been shifting my weight with a hand to the floor, and found my sweaty palm covered in something that felt like cotton candy and smelled like the cheap plastic packaging of cut-rate knockoff electronics. A nearby crate sat slightly cockeyed where one of the seams had split.

Of course it had.

Darnell, meanwhile, had plucked a walkie-talkie from a charger at his station and was murmuring into the handset. "Do you copy? Repeat—do you copy?"

The way things were going? I doubted it.

But then, lo and behold, the static pulsed, followed by the

low murmur of a calm voice coming through from the other end. Darnell exchanged some words, then came back to us and said, "My supervisor says help is on the way, but the roads are a mess and even emergency vehicles are having a hard time getting through. Director Kim took the next flight back to Chicago, but they had to put down in Fort Wayne. For now, the best thing we can do is stay put 'till things settle down."

Even if Laura drove the rest of the way back, it would take two, three hours on a good day. But if weather had everything at a standstill, there wasn't a whole hell of a lot we could do but hunker down and wait. While Darnell worked on the problem of freeing Leonard from the elevator, Jacob and I took stock of the situation given the latest developments.

In a voice just a bit too calm—which let me know he must be freaking out on the inside—Jacob announced, "We'd better keep Dr. Jibben comfortable until they get here."

"Comfortable?" Jibben scoffed. "You don't have to sugar-coat it. I'm hardly a civilian."

Annoyed, I said, "We need to keep you from going into shock. Happy?"

Jibben blinked. "It's that bad?" He then proceeded to try levering up on his elbow to get a better look at his leg, despite Jacob's best efforts to keep him down. Then he ended up in a lightheaded collapse, murmuring, "Oh, I suppose you're right...."

Fortunately, I knew the lab layout pretty well from all the times I'd walked the grid. I told Jacob, "There's a couch in that break room where you found the lasagna. Grab the cushions and we'll prop him up better."

With a quick nod, he hurried off to snag them.

"The shipment," Jibben said weakly.

"Extenuating circumstances," I said. "It'll have to wait."

"But you don't understand. This is the find of a lifetime. The sort of rarity that can unlock decades of inconclusive research."

"What sort of...rarity?" I asked cautiously as the hairs raised on the back of my neck. With everything else going on, I hadn't given much actual thought to the shipment itself. But now I had to wonder if I should have been more concerned.

"It's everything that's left of the Argus Institute."

Relief flooded me faster than a clogged storm drain in a downpour. Between the flickering lights and the awareness of her nearby cadaver, I'd subconsciously convinced myself that it was Jennifer Chance's research in those crates, the guts of a dozen prototype GhosTVs, and a file chock full of my innermost secrets. But the Argus Institute was about as threatening as Captain Kangaroo.

Back when I was a kid—before psychic powers had been unequivocally proven—there were plenty of folks hard at work investigating various psychic phenomena. But half of them were misguided, and the other half were frauds. I wasn't sure which camp the Argus Institute was in. They'd been a TV staple back then, from morning talk shows to late night specials. Whenever something unexplained happened, Luther Hinman, the head of Argus, would show up under the bright studio lights. He (and his massive sideburns) would sit there in orange pancake makeup, with a lapel mike clipped to his tweed jacket, attempting to make himself sound Very Scientific.

But mostly he'd sound like a kook. Especially when he

wrapped everything up with his cheesy tagline: *Exploring the frontier of human potential.*

The line itself was godawful enough, but when it wrapped up one of Argus's late-night info reels, it was overlaid with the graphic of a covered wagon going into space, augmented by the crack of a whip. Despite the fact that a popular dog food had a similar commercial at the time, Argus insisted on using it. Which no doubt caused pets all across America to become unduly excited every time Hinman lit up the TV screen to spew his unfounded psychic theories.

Jibben plucked at his collar. Even flat on his back, he was still squirmy. "You think their work is a sham," he said. I didn't disagree. "The front-facing aspect of the institute...maybe. Research is costly. They had to appease the public to try and keep the funding money flowing in. Of course they'd need to play up the most sensationalistic findings. But their methodology purported to be sound. And their work held a lot of promise. Particularly where it related to telekinetics."

Jacob was back with a couch cushion tucked under each arm and a pillow in either hand...which he promptly fumbled at the sound of that final, fateful word: telekinetics. TKs are exceedingly rare, though not for lack of trying. And the specific eugenics regimen performed by the late, unlamented Dr. Kamal was the only reason Jacob came to be.

Come to think of it...Clayton, too.

Which made me even more desperate to get back home.

It was a relief to get Jibben propped up well enough for me to squeeze out from under his legs. My knees hurt from the hard floor and my quads were cramping up, but given how the massive blunt trauma wound on Jibben's thigh must feel,

I wasn't about to complain.

I was stomping out pins and needles when the heavy stairwell door opened and Alisha came busting out with a tire iron in one hand and a box of granola bars in the other.

"You went through my luggage?" Jacob asked, baffled.

"Well, it was right there—and I figured there might be something we could use."

"Never mind." Jacob was clearly picking his battles. "Did you get through to 911?"

"Help is on the way." With that, Alisha lobbed the keys back to me, then strode toward the elevator doors. But Darnell cut her off at the pass and grabbed the crowbar out of her hands. "Finally," she said. "Somebody actually doin' something."

Oh, Darnell was doing something, all right. He walked the crowbar over to his station and stashed it in the locker.

"What the hell?" Alisha cried.

"I don't care what's going on outside—I won't just let a civilian loose in here with a potential weapon."

"But what about Leonard?"

"Help is on the way. You said so yourself."

"He might *suffocate* by the time they finally show up!"

"I'm okay," called a muffled voice behind the elevator doors.

Up to this point, Jacob had displayed the patience of a saint. But even he had his limit, and when that weapons locker slammed shut, he'd reached that limit. "I'll take my sidearm now," he told Darnell.

"But my supervisor said—"

"I am the ranking agent here." Jacob's tone wasn't just clipped—it was utterly badass. "There's a child at home who needs us. And I say we're leaving. Now."

CHAPTER 8

Every workplace has its culture. The FPMP was no different. And for a sinister government spy organization, when push came to shove, we acted more like one big, reasonably tolerant family. No one pulled rank here. We were just too midwestern for that. Storming in and swinging your dick around was something we'd expect from National. Not one of our own.

But desperate times call for desperate dick-swinging. And as Internal Affairs, Jacob truly was at the top of the spy heap. "You've got this under control," Jacob said. "So give us our weapons and we'll be on our way."

Darnell hadn't been what you'd call affable, even when I recognized him from grade school. But now it was like a barrier had come down. "Yes sir," he said, so neutral it stung, and turned back to the weapons locker....

Only to be cut off by a pair of EMTs slamming through the stairwell doors.

Water beaded on their rescue gear and they moved with the quick efficiency of workers who no longer got joy from knocking things down. Their gargantuan prybar put our tire iron to shame. And they walloped it into place between the elevator doors with a literal sledgehammer. "Good thing you caught us on our way down to the Loop," one of them said between bangs. "You're not the only one with a stuck elevator."

"Lucky it's Saturday," the other one agreed. "Most of the office buildings are empty."

No doubt he was right. But somehow, I wasn't feeling all that lucky.

One thing I can say for emergency workers: they don't fool around. With a few good, solid hits, the elevator doors screeched open. The floor of the elevator was hanging down maybe a foot and a half, and the interior, presumably not on the same power grid as the lab, was totally dark. Darnell swept a flashlight beam through the gap, showing Leonard prone on the elevator floor.

"Sir?" one of the workers snapped, no-nonsense and efficient. "Can you hear me?"

"He's unconscious," the other one confirmed, "let's get him out of there."

Alisha sagged against Darnell, fighting back tears. "What if he's—?"

"They'll take care of him," Darnell said. "He'll be fine."

"Some help over here?" the first guy said over his shoulder as they strained to maneuver Leonard's limp body through the gap. Jacob, Darnell and I hurried over to help. It took all five of us to pull Leonard out, but eventually, we managed.

One medic grabbed Leonard's vitals with a handheld ECG while the other rigged him up to the gurney. "Significant ST-segment elevation," the first one said.

The other acknowledged. "Prepping nitroglycerine—but get him upstairs before we establish a line."

"Understood."

"What does that mean?" Alisha demanded, but Darnell caught her before she threw herself on the gurney, while Jacob cleared a path to the stairwell and held open the door.

I was familiar enough with the lingo to be glad she hadn't asked me. But Jibben couldn't resist being the smart guy. "Sounds like a myocardial infarction."

Alisha's eyes went huge.

"Heart attack," Darnell translated.

Which didn't help at all.

Alisha started wailing something about Leonard being too young to have a heart attack, while Darnell steered her away from the stairwell. The EMTs would have a hard enough time dragging Leonard's bulk up the stairs without her interfering.

Which meant Darnell's hands were full—with our guns still locked in the weapons locker.

Jacob caught my eye and nodded to a corner of the lobby that was semi-blocked from the drama by the pile of crates, and I slipped around Alisha and Darnell to have a word.

"We can't leave our sidearms here," Jacob said. He didn't need to remind me why—not after the time he'd had Laura Kim detained for Roger Burke's murder based on her service weapon. "But there's no reason we both need to stick around."

"You want to split up?" It made sense, I supposed. Jacob hardly needed my help to go home to Clayton. "Fine. Just make sure you don't forget to come get me when this is all over."

Jacob looked puzzled. "No, Vic—I meant that *you* should go home."

"Me?"

"I need to stay. I'm the only one Agent Thompson will take orders from."

True. Darnell was turning out to be a real hardass. "But, with Clayton—"

"He trusts you." Jacob looked into my eyes—a look that would normally have been accompanied by him cupping my jaw or settling a hand on my hip. We were at work, though, and a big fish-eye camera in the middle of the elevator bay ceiling had a clear view of every last nook and cranny, so we had to act professional. Still, I knew his looks pretty well by now—and I could practically feel the hug. "You got this, Vic."

It's the little things. Cliché, but true. Jacob plies me with compliments all the time, from thanking me for cleaning up, to random remarks about my sense of humor, to praise for my bedroom technique (which I still think is basically nonexistent—but if he's happy, I'm happy.)

But Clayton is his favorite kid in the whole world. Even when Clayton was at peak-level obnoxiousness, as far as his uncle was concerned, he could do no wrong. For Jacob to stay back and deal with our guns and leave me to ride to Clayton's rescue hardly seemed like something for me to get all schmaltzy over.

I did, though.

Jacob loved me, I had no doubt. He lusted after me, too, and he missed me when I wasn't there. While most of the time, though he might secretly think he was smarter, he did acknowledge I was the expert where ghosts were concerned.

But him trusting me to be there for Clayton—to be the *responsible* one—took things to an entirely new level.

"Don't worry." I gave Jacob's forearm a quick, semi-professional squeeze. "We're all gonna be fine."

But as I turned toward the stairwell to ride to the rescue of Jacob's precious nephew, the building quivered.

I felt it in my bones, even three stories underground. Something rumbled so low it was practically subsonic.

And then all the lights went dark.

"Are you fucking kidding me?" I hadn't meant to say it aloud, but I'd wager the sentiment was shared by everyone else stuck in the FPMP's sub-sub basement.

I pulled out my pocket flashlight. And as I flicked it on, everyone else produced a light of their own. Jacob and Alisha both had their phones out, Darnell had a massive magnum, and even Jibben had a little pen light going. Jacob aimed his phone's light at the stairwell door, and told me, "Stick with the plan—go home to Clayton."

And get my ass out of the dark basement? He didn't need to tell me twice. But when I tried to charge out the door, I bounced off and staggered back.

What the hell? The paramedics had just gone through.

It was a big steel slab with a pushbar across the middle. Jacob immediately tried again, rattling the bar. But no luck.

"It's an electric strike lock," Darnell told him. "If the power is out—"

Jacob interrupted him. "It should still open from this side."

"It must be jammed," Darnell said. But I wasn't so sure. The FPMP played fast and loose with the sorts of safety rules that other people had to follow. I wouldn't put it past them to trigger a total lockdown if they thought someone was capable of stealing their precious scientific secrets. I might have even thought it was a fine idea, given the types of nut-jobs who'd probably kill for whatever was inside the lab. But not with me trapped down here, too.

Darnell retrieved our crowbar from the weapons locker, and I wondered if Jacob was gonna commandeer it by force. But any potential macho-contest was diverted by a crackle of static on Darnell's walkie, followed by a message.

Attention all security, the building has sustained a lightning strike. Everyone stay in place until further notice and secure the area. We'll update you as soon as more information is available.

Darnell and Jacob both froze and locked eyes. This was uncharted territory. And the protocol was clear: do as we're told, stay put, and await further instructions. But whether or not Jacob was about to follow orders was anyone's guess.

Here's the thing about Jacob and authority. He's all for it... as long as he's the one with all the power. While he may be pretty good at pretending to follow orders, and while his perfect Boy Scout demeanor has most people fooled, ultimately, Jacob does only what Jacob wants to do.

And I think Darnell had his number.

But even Jacob couldn't challenge the weather, and when Darnell set the crowbar aside, he didn't make a lunge for it. "We're staying put," Darnell said to the room at large—but mostly to Jacob.

Jacob nodded. "We're staying put."

But some people just can't let sleeping alpha dogs lie. And through the wedged-open safety glass door, Jibben called out, "Then we might as well get the crates into containment, since we're stuck down here anyway."

"Staying put *in the elevator bay*," Darnell clarified, annoyance threading through his businesslike calm.

Jibben added, "And then, once you square the crates away, I'll show you the emergency exit."

Stunned silence.

Maybe Darnell would finally return our sidearms—once I promised to use mine on Jibben.

Alisha recovered first. She swung around to do a double-take at Jibben. "There's another way out? What the hell's the matter with you? Tell us where it is."

"Not until the artifacts are secure."

For a guy flat on his back with his pant leg cut off and a lasagna strapped to his leg, Jibben was maddeningly smug.

Jacob clearly knew stubbornness when he saw it, because he was the first to give in. "Fine. Where is this storage?"

"Agent Marks," Darnell reminded him, "you agreed to stay put."

"That was before the emergency exit," Jacob said, and stepped over the crate wedged in the doorway to begin shifting boxes. "Give me a hand," he told Alisha and me. "The sooner we get this over with, the sooner we get out of here."

I knew the FPMP. And I knew that under Con Dreyfus's regime, lots of high-tech hidey-holes and panic rooms were installed. Dreyfus's sense of self preservation was legendary. And I couldn't imagine he'd let himself get trapped in a basement with no way out.

The first step was extricating the cart from the door—but we were all very motivated, and with Jibben holding my flashlight on us, soon we had the thing upright and loaded with heavy crates.

No thanks to Darnell.

We could've used another pair of hands, but he just stood beside his post with his mag light trained on us, glaring—following orders to the letter and staying put. And while I understood that a whole team of Jacobs playing by their own rulebooks might be every boss's worst nightmare, there was definitely a time and place to improvise.

As we struggled with a particularly heavy crate, I told Darnell, "Look, this isn't Mrs. Smith's class where you'll get in trouble for leaving without a hall pass."

"I told you, I don't remember Mrs. Smith."

I said, "No one can get in or out of the basement, so you might as well pitch in."

Whether or not Darnell remembered me, I'd like to think I was starting to get through to him.... At least until his walkie let out a loud blip of static and reminded him that his supervisor was somewhere on the premises.

I glanced up at the fish eye camera mount in the ceiling and said, "They can't see us, y'know. Not if the power's out."

Darnell wasn't listening—he was too busy with the walkie. "Break. This is Agent Thompson. Did you have a message? Over."

The only reply he got was a jumble of blips and static.

"Don't waste your time with him," Alisha called to me from the safety glass door. "Ain't nobody gonna change that man's mind once it's made up. We're better off doing this ourselves and getting it over with."

I had to agree.

"You could at least hold the door," I told Darnell, who

grudgingly stuck a foot in to wedge it open while the rest of us worked free the biggest, stuckest crate. He couldn't even be bothered to aim his mag light in any useful way, because he was too busy futzing with his walkie.

"You need to lift the far corner," Jibben pointed out from his vantage place on the floor. "Once you straighten it out, you can work it free."

"He's right," Alisha said. For some reason, I was more inclined to believe her. Not only because she moved heavy stuff for a living, but because she probably had more common sense than Darnell and Jibben put together. "Grab that side. Got it? On the count of three. One...two...."

The fiberglass crate came free with a groan—what the hell was in there, barbells?—but somehow, we managed to muscle it back onto the trolley. Again, with zero help from Darnell. A blast of static caught his attention and he turned away from the door, waving his walkie around as if it might help him catch the signal. "Say again," he barked into the handset. "I don't copy you. Repeat, I don't cop—"

His voice cut off abruptly as the safety glass door closed behind him with an ominous clunk, with Darnell in the elevator bay and the rest of us in the lobby.

Jibben aimed my flashlight at the push bar. The beam danced over the safety glass like a spotlight and landed right on the imposing horizontal hunk of metal.

Alisha said, "Do not tell me *that* door is locked now, too."

I gave the handle a good shove and the door didn't so much as flex. But the bar itself did rattle, which caught Darnell's attention on the opposite side of the glass. He grabbed his side of the handle and tugged. Nothing. And then he reached over his guard station and jabbed uselessly at his powerless buzzer.

I sighed.

Meanwhile, Darnell holstered his walkie...and picked up the crowbar.

"That'll never work," Jibben said. "It's one of the world's strongest polymers. You'd need a jackhammer. And even then—"

Darnell probably knew exactly what that window was made of—so he didn't try to shatter it. Instead, he went for the door frame.

We'd all seen how much effort it took to get the elevator doors open—equipment in the same category as the Jaws of Life. But Darnell was determined to show that door who was boss. He tried to wedge the chiseled tip inside the doorframe, but the seam was just too tight. Undaunted, he went for the hinges. No good.

Finally, he resorted to brute force, and drove the tire iron like he was putting a stake through Count Dracula's heart. If it were me, I'd probably bounce it off the steel frame and put my eye out. But Darnell's aim was true, and the chisel tip wedged itself solidly between the door and the frame, just above the strike plate.

Would the crowbar be strong enough? Hopefully so—it was designed to lift a car, after all.

The only thing left for Darnell to do was use leverage to his advantage and pry that sucker open.

All of this had been taking place by the light of two flashlights and two cellphones—so when the overhead lights flared to life, we were all struck momentarily blind. At least until, with a sound like the pops of distant gunfire, every overhead can light exploded and we were plunged back into darkness.

I blinked away afterimages and snatched up my pocket flashlight from Jibben, who'd been bouncing it uselessly around the ceiling to gawk at the blown out fixtures.

"Give me that," I said, and did a quick check of the room. "Broken glass—everyone okay?"

No one was showered in glass shards, even Jibben lying there on the floor, so I was relieved we'd come through the power surge unscathed.

At least, I'd thought we were all fine....

Until I swung my beam out through the safety glass and saw Darnell lying face-up on the floor with his magnum and the crowbar beside him.

"Did that fool knock himself out?" Alisha demanded. "Tell him to get his ass up."

I soon realized that wasn't gonna happen, given the last lightning strike, the steel doorframe...and the fresh repeater flickering there on the other side of the glass.

CHAPTER 9

I'd seen a lot of death in my time, but I'd never witnessed a fresh electrocution. It had been quick, at least. But in a way, that was even worse. No one saw it coming, so no one could prepare. And now there was yet another repeater in the FPMP collection.

"Somebody help him," Alisha said, voice quavering. She looked from me to Jacob, and even spared a glance at Jibben. "Somebody gotta help him."

"I'm sorry," Jacob told her simply.

"But you don't know—"

Jacob cut his eyes to me, figuring that I probably did indeed know whether Darnell was alive or dead, and I said, "You saw what the strike did to the lightbulbs."

Alisha approached the safety glass, but didn't touch anything. She had more sense than that. "Are you *sure* he's not breathing?"

Darnell's mag light had landed beside him, throwing his face in shadow, but illuminating his body just fine. The palm of his hand was charred. And even though I saw his repeater flickering there, just on the other side of the door, I dutifully stepped up beside Alisha to make sure his chest didn't rise and fall. Jacob, who does comfort much better than I do, flanked her on her other side and put a consoling arm around her. "It was quick," he said. "And it happened while he was being a hero."

Alisha did a slow blink and teardrops trembled on her eyelashes. "It doesn't seem right. I was so awful to him—and it's the last thing he'll ever hear from me." She sniffled. "Why was I so mean?"

Jacob said, "I don't think that's how the people who've passed on remember us. They remember all of it, the bad times, but the good too. And I don't think they hold a grudge."

Says the guy who was stalked by the Criss Cross killer...but, thankfully, instances like that are few and far between, and all that was left of Darnell Thompson was the occasional flicker of a guy trying to free us with a crowbar. We were all staring at his body somberly, trying to make sense of what had just happened, trying to take it all in, when from his spot on the floor, Jibben piped up, "What about the delivery?"

"What *about* the delivery?" I repeated.

"Leaving it out here to be contaminated won't bring Agent Thompson back, will it? Is that what he would have wanted?"

It was a cheap ploy. But I had to admit, I had no clue what Darnell would have wanted. We were seven when we'd known each other, and back then, wants were as simple as Hot Wheels cars and chocolate milk.

If Jacob didn't have access to the ghost-litmus test he'd married—if there were any chance at all Darnell might still be alive—he would have forced the location of the emergency exit from Jibben by any means necessary to go get help. But since Darnell was clearly well beyond that, Jacob grit his teeth and said, "If you're inventing an emergency exit to get what you want—"

"I guarantee, Agent Marks, I want to get out of here just as much as you do."

Given the whole Clayton situation, I highly doubted it. But not only would moving those boxes satisfy that weirdo, Jibben—it would give Alisha something to look at other than her ex's dead body. Or, it *would* have given her something to look at...had the whole place not been darker than my stiffest pot of coffee. And I brew 'em pretty thick.

Jacob held up his phone to shine the flashlight app down the hall, then cursed under his breath. "Low power."

"There's a charger in your suitcase," Alisha offered.

Jacob pinched the bridge of his nose.

From the floor, Jibben said, "There's an emergency kit in the lab. Power bank, flashlight, plenty of things we can use."

Unfortunately, the only one likely to locate this kit in the dark was him. Even though I'd been sweeping through the lab a couple times a week for the past two years, that thing was so full of cabinets, I'd be pawing through them all 'till the cavalry finally showed up.

"I'm not that dizzy anymore," Jibben said. "If you could just bring me to the lab...."

And that's how I ended up pushing around the least popular FPMP Lab Manager on an office chair by the light of my pocket flashlight while Jacob and Alisha started shifting boxes.

Luckily her phone still had enough charge...though the way

the flashlight app ate through batteries, we shouldn't expect it to last long.

Once Jibben and I were alone, I said, "Given the circumstances, you know you're not making any friends by insisting on dealing with your delivery. Right?"

"Friends," he said with a sniff, as if I'd just said something utterly ridiculous.

Guess the whole "Heebie Jeebie" thing was no big secret. But at some point, you've gotta get over the name-calling and pull up your big boy pants. I'd never dream of hijacking someone during a massive emergency to cater to my agenda. Even a neanderthal cop who insisted on calling me "Spook Squad" to my face.

"I do care about Agent Thompson," Jibben hastened to add. "Of course I do. I've known him for a while now—he's been posted down here in the lab for months. Respectful. Efficient. And, don't forget, he died trying to save us. But there was no saving *him*."

Jibben guided me into one of the many labs with locked cabinets lining the walls—mechanical locks, thankfully, not key cards. When he pulled on a thick pair of rubber-coated gloves to fit the key in the lock, I might have accused him of being unduly cautious. But after what just went down in the lobby, I figured he knew what he was doing.

The cabinet doors swung open to reveal wall-to-wall supplies, everything boxed up neatly and Tetrised in solid. It was packed so tight that when Jibben grabbed the box labeled "emergency lamp", nothing else so much as quivered.

The lamp was a square about the size of a lunchbox, a nifty thing with an LED front panel and some charging ports on the side. "It's charged regularly," Jibben said. "But we'll use the lowest light level to conserve battery."

I'd been pushing him back toward the entryway, but I stopped so fast he nearly toppled off the chair. "Why would we need to conserve battery if there's an emergency exit?"

Jibben twitched. "I don't know. Just in case."

I leaned in and pitched my voice low. "If you dreamed up this so-called exit just for the sake of getting your boxes moved—"

"What kind of man do you take me for?"

At this point, I highly doubted he'd like me to answer that.

By the time I shoved Jibben and his chair back into the lobby, all the crates had been taken care of—all but the one that had split open. Jacob and Alisha were staring at it by the light of her phone. "Is this safe to touch?" She shone the light at the weird fluff spilled out onto the floor.

Jibben said, "I'm more worried about you contaminating the contents." Alisha gave him a glare, and he said, "But that's just anti-static packing material. It's perfectly safe."

Alisha gave the crate an experimental shove toward the moving cart. As it moved, Jacob squeezed the back of his neck, while at the same time, Jibben shuddered. Taken separately, neither of these gestures meant anything. Jacob did the neck-squeeze whenever he was stressed out, and good old Heebie Jeebie was always twitching around. But the way they'd happened at the very same time....

I glanced out into the elevator bay.

The only thing worse than seeing a ghost? Not seeing it. So I was actually relieved when a few moments later, the flicker of Darnell's repeater buried an invisible crowbar in the doorframe, got blown back, and disappeared.

But repeaters and ghosts weren't technically the same. Back in Hicksville, I'd even spoken to a deputy's ghost while his nearby repeater repeatedly blew his brains out.

So it was entirely possible there *was* a spirit on the loose.

Or...there might be a reason why Jibben was so hell-bent on getting this delivery into containment. One he'd conveniently neglected to tell us.

"Back away from the box," I told Jacob.

But Alisha'd had enough. She stepped forward, undeterred, to get this nonsense over with and load the final crate onto the trolley. Since pushing did no good, she decided to pull. Once she looped a nylon strap around the box, she planted her feet and threw her whole body weight onto it, and lo and behold, the crate heaved up onto the handcart so she could drag it toward containment. Jacob pushed, and I followed with Jibben in his office chair, eager to get this thing over and done with.

Finally, things were going right. Or so I thought. But in the containment room, the moment Alisha's strap went slack, the side of the crate creaked open. Something rolled out—a *head*, a fucking *head*—and our light beams turned into a laser show as we all backpedaled like crazy in the dark.

Until my flashlight beam steadied, the head rolled to a stop, and I realized it was nothing scarier than styrofoam.

"I do not get paid enough for this shit," Alisha muttered.

You and me both, sister.

You and me both.

CHAPTER 10

It probably says something about me that, had an actual human head tumbled out of that crate, I wouldn't have been surprised. Startled? Sure. But, surprised? Hardly. Between the frozen corpses on the other side of the wall, and Jibben's insistence on getting his shipment into "containment," I frankly considered myself lucky there were no obvious dismembered body parts in my vicinity.

I shone my light on the styrofoam head. The features themselves were very plain, just a couple of divots where the eyes should be and a slight hump for the nose. It was the type of head you might store your hats on, or maybe park your wig.

But the wig in question was more high-tech than any hairpiece I'd ever seen. A cap of sensors surrounded the styrofoam head like some science fiction swim cap.

I'm not fond of electrodes. I've had too many panic attack-inducing episodes involving bleeping monitors and random things stuck to various parts of my body. And despite the fact that this gear was older than I was and looked like something out of a cut-rate student art film, it still made my pits prickle with sweat.

Alisha went right for the head.

"Don't touch that," Jibben snapped.

She ignored him, grabbed the thing, and held it up to the light of her phone. "What's this supposed to be, a Halloween costume?"

"That," he said loftily, "is none of your concern. You might have been vetted by the courier company, but that's where your authorization ends. In fact, you shouldn't even have access to anything other than the lobby so any potential exposure to classified information is limited."

"Let me get this straight," Alisha said. "I can't see but two feet in front of my face, and you want me to go back out to the lobby, alone, in the dark, next to a man I been chatting with lying there dead on the floor. Is that what you're saying?"

"There'd be safety glass between you," Jibben offered.

"And that's supposed to make me feel better? It's not as if I thought he'd get up and start walking around."

Though if she saw some of the things *we'd* seen....

"Who the hell's in charge here?" She swung around and looked at Jacob in his casual clothes. "That'd be you, Cargo Shorts?"

"Agent Marks," he corrected her testily. "And, yes. I'm the ranking agent."

"Then tell this fool I'm not going anywhere."

Jacob nodded. "She's right—unless there's a good reason for us to split up, we stick together."

Jibben said, "This is a classified facility—"

"And there's nothing in your containment room to see but

a bunch of dark monitors and the boxes she transported here." Jacob turned to Alisha and added, "But sticking together means following orders and keeping your hands to yourself. This is no place for a civilian."

She gave an exaggerated shrug. "You don't need to tell me twice. I just wanna go home."

Jacob and I dragged the final crate the rest of the way through the door. The containment room was maybe twenty feet square, lined with empty stainless steel lab tables and empty shelves. I'd seen it plenty of my times during my normal rounds, and generally considered it to be a bland, white room. But by the light of the emergency lamp, the pile of random boxes in the center looked positively sinister.

With Jibben and Alisha still bickering in the doorway, Jacob pitched his voice low and said, "Clayton must be scared to death." God, he sounded miserable.

"He'll be fine," I replied.

Talk about a generic platitude.

I tried again. "Look, Jacob, Clayton's not an idiot. And the cannery's a pretty massive pile of bricks. It's been standing for more than a century—so it would take one hell of a storm to blow it down."

Jacob ground his molars—hopefully his new crowns would stand up to the abuse—then said, "Let's hope that storm isn't already here."

Alisha squeezed past Jibben and reluctantly surrendered the styrofoam head to Jacob. He stuck it on a nearby shelf.

"This isn't your grandma's closet," Jibben snapped as he wheeled himself in, one-footed. "You can't just put things anywhere, willy-nilly." He grabbed a clipboard off a nearby table, pulled a pen from his lab coat, and started scribbling. "There are protocols. Procedures. And—"

I cut him off. "And you promised to tell us about this emergency exit if we moved your boxes." I gestured toward the haphazard pile of crates. "Here they are. Now where's the damn door?"

Jibben set down the clipboard, then slapped the pen on top of it. I was just about ready to knock him off the chair for telling me the emergency exit was just a fabrication when he huffed and said, "Fine. Let's go."

We set off deeper into the lab, with Jacob at the front of the line wielding the emergency light, me bringing up the rear pushing Jibben's office chair, and Alisha in the middle of the pack. I knew these hallways—I'd walked them earlier today. But now I was all turned around, and our lights made shadows jump in every doorway.

It was a long hike to the emergency exit. The FPMP building is big, but I suspected the guts of the beast range farther than they should. Jibben directed us to a closet marked Storage—the type of thing you'd expect to be filled with janitorial supplies. And initially, it appeared to be just that. Until Jacob activated the switch Jibben pointed out behind a stack of paper towels, and the back of the closet clicked open to reveal a cinderblock-and-linoleum hallway dotted with regularly-spaced emergency lights that were currently dark. The hall stretched as far as our lantern could see.

"Hold on," I said. "I've never done any rounds down here."

Jibben gave a twitchy shrug. "It would hardly be a secret exit if everyone knew about it."

I looked to Jacob. "Did *you* know?"

"It's the FPMP," he said simply, in a tone that said, *No, but our secrets have secrets—so what did you expect?*

The passage was long. Not sure which direction we were walking, but the basement's top-secret entrails must've passed beneath the highways, or maybe the railroad tracks—several long city blocks, at least.

I might have caught a whiff of mildew. Were we near the river? Or was it just the normal seepage of moisture through concrete? I hate being underground even at the best of times, but we'd been walking so long that I was starting to feel itchy about all that earth pressing in over my head. And when a distant rumble vibrated up through the soles of my feet, I could practically feel the whole thing collapsing—ten tons of sodden cinderblock—and burying us all.

We'd been walking for what felt like hours through the dank, dark cinderblock hall when the silence was shattered... by Aretha Franklin.

"R-E-S-P-E-C—"

Alisha fumbled with her phone, her eyes wide with surprise. "My son." She quickly grabbed the call, cutting off Aretha mid-respect, then answered with a patently unsentimental, "Yeah, what?"

Everyone else whipped out their phone. No bars.

Figures.

"Nothing," Alisha was saying blandly. "Roads are bad, I might be late...or I might not. We'll see. No, I ain't picking you up no McDonald's, there's plenty of food at home. Microwave a burrito."

"He's got power?" Jacob asked.

Alisha held up a finger, listening, then told her kid, "Well then maybe next time you should tell me you ate 'em all *before* I go to the store. Guess you gotta settle for a sandwich. And don't go saying we're out of baloney, 'cause I know for a fact there's a brand new pack nobody even touched yet—" her brow furrowed. "Kelvin? You there? Hello—"

Jacob leaned in and said to me, "If Alisha's house has power, maybe the cannery does, too. This facility must be on a different part of the city's grid than a residential neighborhood."

If it was even on the grid at all. I wouldn't put it past the FPMP to be powered by a giant underground hamster wheel, if that was part of the convoluted contingency plan Con Dreyfus put in place.

Alisha jabbed at her phone in annoyance. "Nothing."

"I don't understand," Jibben said. "Why didn't you tell him you were—"

"I was what? Trapped in some crazy-assed basement somewhere in a secret government building that doesn't even show up on a map?"

Jibben frowned. "No, I guess you wouldn't want to worry him."

"Worry? Kelvin is a teenage boy—he don't worry 'bout nothing but shooting hoops, texting with girls, and feeding his face. Whenever I'm working a Saturday shift, I stop home to check on him. All different times. No warning. Otherwise, he'd get the bright idea to throw a party while I'm gone. He's done it. And I'm not gonna let him get away with it again."

Was that what parenting a teenager was really like? At least there was no local group of friends for Clayton to invite to an impromptu get-together—and no liquor cabinet for him to raid. As for the porn, well...we'd stashed it all last night. And hopefully he had more pressing matters to attend to than going through our closet.

Jacob locked eyes with me as if he'd just read my mind—not necessarily the porn part, just worrying about Clayton in general—then said, "Let's get moving. I'd like to get out of here sometime today."

We slogged along for another good while—where the hell did this hallway let out, Indiana?—when something other than a vast expanse of endless hallway appeared in the beam of our emergency lantern...and we found ourselves at a door.

It was a simple thing. Flat. Industrial. Fitted with the kind of panic bar that didn't even lock from our side. No keypad, no cameras, no nothing. Just a door.

But it was a steel door—and all of us had Darnell's encounter with the metal door frame fresh in our minds. If Jibben had been able to stand on his own, I would have thought up some reason for him to be the one to try and open it. It was his lab after all. His door. But he couldn't even stand unassisted, and we couldn't expect the one civilian to do it, which left Jacob...or me.

"Jacob," I said—and when he looked at me, it was obvious there was no way in hell he was about to let me anywhere near it. "At least, uh, open it with the chair so you're not touching anything."

Alisha and I lowered Jibben to the floor, I held up the lamp, and Jacob wasted no time in plowing toward the door like a charging bull. I must have expected it to be locked. Given the day we'd had, everyone else was probably thinking the same thing. So we were all stunned when the chair hit the panic bar, and the door flew open wide.

On the other side was a small landing...and a set of stairs going up.

But the best thing about it? The lights were actually on.

We had power.

Jacob forged right ahead...or, at least, he tried. But Jibben had toppled forward to grab him by the cargo shorts—and that guy had one hell of a grip. "Agent, wait! Over there by the stairs—!"

I angled the lamp, and sure enough, in the shadow of the stairwell, a rope of insulated cable was dangling from an electrical panel with its access door hanging slightly askew.

Scary? Sure. Especially with Darnell's death fresh in my mind. But the landing was wide enough. Surely we were all capable of giving the dangling cable a wide enough berth and make our way up the—

Alisha aimed her flashlight app at the floor, which bounced the light like a mirror.

Sonofabitch. The floor wasn't just damp—it was covered in water, as deep as the safety door threshold. A good inch. Maybe more. And the frayed end of the cable?

Just skimming the water's surface.

CHAPTER 11

There was no spark coming from the end of the cable. No tell-tale crackling sound, no light show. But all of us were staring at that damn thing like we'd just found a turd floating in the punch bowl. Eventually Jibben spoke, because the guy just couldn't keep his mouth shut. "Pure water isn't conductive," he said in his know-it-all tone. "But the minerals suspended in it certainly can be. And this water has probably leached plenty of minerals from the concrete. Besides, it's not as if any of us are capable of walking across the surface itself—"

I cut him off. "No one was thinking of stomping through that puddle."

"But maybe we can jump," Alisha said. I eyeballed the distance from the threshold to the stairs.

"It would be some jump," I said. I do have a long stride. If circumstances were different—and if no one was watching me—I might even attempt it. But when failure meant death, I wasn't about to put my jumping skills to the test. "Besides," I glanced down at Jibben. "Not all of us can even walk. We need to stick together."

The only one who hadn't weighed in was Jacob. Which was odd. He tends to have an opinion, and that's putting it lightly.

He was just staring at that hanging cable, though, as if it held some sort of secret he might unlock, if he just tried hard enough.

"Jacob," I said, "it's not worth the risk. Right?"

Reluctantly, he cut his eyes to me. "Agreed. If no one's got any phone signal, it's best to get back to the lab."

"To containment," Jibben amended. "So many unauthorized people. And all of our environmental controls down. It's the best place to be to make sure your electromagnetic fields don't contaminate anything."

The scientists around here were obsessed with their work. I got it. But I was more concerned about staying alive than preserving their precious experiments.

Still, the containment room probably was our best bet. I might not give a rat's ass about contaminating any psychic experiments, but I sure as hell didn't want any of them contaminating me.

We trooped back up the long dark hall. Containment was exactly as we left it, with a bunch of haphazard crates piled in the middle. I said, "I'll grab some chairs from the break room so we're not just sitting on the floor."

"And food," Jibben said, "bring all the food you can find. We need to assess our situation and catalog our resources. We don't know how long we're going to be here, so we'll need to take stock."

I fully expected the power to come up any minute now, or at the very least, be found by a rescue crew. He made it sound like we were heading into a Donner party situation.

"I'll get the chairs," I said blandly, and headed for the door. "Come on, Jacob. I could use a hand."

And I could use some moral support. The lab was creepy enough on a good day. Walking through the darkened halls by the light of my flashlight gave *me* the heebie-jeebies. Still, I knew the layout well enough to get to the break room without stumbling into any mysterious and uncontained psychic experiments. And it was a relief to finally be alone with Jacob.

The break room looked ransacked, with its couch cushions missing and a chair knocked askew. But when I opened the refrigerator door, at least all the contents were still cold. So hopefully, right down the hall, Jennifer Chance's body wasn't thawing too rapidly, either, and Jacob's worst nightmare of wrangling her thrashing corpse wouldn't come true...again.

Should I break the news that the body was back—or wait until we were far enough away from it that he wouldn't have to freak out? I cut a glance in his direction, realizing he was still awfully quiet, and found him staring at the plug of the coffee maker.

"Okay," I said, "you wanna tell me what's going on?"

He sighed. "You saw that electrical cable."

"I did."

"It was just touching the surface of the water. Barely even skimming it."

"Yeah...."

"Well, that's exactly the type of situation telekinetics were bred for. Land mines, bomb triggers, anything too volatile to touch—"

"Whoa, hold on, mister. Are you saying you thought you should have been able to move the wire out of the way *with your mind?* You are, aren't you? I'll have you know, the strongest telekinetic I've ever encountered got a nosebleed from sliding a freaking penny across the table. Besides, that's not how your abilities work, and you know it. If there was a habit demon floating around in the water, then yeah, I'd expect you to step up to the plate. But there wasn't a damn thing you could have done different."

Jacob clenched his jaw and looked away.

"Look," I said, "I know it's killing you to not be able to do much of anything right now. But we all saw what happened to Darnell when he tried to play the hero. So the safest thing to do is just hunker down and wait."

"Is it?" he asked. "What if no one knows we're down here? Most of the staff is out in Nantucket. And Laura Kim is probably stuck on the expressway in bumper-to-bumper traffic. Is it really safe for us in the lab? We don't know what they're working on—and we don't know what it would mean if any of their safety devices lost power. Besides, someone needs to let rescue workers know where we are."

"That someone being you," I said dryly.

"There's got to be a way to get through that safety glass. It's resin, right? This is a lab. I'm sure there's a tool here capable of cutting through it. We'll cut through the glass, and I can climb up into the elevator—"

"Are you serious, Jacob?"

"There's a hatch in the ceiling. I can make my way up the shaft—"

"That's an even shittier plan than jumping over the electrified puddle. We're at least three stories underground, so even a stuntman would think twice about making that climb. Plus, the entire shaft is made of metal, so another lightning strike could fry you. I know that sitting on your hands is making you nuts. But seriously, I'd never in a million years let you risk your neck like that." I turned Jacob to face me, pulled us both together, and carded my fingers through his hair. "Got it?"

With a long sigh, Jacob pressed his forehead to mine. "You're right. I know you are. I just need to do *something*."

"Sometimes there's nothing to be done." Yeah, it was definitely for the best that he didn't know about the body.

I held Jacob for a moment, wishing there was any way at all for me to make him feel better. Watching someone you love suffer is so much worse than suffering yourself. But if there's any way to ease the burden by taking on someone else's pain, I've never figured it out.

"What's really eating you?" I said softly.

Jacob turned away. "I keep looping back to the sight of Agent Thompson lying there on the floor with his eyes half-open. And me, hoping he was just unconscious...but then seeing the look on your face, knowing you'd *seen* something... and realizing he was never getting up again."

"It's just his repeater," I said. "He's not haunting us."

"That's not it." Jacob huffed in frustration. "The last thing I said to him...I was such an asshole. And now there's no way to make it right."

"Sometimes, when you do what you gotta do, you make some enemies." Jacob had been a cop even longer than I had, so that should come as no surprise to him. But it was the only comfort I could offer.

"I didn't have to take that tone. I was the ranking agent. Full stop. He would have respected my authority. No reason for me to act like a dick."

"You were stressed. We all were."

Jacob shook his head. "I was being reactive. And the worst part? It wasn't even Agent Thompson I was reacting to. It was Barbara."

Oh boy.

"If only I'd stood up to her last night—if only I'd told her not to loop us into this standoff she was having with Clayton—"

"Stop." I stepped in front of Jacob again and took him by the shoulders. "Just...don't. You can't change your sister any more than you can change the weather—and good luck trying to control either one. Second-guessing the choices you made won't help us now."

I pressed a kiss to his temple, hoping to drive my point home. That I loved him. That I supported him. And that I sure as hell wasn't gonna let him blame himself for Clayton being stuck at the cannery alone.

People have certain smells to them, and the scent of his hair—which was the smell of his pillow, our bed, the cannery, us—made me realize exactly how much I'd come to rely on him. Maybe, before, I'd been ticked off at him for checking up on me. But now I wasn't just okay with the decision he'd made earlier today to ride that shuttle back to HQ. I was beyond relieved he'd done it.

I nudged Jacob's jaw. He put up a token resistance, but eventually he let me turn his head so my kiss skimmed along his cheekbone. He angled his mouth toward mine, and my lips found his.

And kissing him was like coming home.

Tension drained from both of us as we sank into the kiss. Such a simple thing—something we'd done a million times before. But the kiss was a powerful reminder that the two of us were solid. A true partnership. So much stronger together than either of us could ever be on our own.

The kiss deepened. I cupped his face while his hands found their way to my hips, pulling me closer as we lost ourselves in the moment. It was oddly poignant finding comfort in Jacob, yet not knowing when we'd manage to get back to the cannery...and if it would even be standing by the time we got there.

Time went funny in that way it sometimes does, and the stolen moment felt both extravagantly long and pitifully short. I was debating whether I should let myself linger with my husband for just a few more seconds...when the sound of distant squabbling made us jerk apart.

"Get back here! You are *not* authorized to leave containment—"

"Keep your pants on—I said I would just be a minute!"

Jacob and I locked eyes, then hustled back to see what the problem was now.

We found Jibben one-leg scooting his way down the hall, on his office chair, in the dark. Up ahead and around a corner, light shone—the big emergency lantern, judging by the size of the glow.

"This is a nightmare," Jibben sputtered. "While the two of you were gone, the civilian decided to go on a treasure hunt!"

I told him, "Calm down, there's nothing to see but a bunch of dark, empty rooms with blank monitors. And even if she did glance in, it's not like she'd even know what any of the equipment was." I *traipsed* through there all the time, and I sure as hell had no clue what they were doing.

"She's got a phone," Jibben whispered. "In other words, a camera. If she were to document the lab, do you know what she'd get for those photos on the black market?"

Alisha had expressed zero interest in the workings of the lab, so I doubted any scientific espionage was taking place. But I jogged out to see what she was up to, anyhow, figuring she probably just had to use the can.

I followed the light—but soon discovered Alisha wasn't going through anyone's office. Instead, she stood there in the lobby, with a jumble of couch cushions at her feet and Jacob's box of granola bars in her hand. She'd gone still, staring out through the safety glass, transfixed at the sight of Darnell's body out in the elevator bay.

When I paused beside her, she said, "I almost didn't take a shift today. But someone called in sick, and my son wants a new gaming computer—have you seen how much those things cost?—so I said, sure. I'll cover it." She shook her head sadly. "Maybe if I hadn't, Darnell would still be alive. If it was just the folks who work here trapped inside, maybe he wouldn't have been so hell-bent on busting down that door. Maybe he would've just let y'all wait this whole thing out."

I shook my head. "I think Darnell would've gone into rescue mode for anyone. That's just the kind of person he was." Mind you, I hadn't known the guy since we were both seven. But given the amount of guilt everyone was wallowing in, I figured it was something she needed to hear.

Alisha finally tore her gaze away from Darnell's body and spared me a wistful smile. She shook the box of granola bars at me and said, "You might wanna take some now. That twitchy guy's gonna start rationing soon."

If Jibben were a normal person, I would've assured her it wouldn't come to that. But given what a control freak he was, Alisha might've been onto something. I stashed one in my jacket and she shoved a couple in her pocket, then we gathered up the couch cushions and headed back to containment.

"You can't possibly be serious," Jacob was in the midst of saying.

Alisha gave me a meaningful glance as if to say, *This oughta be good.*

We found Jacob beside Jibben at one of the stainless steel lab tables with the formerly frozen lasagna between them. Jibben was scrawling stuff on a clipboard. "The meal contains 320 calories. The average man needs 2500 calories a day, but the average woman only needs 2000. And with your frame, you probably need more. So if we divide it off-center—"

"I'm not eating something that was strapped to your leg," I said. Those things were so small, a quarter of a lasagna would barely be a mouthful, anyhow.

Jibben said, "If you don't consume your share of the calories, your cognitive abilities might be compromised."

"Fine, I'll eat a granola bar." I snatched one out of the box.

"Not *now*," Jibben said in horror. "We need to take a thorough inventory first."

"No one needs to do inventory," I said. "Even if it took them 'till tomorrow to dig us out—"

What I'd intended to say was that I doubted anyone would starve. But Alisha grabbed my arm and said, "You think we're gonna be here all night?"

I already regretted saying anything at all. "Worst case scenario."

Jibben "helpfully" added, "Actually, there's no telling how long it'll be."

"Storms don't last forever," Jacob said—thankfully, he'd recovered his uber-calm "everything's fine" voice. And the sound of it made me feel better, even though I knew it was total bullshit. "Maybe we can't see or hear what's going on from down here, but when the larger strikes hit, we felt them. We haven't felt any rumbling for a while, though. So it stands to reason—"

I think whatever Jacob was planning to say might've been a pretty good closing argument, had Jibben's pen not chosen that particular moment to roll slowly across the countertop of its own accord....

And clatter to the floor.

CHAPTER 12

"Did that pen just move by itself?" Alisha demanded.

"Of course not," Jibben said. "In all likelihood, another lightning strike created a faint vibration that propelled it. Something too subtle for us to feel that was amplified by the stainless steel table. If any of us had been touching the table at the time—"

"Okay, fine, Mr. Wizard," I said, already annoyed. Maybe I was getting hangry. "We got it. No self-moving pens."

But Alisha wasn't convinced. She backed away from the pen as if it might jump up and bite her...then jerked around, looking at the floor in accusation. "What the hell?"

I shone my flashlight down where she was looking and saw a long, murky puddle snaking out from one of the crates.

"Step aside," I told her.

"What is that?" Jacob asked.

But Jibben didn't know. "I'd have to check the manifest."

Jacob locked eyes with me and said, "It could be anything." Meaning, it's probably something *really* messed up. "And Alisha stepped in it. We need to get the boots off her."

Those office chairs we'd retrieved were coming in awfully handy. Alisha sat herself down and immediately got to shucking off her steel-toed work boots. No clue what she'd stepped into, but at least she wasn't wearing flip-flops.

Gingerly, I picked up the boots and set them aside well away from the rest of us. Then, as Jibben flipped furiously through the manifest to try and identify what could possibly leak, Jacob crouched down beside the puddle.

I said, "Don't you dare even *think* of touching it, mister."

There must have been something in my tone. Alisha looked at me sharply. "You two know each other pretty good?"

"Oh, you could say that."

I flashed her my wedding band, and understanding dawned. "Okay," she said, as if the situation had only just now progressed into super weird territory.

"This is bad," Jibben said. "Very bad."

"Am I gonna lose my foot?" Alisha cried.

Jibben waved it off. "I'm sure your foot is fine. But if we can't contain whatever's leaking out of there, it will evaporate before we have a chance to study it! That crate needs to be unboxed, ASAP."

The rest of us looked at him like he was nuts.

"Fine. I'll do it myself." He one-foot-wheeled himself over to a cabinet and pulled out a white plastic packet the size of a small throw pillow and shoved one toward each of us. "But if we're going to expose the artifacts, we'll all need to suit up so you don't contaminate them."

The packet contained a single-use hazmat suit. Not that I'm any kind of fashion plate, but normally, I'd tell him where he could shove his white plastic outfit. But since they would likely protect us as much as they did the so-called "artifacts," I figured I should probably swallow my pride and don the jumpsuit.

Jacob seemed even less thrilled with the prospect of wearing a clean suit than I was. At least there were protective booties included, so Alisha didn't have to go around in just her socks.

I fully intended to sit this one out. But when Jibben wheeled over to the crate and started struggling with it, he was so pathetic I couldn't help but go over there and put him out of his misery.

"Here," I said, "hold it steady." Our crowbar would have been helpful, but given that it was lying out there next to Darnell's dead body, I didn't point that out. But we were able to dredge up some basic tools from one of the cabinets—a box cutter, a small pry bar, a screwdriver—and get to work.

Soon, it was pretty obvious that Jibben was just in the way. I was none too eager to pop open that crate myself and be sprayed with mysterious fifty-year-old fluid. But at least I could get out of the way quicker without tripping over him.

"Go read the manifest," I said. "We got this."

He wheeled himself back to the table and took up the manifest. Meanwhile, Jacob eased up to me and met my eyes. Speaking low, he said, "There could be anything in here."

"But it's the Argus Institute," I said, semi-hopefully. "Probably nothing worse than a broken fish tank." Because it would have been totally normal for someone to pack a fish tank, complete with water.

Jacob quirked an eyebrow, but didn't indulge in any snappy comebacks.

We futzed with it for a while, but the seams on the crate were tight. I was about to suggest searching for a sledgehammer when finally, Jacob managed to wiggle the screwdriver into a crack. With a loud creak, the side of the crate popped open.

Jacob and I held our breath as we peered inside, and Alisha hurried over to hold the light—probably more out of curiosity than any desire to help. At first, it looked like a jumble of junk inside—a few rusted tools, some ancient wiring, and what looked like a broken radio. "Be careful," Jacob said. "If there's a leaking battery, it could be acid."

I lifted out a box vaguely marked as "Samples," and then a stunningly old computer (that probably cost more than my car, back in the day) that I set carefully aside. There were dozens of boxes of floppy discs, a lot lighter than I expected, and a weirdly shaped desk fan with no power cord, an overlong neck, and too many fan blades. Eventually, when we got to the bottom....

"It *is* a fish tank," I said. You can't make this shit up.

"Not a fish tank." Jibben wheeled over to see for himself. "According to the manifest, it's a Saline Transference Environment."

"So, a *saltwater* fish tank," Alisha said.

Loftily, Jibben said, "Don't be ridiculous. Dr. Hinman theorized that a saline environment could amplify the range and dynamics of telekinetic ability."

"Dr. Hinman?" Alisha repeated. "You mean the old white dude with the crazy sideburns?"

Jibben was surprised. "You've heard of him?"

"Everyone's heard of him. He was on every other episode

of Psychic Mysteries." She frowned. "Okay, maybe more like once or twice a season. But those sideburns...." She shuddered dramatically.

Jibben twitched, too—and then Jacob got in on the act, chafing the back of his neck.

Apparently the heebie-jeebies were contagious. Kind of like yawning.

"So, what about the puddle?" I asked.

Jibben scrounged a swab from one of the cabinets. "Obviously, I can't run it through a spectrometer without any power." He swabbed and gave it a sniff. "But I suspect it's just saline—tainted with five decades of corrosion. But bag it up, all the same, I'll need to run it through several tests—and it's evaporating even as we speak."

Even with half the juice leaked out, the tank was still pretty heavy—plus, neither Jacob nor I was eager to spill something on ourselves that turned out to be full of hungry flesh-eating 70's nanobots...or, more likely, dysentery.

Once we wrangled it into a giant plastic bag and sealed it up tight, Jibben said defensively, "Dr. Hinman's public appearances were a necessary evil. TV paid well for the right experts, and there was no government funding for this type of research."

I dunno about that. Uncle Sam probably had Dr. Kamal and his crew on the payroll—not that there'd be any paper trail left behind to prove it.

Jibben went on. "Dr. Hinman was a true pioneer, mark my words. Interviews can be spliced to say whatever the media wants them to say. So take anything you've seen on those garbage documentary shows with a hefty grain of salt."

"I *like* those garbage documentary shows." Alisha crossed her arms in annoyance and turned away from him, and her gaze fell on the goofy fan. "Hold up, now. Is this the…whaddayacallit? Wait, don't say. It'll come to me."

"I highly doubt it," Jibben said.

Alisha swung the full force of the emergency lantern at the fan. "It will. I seen it before. In the episode where they were trying to see if that spoon-bending guy was legit. He showed how it was supposed to move when it picked up on psychic shit going on." She snapped her fingers a few times, then looked back at Jibben triumphantly. "Rotational Indicator. See? Not so garbage now."

Huh. It all looked like a big pile of junk to me. Clearly, I needed to watch more TV.

The cupboards in containment were as well stocked as the rest of the lab—since lack of government funding was no longer an issue like it was in Hinman's time. We were able to soak up the leaked fluid with a weird gelatinous sheet, which we then tucked away in yet another bag. It was a lot like collecting evidence. And while the Chicago PD left it to the experts to run through a crime scene with a fine-toothed comb, I was versed enough in collection basics, in case I arrived at a scene full of transient evidence and had to grab what I could before something important was lost.

I thought we did a pretty good job with the cleanup, but Jibben wasn't satisfied. "Who knows what else might've been damaged when the shipment fell." When *he* pulled it over monkeying around with it, to be precise. "We need to inventory the whole crate."

"We need to get out of here," Jacob said.

But since his plan for getting out of there involved spelunking in an electrified elevator shaft, I had to side with the annoying scientist. It was a prime opportunity to give Jacob something to do—something that didn't require a resin cutter, a safety harness, and a frantic Hail Mary—so I gave Jibben's plan my vote. "We all decided we would stay put. So we might as well keep ourselves busy."

We got to work taking inventory of the crate, using the manifest to identify the items we pulled out. We proceeded carefully, careful to document each item and its condition. There were no more specialized gizmos that made an appearance on a sensationalistic pre-Ganzfeld-Report TV show. Just stacks of file folders and ledgers crammed with yellowed papers, and a bunch of archaic phones from a putty-colored multi-line office phone system that was doubtlessly ultramodern at the time.

I've heard most kids these days who grew up with cellphones are incapable of operating an actual telephone... though maybe that's just rotary. Would Clayton take it into his head to start monkeying around with our landline? And wasn't it possible for lightning to travel through the wires?

Normally, I would have thought that notion was beyond paranoid. But after watching what happened when a strike traveled through a steel doorframe and a crowbar, I wasn't so sure anymore. The thought of finding the kid sprawled on the kitchen floor, staring up at the ceiling with half his face blackened was enough to make me hope that porn was the only thing he snooped into.

Generally, Clayton was a fairly incurious kid, and was happy enough to sit and play Xbox while the grownups did grownup things. So hopefully he wasn't overcome by the sudden urge to master a new phone.

Unless he thought it might get through to us when his cell phone didn't.

I pulled out my cell and thumbed in a message. *We're running late. Just hang tight.* Not that I thought he'd actually receive it. But the call from Alisha's kid came through, so you never know. A gap in the clouds might align just right and let my tiny, inadequate text wing its way to the cannery.

Unfortunately, constantly searching for a signal that didn't exist was doing a real number on my battery—and I hadn't even been using the flashlight app. I'd started the day fully charged but was already more than halfway down.

Alisha, meanwhile, was thumbing through one of the binders from the crate when a photo slipped out and fluttered to the floor. She picked it up and turned it this way and that. "Look at these old farts," she chuckled, holding the photo out for me to see.

I caught a glance of very 70's looking middle-aged guys in stark white lab coats and oversized safety goggles.

But before I could take a closer look, Jibben rocketed over on his office chair and snatched the picture from her hands. "This is classified information," he huffed, as he crammed the photograph back into the binder. "Not TV Guide."

She said, "How can it be classified if it's all on Psychic Mysteries for everyone to see?"

Jibben held the binder close, wheeling backwards with one foot as if he thought Alisha might fight him for it. "Dr. Hinman did important work. Historically significant work. Never mistake it for a trashy, sensationalist documentary designed for mass consumption."

Alisha turned to Jacob. "You're in charge. You gonna let him talk to me like that?"

"Look, both of you. We're all in this together, and it's important we treat each other respectfully and work like a team."

"Fine," said Jibben. "Then use that teamwork to put everything back in the crate. And, respectfully...try not to break anything."

CHAPTER 13

Repacking the box we'd just unpacked was nothing short of busywork. But if it kept Jacob from crawling out of his own skin, I was all for it. We packed the boxes of floppy disks first, since they formed a pretty good base. And then we carefully stacked in the remaining office equipment and other random crap.

We were getting to the last oddball, weirdly shaped things when Alisha announced, "I gotta pee."

"You can't just go gallivanting around the lab alone," Jibben said, "it's a security risk."

"Gallivanting?" she said. I supposed it was even worse than *traipsing*.

"I'll take her," I said, since I was eager to put a little distance between Jibben and me before I said anything I'd regret.

Alisha and I stepped out into the hall and I switched on my pocket flashlight, and the beam flickered a couple of times before it went solid. No doubt there were fresh batteries around here somewhere. Though finding them would be another matter.

We made our way up the hall, and Alisha broke the silence with, "So...you and Cargo Shorts are married, huh?"

"For the record, coming into work today wasn't on his agenda. He'd normally be wearing a suit."

"He's fine. For a white guy."

"Yeah. I think so, too."

By the time we reached the restroom, a small and unassuming unisex deal, my flashlight was still holding steady, but thanks to that flicker, I didn't trust it now. So I switched to my phone.

"Pee fast," I said, "or else we'll end up in the dark."

Alisha hurried into the can to do her business while I considered my phone. The icon for the app I normally used to calm down, a kids' game called Mood Blaster, beckoned to me from my first screen. But it needed earbuds to work, and my earbuds were back in the car. Probably for the best, given the fact that my battery was now draining faster than our shower after a good solid session with the plunger.

Once Alisha finished her business, we headed back to containment, where the last few electronics were lined up on the table while Jacob puzzled out how to best fit them into the crate. I picked up the emergency lantern to check out the various ports and connections on its side, throwing shadows around the room as I turned it in my hands. "This thing is a power bank, right? I need to charge my phone."

Jibben wheeled over and snatched it from my hands. "Do you? There's only so much charge here, you know. And this lantern puts out more lumens than your phone for a longer amount of time. We don't know how long we'll be trapped down here, after all."

Alisha made a small sound of distress.

Jibben went on, "And with the repeater offline, it's not as if you're going to get a signal anyway. We're best off shutting down our phones completely and conserving whatever charge is left."

While all of that was technically true, powering down my phone made the whole situation seem awfully grim. But I did shut down, and the others did the same.

Jibben said, "In fact, we need to start rationing more than just the power—to catalog everything we could possibly use and see what we're working with."

As he paused for a breath, my stomach chose that moment to interject with a long, low rumble.

Jibben said, "We'll start with the food."

Leaving the last of the electronics scattered around containment, the four of us trooped off to the break room, where Alisha flopped down on the cushionless couch. She said, "I don't see why we can't stay in here. It's a lot more like a real room."

"You're absolutely right," Jibben said. "Containment isn't just any old room. It's special. It's shielded. So it's exactly where we need to be...just as soon as we gather our resources."

In terms of so-called "resources," the fridge was slim pickings. Two bottles of salad dressing—Italian and ranch, both low-fat. Two creamers: one half & half, one soy. Three cans of diet pop. A piece of individually wrapped string cheese. A nearly empty bag of hazelnut coffee. Half a jar of pickles. And a container of hummus with a sticky note on it that said, *Toss this and I will hunt you down and kill you. Love, Patty.*

Jibben shook his head. "We clean it out on Fridays. It was

practically overflowing yesterday."

"Great," I said. "Good to know. Now, give me my pickle."

"This counts against your share."

"Fine."

"And it'll offer you precious little by way of calories. No protein, no fat—"

I reached around him and screwed off the lid. "If it fills my gut, that's all I care about."

"But the average adult male requires 0.8 grams of protein per kilogram of body weight—"

As if I even knew what a kilogram was...let alone how many grams of protein were not in that pickle. I just knew that the longer we talked about rationing our food, the more I was kicking myself for scarfing down a breakfast that consisted of nothing but a strong cup of joe and a random hamburger bun.

Jibben said, "Too bad the microscopy lab is magnetically locked. The agar culture plates are edible, technically. They'd at least provide a feeling of satiety."

I didn't plan on being stuck down there long enough to start chewing on the lab supplies, thank you very much. As I crunched down on a fairly unsatisfying pickle, Jacob wheeled in the delivery cart so we could raid the supply closet and take it all back with us. I was fairly sure we wouldn't have any use for the emergency foil blanket or the spare lightbulbs. But better safe than sorry.

We did manage to come up with a few helpful things, though. Bottled water, duct tape, a small first aid kit. But very little by way of batteries that would fit my flashlight, other than the ones we managed to pull from a TV remote.

With the remaining break room chairs and couch cushions

in tow, we headed back to containment. Jibben immediately started divvying up the food. "We need to take our individual dietary needs into account. Preferences?" he asked. "Particular aversions—"

I eyed him dubiously. "I'll eat whatever."

Jacob added, "This level of micromanaging really isn't necessary."

But Jibben was in his element. He gave the remaining half-jar of pickles a shake. "High sodium, but some of us might need to replenish our electrolytes soon enough. You can have one more pickle, Agent Bayne." I reached towards the jar. "One."

"I'll try not to eat it all in one place."

Jacob got a packet of something snacky and Asian—maybe wasabi peanuts, though it was hard to say, as the writing was most definitely not in English. Alisha got the string cheese. The hummus and salad dressing were divided among us all. I silently apologized to "Patty." I hoped that wherever she was, she could find it in her heart to forgive us for confiscating her hummus.

"Any vegans among us? No? Good. Then this creamer is for everyone." Jibben rationed it out evenly among small plastic specimen cups, then counted out a granola bar for each of us from the open box. There were originally eight inside— Alisha and I had taken three—and my hoarded granola bar sat heavy against my chest as Jibben got to the last bar and puzzled over what to do with it.

"The hummus, granola and pickles should keep," Jibben said, "so I recommend you all start with the perishables. The lasagna shouldn't spoil right away—it's phenomenally processed—but it may start getting rubbery around the edges. And the creamer is already warm." With that, he slurped down his hunk of room-temperature lasagna and followed it with a half-and-half chaser.

Miraculously, he didn't even shudder. Though I did.

Jacob eased up beside me and said, "Did you want my lasagna?"

"No thanks. I'll pass."

But Alisha had zero qualms. "If you're not gonna eat it, I'll take it."

Jacob and I both slid our portions her way, while Jibben grumbled about the fact that redistributing our food put a serious dent in his carefully orchestrated plan to keep us all fed.

With nothing else important to do, we ate. And while I can't recommend half & half without any coffee, the combination of pickles and hummus was surprisingly okay.

As I scraped up the last bit of garlicky chickpea paste with the pointy stump of the pickle slice, Alisha announced, "I gotta pee."

Again? It had only been maybe an hour. Though with Jibben waxing eloquent about dietary requirements, it seemed like a lot longer—and I was eager enough to get away from all those meaningless numbers.

"We'd better hustle," I told her. "I dunno how much longer my flashlight is good for."

We hurried back to the restroom, where Alisha paused outside the door and said, "Are you gonna eat that granola bar I gave you back in the lobby?"

I could've pointed out that it wasn't communal food, since

it had originally come from the trunk of *my* car, but I was in no mood to split hairs. "Maybe."

"'Cause I thought I'd be home by now, and I didn't eat breakfast...."

"Fine." I'd felt guilty for not offering the thing up for inventory anyhow. I dug it out from under my hazmat suit and handed it over. "But hurry up and pee before the flashlight goes kaput."

Alisha went into the bathroom and immediately turned on the taps full-blast. Because she was worried I'd hear her peeing? Or eating? Or...who knows. Maybe she had to take a dump and didn't want the sound to carry.

In terms of the water, though, was electricity required to keep it flowing, or was it more of a gravity thing? I didn't know if there was a pump involved, or if it was just forced through the pipes by municipal water pressure.

Maybe there was a secret storage tank somewhere in the building—I wouldn't put it past Con Dreyfuss to have something like that installed. If so, there'd probably be more than enough water for four people—even if someone insisted on running the tap the whole time they were in the can. Though if someone were to sabotage the FPMP, tainting the secret water tank would be a pretty good way to go about it—

Alisha yanked open the bathroom door. "Let's get back before your light goes out."

Multiple bathroom trips, running water. Was she being weird? I didn't know her well enough to say. And if she had a stomach issue going on—or, god forbid, her period—then I really didn't need to know.

Still, the perfect time to sabotage the building was when it was running on a skeleton crew.

As we turned the final corner leading back to containment, we were greeted by raised voices. Jibben was saying, "—just because you're uncomfortable is no reason to break protocol. If anyone should play by the book, it's the ranking agent on scene."

Inside, we found Jacob standing with his clean room suit open to the waist, hands on hips, looking sweaty. "You said yourself the room is shielded—and we've all handled the shipment by now. What more do you possibly think we're going to contaminate?"

Jibben swung around to look at us. "What with all this to-ing and fro-ing—" He'd been gesturing to make a point, and ended up backing into one of the steel tables where a 1970s Rolodex from Argus Institute rattled and nearly toppled off the table.

It *was* getting awfully stuffy in there, but flailing around and arguing wasn't going to make it any cooler. And it would be a shame if we managed to screw up the shipment we'd gone through so much trouble to preserve. "We'll keep the suits on," I said, "for now. But if we start running out of air...."

I'd been exaggerating, obviously. So I was none too comforted when Jibben said, "We'll cross that bridge when we come to it."

Well, shit. Water pressure might not depend on electricity, but the ventilation system did. I glanced up at a grate in the ceiling as if glaring at it might make a wisp of air come out. I couldn't feel anything. Although...the blade of the weird fan-looking piece of equipment beside me was spinning in a lazy rotation. So who knows, maybe some other part of the building had power and was pumping breathable oxygen our way.

And if it wasn't...hopefully Jibben wouldn't start trying to ration the air.

CHAPTER 14

Our meal was meager by anyone's standards, but at least it gave us something to do besides sit around and stare at each other by the light of the emergency lamp. Which was exactly what we'd been doing for the past five minutes...and which, naturally, seemed easily like five hours.

Alisha said, "We need to do something to pass the time. Let's play a game."

Jacob has a competitive streak a mile wide. You know he's in a bad headspace when he doesn't jump up and start picking teams, calling dibs on the red piece, and planning out his victory dance.

"What game?" I said, since no one else did.

Alisha surveyed the room. "We got paper. We got a pen. How about tic-tac-toe?"

"What's the point?" Jibben said. "The optimal first move is the center square. And once that's taken, there are only eight possible moves left. Ultimately, the best you can hope for is a draw."

Alisha rolled her eyes. "Okay, then, smart guy. What kinda

game can *you* make with nothing but a few pieces of paper?"

"Chess, obviously."

Obviously.

Jibben shuffled a blank sheet to the top of the clipboard, then folded another into an impromptu ruler to create an exacting grid. Where were these MacGyver skills back when we stood some chance of actually getting out of here on our own? "Unfortunately, my drawing leaves something to be desired. Does anyone else care to draw out the pieces? No one? Well, that's fine, I'll just write the names of each piece on a square of paper. And I'll differentiate the black from the white with either a circle or a box...."

I found myself wishing someone had suggested making our own chess set sooner. Jibben was not nearly as annoying when he was putting the thing together. But, all good things must come to an end, and as he jotted down the final square pawn, he said, "We can play tournament-style. Anyone care to go first?"

If there'd been a cricket in containment...it would've been chirping.

"Don't be shy," Jibben said. "We can draw lots if that seems more fair."

"Actually, I don't play," I admitted. Too much paying attention involved for my taste, not to mention too many goofy rules.

Alisha said, "Neither do I."

We all looked to Jacob. "Never did pick it up," he said.

Jibben was affronted. "Seriously? None of you? You could've said something before I wasted all that paper. We might end up needing it—"

"What for?" Alisha said. "Writing all the help messages in the world won't do us any good if the paper's stuck right down here *with* us."

Jibben considered. "Maybe not...but we could jot something down and tape them up by the security cams for when the power comes back online." He turned over his "chessboard" and wrote, S.O.S - 4 TRAPPED - LAB on the back, then repeated it with three other pages.

He handed the stack and a roll of duct tape to me, saying, "Aside from me, you're the only one who's familiar with the layout. Hang them in different locations so they have a better chance of being seen."

I cocked my head for Jacob to join me. "C'mon. I need you to hold my tape."

We went toward Dr. K's office first, figuring the most prominent camera would be aimed there. Sure enough, we found a fish-eye mount just outside his locked door. "Tape," I said, holding out a hand like we were doing surgery. I kept my tone light. Playful, for me—though you'd probably only get that if you knew me phenomenally well.

Jacob knew me better than anyone in the world. And even so, the pensive crease between his eyebrows didn't ease in the slightest as he tore off a piece.

"Gotta admit," I said, "I had you pegged for a chess master. So, you don't play at all? Or you just didn't want to play with Dr. Spreadsheet?"

As Jacob stuck the tape-square to my finger, the corner of his mouth twitched, and the eyebrow crease smoothed out some. "No, I just never got into it."

"Huh. Chess club seems like it'd be right up your alley. All that strategic mental flexing, not to mention trouncing your opponents in a socially acceptable public setting."

"Chess club met the same time as wrestling, so...."

Ah, that made more sense. Just as much competition—but more skimpily-clad teenager eye candy. Not to mention all the male grappling.

"Pardon the pun," I said, "but back in containment, you seemed kind of off your game."

Jacob tore off another hunk of tape and smoothed it across the bottom edge of our S.O.S. "I don't know if it's the lack of ventilation, lack of food, or the stress of the whole situation. I've got this nagging headache that just won't quit."

"Then don't be a hero. Raid the first aid kit and find some aspirin."

We stuck another sign up by the camera at the main inter-section between the research area and the offices, one by the break room, and then, finally, headed toward the entrance.

My flashlight beam was steady now, and I kind of wished it wasn't, as it illuminated the body of my old classmate still sprawled on the floor on the other side of the safety glass... and his repeater getting blown back from the door. I'd won-dered if the repeater might have faded a bit over the past few hours, but it looked the same as it had when it first jolted out of Darnell's physical form. Repeaters don't fade easily, not without intervention, and I've got no idea what their normal half-life might be.

Jacob eased up to the door and placed a hand on the glass. "Don't risk it," I said. "Supposedly lightning can't strike twice, but why tempt fate?"

Jacob let his hand drop. He was scowling hard again, I saw...

no doubt searching for that repeater.

"Not great for your headache," I warned.

"No, it's okay. It's easing up. I just needed to get up and walk around."

I slapped up the final S.O.S. in plain view of the lobby cam and turned to go, but Jacob didn't follow my lead. Sighing, I turned back and planted myself beside him.

Eventually, he said, "What do you think Clayton is doing right now?"

"In all likelihood...same as us, scavenging up a meal. But look at it this way: we've been meaning to clean out the cupboards for a while now and never got around to it."

"I should never have left—"

"Come on," I said gently, and slipped an arm around his waist and bumped our hips together. "First of all, he's probably got power. I can't imagine a city the size of Chicago would be totally down from one end to the other. And, second...neither one of us is even remotely motivated enough to clean out our fridge every Friday. Clayton might have to gnaw through some incredibly stale bagels, but he's not gonna starve."

While Jacob pondered that, I double-checked the position of my note, and decided it would be seen wherever I'd managed to stick it. When I turned back around, I found Jacob staring at the soles of Darnell's shoes. I said, "He didn't suffer. And his etheric form didn't stick around. So, don't worry. No one's here but Alisha, Jibben, you, and me."

We headed back to containment, where Alisha greeted us with, "Finally." She seemed awfully relieved, or annoyed, or both. "Maybe you can explain it better than me."

"Explain what?" I asked cautiously.

"Never Have I Ever."

Jibben said, "I just don't see the point."

"The point," Alisha said, "is to pass the time before we all lose our damn minds."

Jibben said, "It's a drinking game, yet we have no alcohol—and it would be silly to squander the bottled water—"

Alisha interrupted. "We don't need to drink, I already said that."

"And there's no way of fact-checking anyone's answer. So what's to stop us from lying to score a point?"

Most of my experience with this particular game took place during my Camp Hell years. The questions were vicious. The prizes were meager. And if you so much as thought about fudging your answer, a telepath was sure to pipe up and tattle on you.

"If you lie, it's on you," I told Jibben. "But we don't need to drink, we just keep score. Hold up your hand. For every statement you can't agree with, lose a point and fold a finger down."

Alisha said, "And the first one to make a fist has to be quiet for half an hour, and not say a word." Three guesses as to who she was trying to knock out—two of which, I didn't need. "I'll go first." She held up a hand, fingers spread wide. "Never have I ever cheated on my taxes."

The rest of us looked at her blankly.

"Really? None of you? I thought that was something old white dudes did all the time."

It was Jibben's turn next, and clearly, he thought the game was the most pointless thing he'd ever heard of. But he decided to play along...or at least try to. "Never have I ever... used a pen."

Alisha gave him a bland stare. "We all just *saw* you use a pen."

"Oh."

"We are not counting that one—and you lose your turn."

Jibben shrugged, and play moved on to Jacob. He stroked his beard and said, "Never have I ever eaten a frozen lasagna without heating it up." I caught that sharky glint in his eye—the competitive spirit he'd been hoping to flex this weekend—and was immensely grateful to Alisha for dreaming up such a workable distraction.

"Never have I ever skinnydipped," I said, thinking that Alisha seemed like she might've been pretty daring in her younger days.

Unfortunately, Alisha hadn't...but Jacob had.

Alisha narrowed her eyes at me and said, "Never have I ever shaved my face."

Jacob and I each lost a point, and so did Jibben. As an educated man of science and elite researcher for a top-secret government agency, he clearly thought this little game was below him. And yet, since the rest of us were all gung-ho about it, he gave it the old college try.

Not *well*, mind you. But he did make an effort.

"Never have I ever won a Ganzfeld Endowment Grant."

Right. Moving right along....

Jacob considered the room, and said, "Never have I ever had an allergic reaction."

I said, "Wait a sec—that time we were cat-sitting and I got all puffed up—?"

"It counts."

If this game mattered whatsoever, I'd be affronted that he was using his knowledge of me to deliberately knock me out.

Affronted, though not exactly surprised. Winning means so much to him, he'll resort to any means necessary to come out on top.

Alisha lost that round, too. "Shellfish," she said. "Shrimp makes the roof of my mouth all itchy."

My turn. And since Jacob was gunning for me, I figured I'd return the favor. "Never have I ever left a pair of socks on the front stoop."

"I told you, they were wet."

"We've all had wet socks. And yet, you don't see anyone else here airing them for the whole block to see."

"Actually, I live in an apartment," Jibben said, "but Agent Bayne does have a point."

"Never have I ever kissed a girl," Alisha said, earning a raised eyebrow from me. Jibben folded down a finger, though I had to wonder if maybe he only did so because the alternative— admitting to being a forty-year-old virgin—was too embarrassing. Then again, I'd never kissed a girl myself, though back when I was too young to drive, I'd been giving out hand-jobs behind the gas station.

Jacob, however, lowered a finger as well....

I filed that tidbit away for later discussion.

Jibben—finally getting the hang of things—went next with, "Never have I ever forged a signature." I strongly suspected Jacob was lying when he didn't cop to that, but since he wasn't hooked up to a polygraph, no one could prove otherwise.

Alisha and I both took a hit. We were all tied, with two fingers left...except Jacob, who trailed the rest of us with only one remaining strike. But it was his turn to even the score. "Never have I ever recited pi past four digits."

Good to know my husband was on my side again. The only one who admitted to that nerdism was Jibben.

My turn again. One more hit would take Jacob out—and since he was the only one I didn't want to shut up, I'd need to be more strategic about dinging someone else. What did science-y guys like Jibben do that the rest of us mere mortals would never even consider? Everything I presumed would interest Jibben, from learning Latin to reading the encyclopedia, were also things Jacob had probably done at one point or another, since he gets off on being the smartest guy in the room. Though Jacob was such a good liar, if he didn't want to admit doing something, he could just pretend he hadn't, so I really shouldn't overthink it—

"Say something already or lose your turn," Alisha snapped.

Damn. "Never have I ever, ah...discovered something and shouted, *eureka*."

Even as it left my mouth, I knew how pathetic it was. No one lost a point. Not even Jibben.

Alisha must've been cooking up a really juicy question, because she hunkered down, leaned in, and lowered her voice dramatically to say, "Never have I ever...seen a ghost."

What the hell had possessed her to ask that?

Suddenly, second-guessing looked more like simple arithmetic as I waffled between third, fourth and fifth guesses. She shouldn't be able to read the codes on our ID badges. Did she know I was a medium? Had I said something in passing? I didn't think so. Only to Jacob—and only out of her earshot....

Unless she'd been eavesdropping.

But before I got defensive and blurted out an accusation I'd later regret, Jibben twitched a few times, then said, "I have."

The rest of us looked at him like we'd all just now seen a ghost ourselves. "It's true. I have. Or, at the very least, I've seen the evidence of a noncorporeal being. In fact, the house I grew up in was incontrovertibly haunted."

CHAPTER 15

The whole point of all the "never have I ever" rigmarole we'd just gone through was to shut Jibben up. But now we all wanted his story. And so, naturally, we let all those awkward questions and answers go totally to waste and allowed him to speak.

"We moved into the house when I was thirteen. I remember it well because it was my birthday, and my parents claimed the house was my birthday present. Obviously, they'd just been too busy and preoccupied to shop for a gift. But a boy that age gets a real charge out of thinking the place belongs to him—even if that house turns out to have a second mortgage on it and is essentially worthless...." He twitched a few times, then fell silent.

Alisha, being the sensationalist junkie she was, couldn't let Jibben leave it at that. "Was it a spooky old Victorian with boards on the windows? A gnarly tree out front with a swing that moves by itself? A scary basement full of a dead kid's toys and a bunch of broken dolls with eyes that just stare right through you?"

Jibben blinked. "No, none of that. It was a 1960s split level with an avocado green kitchen and wall-to-wall shag carpeting."

Alisha shuddered. "Well, that's nearly as bad."

Jibben said, "I had a funny feeling about the house, but I just chalked it up to my excitement. It was *my* house, after all—at least as far as I was concerned. Of course I was excited. But soon enough, strange things began to happen. At first, it was just small things, like finding my homework slid down behind my desk, or coming across an open door that I was sure I'd closed. Nothing too out of the ordinary, but enough to make me feel uneasy. Then, it got worse."

He took a deep, shuddering breath and his eye gave a spasm that made the rest of us wince.

"Keys started going missing. It was as if the house didn't want us to leave."

"I take it back," Alisha said. "The shag carpet wasn't the scariest part of the story."

Jibben seemed surprised. "You believe me?"

"Why wouldn't I? Stuff like that happens on Psychic Mysteries all the time." When Jibben scoffed, Alisha plowed ahead. "No, hear me out. New house. Just moved. Stressful situation. And you were thirteen—an adolescent. Just the right age for a poltergeist to attach itself to you."

And just the same age I'd first spotted a transparent guy in a bloody hockey jersey staring at me through the window of my junior high social studies class.

Alisha leaned forward, her eyes wide with excitement, asking, "What did you do?"

Jibben shrugged. "What *could* I do? I was just a kid. I tried to tell my parents what was going on, but they didn't believe me. They said I was just having nightmares."

He'd likely dodged a bullet. After all, my foster father Harold hadn't necessarily believed some bloody guy was peeping into my classroom, but he definitely thought something was wrong with me. The resulting trip to Dr. Kleinman ended up with me never seeing him or Mama Brill again...and moving into a new house of my own.

And no one tried to bullshit me into thinking it was my birthday present.

"The experience left a mark on me, to be sure," Jibben said. "It would be a few years before the Ganzfeld Reports came out—before any hard evidence existed. And by then I'd made it my life's work to prove the unprovable. Unfortunately...I've never been able to document a poltergeist. In fact, there's not a bit of mediumship evidence to support their existence."

He cut his eyes to me, as if hoping I might contradict him. A new finding of some kind, a twist on an existing theory. But all of my work was right there on the FPMP servers for anyone with proper clearance to see—not counting the stuff I got up to with Jacob, obviously, but everything that happened on the clock. So, Jibben would be just as up to date on any new findings on nonphysical entities as I was.

"This is a discussion for another time," Jacob said, since it was his job as ranking agent to handle the scene—and although Jibben was talking in vagaries, things were getting too close to classified for comfort.

So, of course, Alisha was having none of it. "Another time? Like when? Ain't like we got nothing better to do than sit around and tell our ghost stories."

Smooth operator that he was, Jacob took the opportunity to turn things around on her. "Well, then, how about you take a turn?"

"All right," she said loftily—and grabbed the emergency lantern to cast an uplight on her face as she settled in for a dramatic ghost story. "Picture this: a crummy old apartment complex, you know the type, where the walls are covered in graffiti and folks mind their own business.

"I was up past my bedtime, reading, when I heard footsteps coming from the apartment upstairs. Nothing strange about that—you hear all kinds of stuff in those kinds of places. But they were so damn loud—like Frankenstein was up there stomping around in his platform shoes. I was hoping it was a one-time thing, but it happened the next night, and the next.

"Always at midnight.

"I was scared to tell Momma, of course—'cause I wasn't supposed to be up that late. But eventually, I got so sick of the noise, I went and got her at 11:55 and had her sit in my room and listen. And sure enough, soon as midnight hit, the stomping started up again."

She paused for effect, her gaze steady on the rest of the group. "So, you know what my momma did? She got fed up and went flying upstairs to tell them to shut the hell up. But when she got there, the apartment was empty. No people, no furniture. Nothing."

We sat with that story for a long moment, then Jibben said, "But...the door was unlocked?"

"I dunno. I guess it must've been."

"So someone could have been walking around up there. You said yourself, it was an apartment complex. Other people lived there. It wasn't as if you had a single-family home and observed inexplicable noises coming from the attic. And the fact that it happened on a routine makes it more likely that it was tied to some other event—a person coming home from work, for instance. Or even an OCD sufferer performing some sort of ritual—"

"It figures," Alisha snapped. "I heard out your story, gave you the benefit of the doubt and everything. But then I tell you mine, and suddenly I'm making it all up."

"That's not what anyone is saying," Jibben insisted. "But Occam's razor does suggest that the simplest explanation is also the most likely."

"Yeah? I don't know about him, but I'll bet Luther Hinman wouldn't be so quick to back you up. I was in a stressful situation, same as you. I was thirteen, same as you. And Luther Hinman always said that's exactly when a poltergeist can latch on!"

Frankly, I wouldn't put much stock in conclusions drawn by any of the pre-Ganzfeld psychic researchers, but I *was* in the unique position of seeing both sides of Alisha's poltergeist situation. While my own psychic powers had reared their head at puberty, I'd never known a ghost to make enough noise to bother anyone but a medium. Alisha's mom had heard it too, though. And while she might very well be psychic herself...the ex-cop in me was a lot more apt to believe that some idiot was just stomping around the upstairs apartment for reasons apparent only to them.

Hoping to smooth over the ill-will, Jacob said, "Even with all the recent advances in psychic research, there's plenty they still don't know. Was there anything else that led you to believe this was a poltergeist?"

But Alisha had decided the "old white dudes" were just humoring her now, and she put down the emergency lantern in a snit, crossed her arms, and glared pointedly at the wall.

Jacob sighed heavily and gave his forehead a swipe with the sleeve of the hazmat suit. By the dubious light of the emergency lantern, he was glistening. I stood up and said, "Now I gotta use the can—" hoping that Jacob would come along, and a brief walk with me down the hall would let him air out some.

But Alisha snapped out of her bad mood and said, "I'll come with you."

Well, what could I say to that—without looking like a total asshole, anyhow? I'd have to start limiting my trips to the bathroom, given the way my flashlight beam started flickering the second I turned it on. Luckily, once we were within eyeshot of the can, the flashlight rallied. I probably should've just come out and said I wanted to talk to my husband alone. But that might make the other two wonder what I had to say that couldn't be said in front of them.

And I couldn't have gone around announcing to the room in general that I wondered if Alisha was really a random delivery driver...or something more.

Alisha nodded at the bathroom door. "I'll go first. Unless you need to go bad."

I waved her off. "I just wanted some air. I'm not what you'd call a people person...and I wasn't in the mood for a lecture on squandering our limited resources by taking an unnecessary walk."

"I was thinking, anyway—this is a big place, there must be

more than one washroom on this floor. Right?"

"I guess."

"Maybe this one could be the official Ladies' Room. You know. So I can leave out my tampons—"

"Yeah, say no more. Fine. It's yours."

As Alisha ducked into her own newly-christened private bathroom, I considered the slim possibility that she wasn't lying. That she just happened to be in the thick of things when the power went out. That it was entirely random all this occurred while we were severely short-staffed. And that she actually did need to pee every half hour.

My current theory? We were being tested to see how strictly we'd adhere to emergency protocol in a dire situation, and she was doing some kind of reporting in the can...maybe on the phone that just so happened to work when the rest of ours were down.

But who was pulling her strings? That was the question.

If it was Laura Kim, Jacob would've caught wind of the plan in the Oversight Division. So it must be National. And I liked them even less than I liked the thought of being accosted by a surprise tampon.

The only comfort I took was that Jacob wasn't the intended target, since no one could have predicted he'd turn around from the airport and come back. Frankly, since I could've done my lab walkthrough at any point during the day, I doubted I was the target, either.

That left Jibben under the microscope. Tough break for him. But I'd need to watch myself if I didn't want to get caught up in whatever mess he was in.

At least my flashlight was holding up. It was nothing like

the whopping 2-pound maglite bruising my hip, back when I walked a beat. This thing was hardly bigger than my palm. But for all that it rode along in my pocket as unobtrusively as a pack of gum, the LED bulb cast a pretty good light, and it's helped me out of plenty of scrapes. But while I changed the battery on the regular, you never know. Sometimes you get a bad one right out of the package.

...as evidenced by the fact that it started flickering again two minutes later on our way back down the hall. But at least we were within sight of containment when it happened—and at least it was just a flicker, and not a total flashlight failure, since the door to that room was sealed so tightly, not even a hint of light could squeak out around it.

I quickly discovered that seal was doing Jacob no favors. He'd chucked off the clean suit, much to Jibben's consternation, and was sweating through his polo shirt. I found the room stuffy, no doubt, but nothing I couldn't handle—but Jacob has always run a lot hotter than me.

Lucky for him he had on those cargo shorts, and not a wool suit.

"The crates are fiberglass," he was saying, "and they're a good size. The lids are removable. So we stack them up at the foot of the emergency exit and walk across to the stairs."

"What about Jibben's leg?" I asked.

"I want no part of this," he said. "Agent Marks outranks me. And if he insists on this fool's errand—which may very well get him electrocuted—there's nothing I can do to stop him. But unless he orders me to go, I'm staying put right where I am and waiting for rescue. Which we should all be doing."

"You don't have to come," Jacob said. "I'll send help."

Jibben twitched, a sudden, awkward blink. "I'm sure it's already on the way. Unless you plan on single-handedly restoring the power grid, forging your way out of here accomplishes nothing at all but putting you at risk."

Well, that's where Jibben was wrong. Because extricating himself from this mess would also bring Jacob one step closer to Clayton.

CHAPTER 16

Obviously, I wasn't going to let Jacob embark on this fool's errand alone. "Hold on, I'm going with you. Just lemme grab a fresh battery." I pried a couple out of the remote we'd found in the break room, hefted a fiberglass panel, and followed Jacob out the containment room door.

As we hustled down the hall, I considered suggesting we slow down. But since Jacob was capable of jogging in 90-degree Chicago weather (with a million-percent humidity) I plowed on ahead. We didn't pause 'till we got to the janitorial closet with the false back...and Jacob grabbed a towel from one of the shelves to mop his sweaty brow.

"Are you sure you're okay?" I asked as he toweled the back of his neck.

"I don't know. Maybe I'm coming down with something."

I pressed the backs of my fingers to his forehead, then checked mine for comparison. "Huh. You don't feel all that hot."

"I can't tell if I'm too hot or too cold. I've never felt anything like it."

Uh-oh. I sure hoped Big Boy Leonard wasn't the only one having a heart attack. "We should sit down. Just for a couple of minutes."

"We have to keep going." Jacob considered what he'd just said, then amended it to, "*I* have to keep going."

I reached for him again, but this time instead of checking his temperature, I cupped his jaw and encouraged him to look at me. "I get it, Jacob. Believe me, I do. You're not the only one kicking yourself for leaving Clayton to fend for himself...."

I'd been about to add that the cannery was a safe place for him to be, but before I could finish my thought, Jacob said, "Then you understand why I need to do this," shoved open the secret door, and went striding off down the long, dark hall to the exit.

The hall was narrow and the fiberglass slab I carried was ungainly. It smacked against the wall as I hurried along behind Jacob, flashlight beam bouncing around wildly, hoping to make him see reason. "What are you going to do once you get out of here?" I demanded. "You'll have no car. It's stuck in the lot. I guarantee no one's going to let you flag them down for a ride. So, what then? You're going to walk home? That would take a couple of hours even on a good day, let alone this crazy monsoon."

But Jacob had his mind made up, and damn it, he was determined to see his ridiculous plan through. We banged along down the hall 'till the final doorway. Jacob set down one of his two panels and used the other to shove open the door. I supposed I should count myself lucky that he didn't just bound out of there and leave me in the dust, but I was the one carrying the flashlight, and he let me catch up.

Good thing he did.

The stairwell looked the same as we'd left it—a couple of inches of water, stairs leading up, and a single frayed power cable hanging to one side, threatening to make repeaters out of both of us.

But something new greeted us this time: a single rat floating on its back. Very big. And very dead.

Better than a live one, no doubt. Yet the possibility that it had been electrocuted gave even Jacob pause about splashing through the puddle.

"Listen to me," I said. "The situation sucks. Neither of us wants to be here. And we're freaking out about leaving that poor kid to deal with this whole shit show on his own. But you know how you'd feel if anything happened to him? Think about how I would feel watching you charge off to the rescue and having you end up like Darnell."

Jacob was very still, tracking the movements of the rat as it circled gently in the current of the seeping water.

Was he seriously still considering vaulting those stairs?

Fine. I'd bring out the big guns. "You think Clayton's traumatized now? What if he found out you died trying to get to him?"

Even by the light of my trusty pocket flashlight, I could see Jacob blanch as he stepped back to let the emergency door swing shut. "Come on," I said. "Let's get going. It's a long walk back."

"Wait. Let's stay put—just for a minute."

"I hope you're not getting any bright ideas about rappelling up that stairwell with nothing but your car keys and a spool of dental floss."

"No, nothing like that." Jacob rolled his shoulders. "I'm just starting to feel a lot better now that I'm out of that stuffy room."

And I was feeling a lot better without the constant peopling required of me in close proximity to a couple of opinionated strangers. I leaned back against the wall and slid down to sit on the floor, and Jacob came and sat beside me.

I looped an arm around him and pulled his head onto my shoulder. He did seem a lot less sweaty now. What a relief he was feeling better. "We are getting out of here," I said. "We just need to make it through the wait."

He settled more snugly against me. "First thing I'll do when I get home is put Clayton in the car and drive him straight back up to Wisconsin."

Normally I would have agreed. But was it really fair to the kid?

"Hold on now," I said. "We don't want his memory of his first overnight in Chicago to end like this, do we? We should at least get him a hot dog and let him show us his stupid video games. Besides, did it ever occur to you that Barbara had a reason for dropping him off—other than to prove a point?"

"Like what?"

"Like maybe she needed the house to herself for a few days because she wanted to hook up with a guy. And maybe she didn't drop Clayton off at your parents' because she didn't want them asking any questions."

"But Barb isn't that good of an actor. She really was ticked at Clayton and trying to prove a point. Too bad, though. Maybe if there was a man in her life, she'd be a little less tightly wound."

Or differently wound, at the very least.

I sure as hell was, now that I had Jacob. I wrapped my arm around his head so I could work my fingers through his thick hair and pull him even closer. Even at a goofy angle, we managed to fit together.

My other hand was on my knee, gripping the flashlight loosely. Jacob reached over and toyed with my wedding band—a habit he's picked up this past year that secretly makes me unaccountably proud of myself.

"I've got an idea," I said. "I know exactly how we can pay Barbara back. Doodlebug, or whatever his name was. What if Wisconsin was his forever home?"

I felt Jacob's silent laugh against me. "That dog must be going nuts. Poor thing. I can't imagine what this thunderstorm would sound like to him—probably the whole world coming to an end."

While Jacob was displaying sympathy toward the dog, I noted that he didn't suggest adopting it ourselves, for which I was profoundly grateful.

"What about you?" he asked. "What do you want to do when you get back?"

I considered the question.

When it came right down to it, my wants were pretty simple. Just the desire to be left alone, to my own devices, with the man I love...though I *was* serious about giving Clayton at least one decent Chicago memory to take back home with him. He'd been to Navy Pier plenty of times before, so that was out. Then, what—the Blue Man Group? If there were tickets to be had on such short notice. There'd been nonstop ads playing for a new escape room in Bucktown...but given the current situation I was in, could I even trust myself to find my way out of a cardboard box?

I was pondering if a trip to Chinatown would pass muster when Jacob jerked away from me with a sudden hiss. "Get up," he said urgently.

Cripes—more rats? I swept my flashlight beam up and down the hallway as we scrambled to our feet. Nary a rodent to be found...but then I spotted something even worse: A puddle creeping out from beneath the emergency exit door.

"We're well below the water table." Jacob wiped a wet hand on his shorts. "And any pumps that keep the place dry would run on electricity."

Which meant we might soon find ourselves ankle-deep in lightning-infested water.

I was so freaked out by the thought of having my subtle bodies zapped out of my physical shell by a fucking *puddle* that I forgot to be impressed by what a trooper my flashlight had been all this time. It didn't start flickering again until we were within sight of containment.

"We're taking on water," I announced to Jibben as I slammed through the door. "That soaker-upper stuff you used on the saline—how much more do you have?"

"There's a whole case of spill mats in the cupboard right behind you."

Hopefully we wouldn't need any of them at all, let alone an entire case, but better safe than sorry. I opened the cabinet and was greeted by a wall of unreadable boxes, and when I aimed my flashlight at the massive pile of cardboard, the beam started to flicker in earnest. We found the spill mats by the strobing beam, and Jacob got to work tearing open the box. Meanwhile, I paused to switch out the battery with the one from the remote.

Better.

For a few minutes, anyhow. Once we trooped back out into the hall and barricaded our position with gel pads, the damn thing was flickering again. Jibben didn't need to tell me to conserve what was left of the battery. With a muttered curse, I hurried back to containment, flicked it off and stuck it in my pocket.

To say the others were looking a little worse for wear would be putting it mildly. Jibben's leg was black and blue for the span of his entire thigh, and it was swollen about half as big again as the other one. He had one of those emergency cold packs pressed against the massive bruise now, but it seemed inadequately small.

Alisha, meanwhile, was huddled in the far corner, hugging her knees to her chest. Her eyes were so big I could practically see the whites all around. "How far along is that water?" she demanded.

"Nowhere in sight," Jacob said in a calming voice. "We're just taking precautions."

"Well maybe you should take some more. Do you know how far underground we are? This place'll fill up faster than a port-a-potty at a free kegger."

Jibben said, "It's statistically improbable that the flooding will last much longer. I'm sure repair crews are already on the scene. It just makes more sense to utilize what time, energy and resources we have to prepare for the worst than to sit here and do nothing."

That probably would've sounded a lot more comforting,

had his right eye not been winking like all get-out while he said it.

Like Alisha, I was none too keen to be stuck in a freaking basement, either. Especially knowing what else was lurking around down here. Two dead bodies: Darnell, relatively fresh. And Dr. Chance, long dead and frozen...hopefully not starting to thaw.

And those were just the ones I knew about.

I'd bet there was valium to be had somewhere in this underground warren. Not for me—I didn't intend to give a stray habit demon anything to latch onto—but for Alisha. It was a stretch to think a spy from National had been lying in wait for months, moving boxes and sexting with Darnell while she counted down the days to infiltrate the building. And yet, I'd done my own share of spying—so, how sure could I be that she truly was a civilian, and not just a phenomenally dedicated spy?

I'd need to play it cautious with her. Just in case.

But if Alisha was nothing more than a random courier—she was having one hell of a shitty day.

"Help me with these boxes," I told her, mostly to get her mind off the situation, but also because the clutter was starting to get to me. For every useful item we'd dredge up, it seemed like there were a dozen more entirely useless things to wade through. Hopefully, we wouldn't be down here long enough to discover a use for dozens of boxes of rubber gloves and a bunch of old electronics manuals, and I was eager to get them back in the cupboards where they belonged.

I felt better once the cabinet was repacked and the room had some semblance of order. I'd moved on to straightening out the papers on the stainless steel work table when the light began to flicker.

Only it wasn't my flashlight this time.

It was the emergency lantern.

"I don't *think* so," Alisha said, as if she could intimidate the light into behaving.

We all held our breath, hoping against all hope it was a fluke of some sort. It stayed steady for a moment...then flickered again.

Reluctantly, Jibben said, "We should turn it off and conserve power."

"And sit here in the dark?" Alisha demanded—and given how she and I were on the same page about so many things, I really did hope she was just a regular person caught in the wrong place at the wrong time. "If a puddle creeps into the room, it won't go announcing itself, now—will it?"

Jacob pulled out another gel pad and laid it across the threshold. I'd wager the seal on the door was tighter than the one around our shower, but why take chances?

As we all stared at the gel pad expectantly, the emergency lantern flickered again. "I thought that battery was supposed to last all night," I said with no little annoyance.

Jibben gave a helpless shrug. "So it claimed on the box, but there's no telling if a battery is defective until it's put to the test."

From here on out, I was never leaving the house again without a backup and a spare.

No one was happy about the plan to switch off the lantern, but if we didn't do it voluntarily, battery drainage would take the decision out of our hands. So we pushed all the chairs toward the center of the room in case the seams around the walls began to seep, and we gave Jibben the go-ahead to cut the light.

CHAPTER 17

Holy fuck, it was dark.

Not "making my way to the fridge at midnight for that last piece of pizza" dark, either.

No, it was completely and utterly black.

And somehow, the darkness made everything louder. I heard Jacob's molars squeaking together. I heard Alisha sigh through her nose. And I heard the click in Jibben's throat and a subtle squeak of his chair as he finally got a chance to let his raging tics fly loose.

I became aware of my own heartbeat, a thrum in my ears that was slowly but surely picking up speed. I may not be susceptible to panic attacks, but the prickle of sweat in the small of my back had Camp Hell PTSD written all over it.

"We should work on keeping our breathing even," Jibben said.

It took me a second to realize the suggestion was aimed at me.

But then Jacob's hand groped its way across my thigh, and I gratefully grabbed it and gave it a squeeze. I didn't need a light to recognize his hand. I knew it by the way it felt—broad, square, capable—and the feel of it sliding home was as familiar as my side of the mattress or my favorite pair of jeans.

But what if I only felt what I wanted to feel? And what if the hand I was holding had been on ice up until a few hours ago, but was rapidly thawed in the stuffy atmosphere of the airless basement lab…?

I flicked on my pocket flashlight.

Jacob blinked. But he didn't let go of my hand.

And the room was just as tight and orderly as we'd left it.

Jibben said, "We all agreed to conserve—"

"I know, I know," I said, irritated with myself for getting wound up over nothing, and flicked it back off before it had a chance to flicker.

The room went dark again. I was struck not just by how dark and silent it was, but how uncomfortably stale. When the whole fiasco had begun, the room had held the vague basement smell of disinfectant and concrete. But now there was the sweaty, salty funk of four people breathing up all the air.

The urge was strong to breathe fast and suck down all the oxygen I could. But since I'd be competing with Jacob, I reined myself in.

Jibben said, "We're all under a lot of stress right now. That means increased heart rate, elevated blood pressure, and rapid breathing. The body diverts blood flow away from non-essential functions toward the muscles and vital organs, so we're primed for quick physical action. In an uncertain situation like this, the effects of stress are magnified. How long we'll be down here, what's safe to touch, whether or not help is on the way. The constant anticipation of danger heightens our anxiety levels and creates a state of hypervigilance. And it's all rough on the body—not to mention what it's doing to the mind."

More oxygen left the room as the rest of us indulged in a sigh.

"How about some brain teasers to take our minds off the stressor?" he suggested. "The more I take, the more I leave behind. What am I?"

"A shoplifter," Alisha said immediately.

"Well, no...that's not—"

"Show me a shoplifter who can stuff more down their pants than they leave on the rack."

Jibben huffed. "You're neglecting to take into account the logical structure of the puzzle. It's not *I must take less than I leave*. It's the *more* I take—"

"Footsteps," Jacob said.

With an eye-roll in her voice, Alisha said, "Oh. It's one of those."

"Very good, Agent Marks," Jibben said. "How about this? What five-letter word becomes shorter when you add two letters to it?"

Un...tall? No, that was only four letters. Untall-y? Ish?

"Guesses?" Jibben said. "Anyone?" When no one volunteered an answer, he said, "Short. Add an -er...."

Alisha flicked on her phone and the light cast by her lock-screen lit her face. "Yeah, we get it. We're not stupid, y'know."

"I never said you were."

The lockscreen put out a fair amount of light. I congratulated myself for tidying up the room before we went dark. At least I wouldn't be worrying about the clutter.

"Now, please," Jibben said, "conserve your battery." The phone went dark. A few moments of sullen silence, then he added, "I was just hoping to provide some distraction."

Alisha said, "That wasn't a riddle, anyways. It was more like a trick."

"You'll note I introduced it as a brain teaser—"

"Enough," Jacob said. "The situation is already stressful without us squabbling over a word choice. Look, no one planned to spend the day like this. We're all on edge. We all want to get out of here. So, let's focus on ramping down our anxiety. Calm, even breathing. Help is on the way. Let your mind drift. Relax."

It wasn't so different from the yoga I endured a few times a week to keep my crown chakra limber—except now I got to be sitting down and not wobbling around in a warrior pose, so that was a plus. My office chair creaked as I settled back, throwing my weight into it, and tried my very best to follow Jacob's advice and relax.

Just fucking relax.

But the mental image of all the corpses in the vicinity just wouldn't give up the prime-time spot in my mind. Was Darnell really just a repeater? And was Jennifer Chance nearly thawed? And what about the rest of the vaults in cold storage? I had no idea who else was stashed in those long metal compartments....

"I can't do this," I said.

"I'm here for you," Jacob said quietly—and with such sincerity it plucked at my heartstrings.

I might've considered trying to stick it out and work through my panic, but then Alisha piped in. "I'm with the tall guy. I can't just sit here in the dark."

I said, "There's gotta be more light down here we haven't tapped yet—look at all the equipment at our disposal. We could light a bunsen burner—"

Jibben put the kibosh on that idea. "Using an open flame would deplete oxygen and potentially compromise our safety." So much for that. If I had to pick between light and air, I'd have to go with air. "No doubt we have the chemicals to create a luminescent compound..."

"Like a glow stick?" Alisha asked.

"Exactly. Though I don't know the formula off the top of my head. It would be on the server."

"But you could *try*," Alisha said testily. "I'm sure you've got some idea—you're *supposed* to be a scientist."

Jibben huffed. "Slapping together a bunch of random chemicals with no formula and no ventilation is an even worse idea than an open flame. It's uncomfortable to sit in the dark—I'll concede that much—but it's no excuse to asphyxiate us all."

Voice edgy, Jacob said, "No one wants to suffocate. But Vic is right—there's bound to be something else we can use as a light source, something that hasn't occurred to us because it's not a traditional light. Clocks, sensors—plenty of things that will cast enough glow that we don't have to sit here in total darkness."

"I'm sure there are plenty of things that might cast a bit of light," Jibben said. "But how many resources will we squander searching for them? You'd likely burn through a flashlight battery looking for something that only casts a minimal amount of lumens."

Thinking back to the brief stint where Jacob wore a fitness tracker to bed—and a blinding light from his wrist woke me up every time he rolled over—I thought some small, constant light would be better than none at all. "What about a tablet?" I suggested. "We could all see just fine by Alisha's lockscreen now that our eyes are adjusted to the dark. This place must be stupid with tablets."

"The tablets are classified," Jibben said with dismay, as though I'd just suggested sacrificing a puppy—a pathetic rescue-puppy.

"Fine," I said. "Then you hold onto it and the rest of us promise not to read over your shoulder."

As far as I was concerned, that settled the matter—so I stood up and flicked on my flashlight....

Only to discover that the papers I'd just piled so neatly had been scattered from one side of the work table to the other.

CHAPTER 18

White light.

I opened up my crown chakra and it flooded on down, thundering through the veins of my subtle body like a shot of pure adrenaline. Maybe I'd never seen a ghost move something in the physical plane—but I didn't give a flying fuck if I was being logical or not. I was trapped in the basement of a clandestine psychic facility in the dark with no way out, and I needed my white light locked and loaded.

Outwardly, I sucked in a breath. Jacob went very still. Alisha made a small whimper, but it was Jibben who spoke. "Obviously, there must be a draft."

Silence.

"That's good," he said. "Don't you see? It means there's ventilation."

I cut my eyes to Jacob. There'd been no draft. We would have felt it. There'd been nothing else to do while we were sitting in the dark but feel a wayward draft that didn't exist.

"Occam's razor," Jibben said. "It's the most obvious explanation."

Jacob stood, giving me a look. He wasn't buying the air current either. But before he could demand to speak to me alone, Alisha said, "Y'all think this is funny?"

"No one's laughing," I said.

"Sit me in the dark, moving shit around—"

I said, "We were *all* sitting in the dark."

"Just 'cause I watch Psychic Mysteries—yeah, I know how bad it is—y'all think I'm some kinda dumbass?"

"Ma'am—" Jacob began in his "calm down" voice.

"Don't you *ma'am* me! I might not be Dr. So-and-So or Agent Cargo Shorts, but that doesn't mean I'll fall for this bullshit."

Jibben gave off a violent twitch. "I would *never*—"

But Jacob stepped in, doubling down on the calm. "No one is implying anyone is gullible, and no one is pranking anyone. We can all agree that airflow is a good thing. So let's not use it up arguing with each other."

I wanted a breath of fresh air as much as anyone...but now that I was pumped with white light, the hairs on the nape of my neck bristled and my lower back went clammy. Unfortunately, that didn't prove much of anything, other than the fact that I was stressed out and jumpy. I might be the most accurate piece of ghost-sensing equipment in the FPMP's arsenal, but I was still plenty glitchy.

And if Darnell was haunting us, I would have seen him.

Unless his ghost needed time to reassemble itself after the lightning strike, and was now lurking around containment.

Even as the thought occurred to me, I knew I was just getting caught up in the stress of the situation. Yes, ghosts most definitely did exist.

But they didn't move things.

So, who'd scattered those papers?

I hadn't done it myself, and I hadn't felt any air coming out of the overhead vents, either. If Jacob had a strategic reason, he'd have no qualms about mixing things up and then lying like a rug to cover his tracks. We'd been holding hands the entire time, though, so Jacob was out.

I didn't know Jibben very well, but he didn't strike me as a very good liar. Too many twitchy tells. Besides, it wasn't as if he could fake the swollen leg keeping him in that office chair.

Which left...Alisha.

And covering up the fact that she'd done it with a plausible display of anger was exactly the type of thing a pro would do.

Damn. I'd wanted so badly to like her—probably because she acknowledged my husband was "fine." But it was more than that. Alisha had struck me as a straight-talking, no-non-sense, take-no-shit person—and nowadays, people like that are few and far between.

It was disappointing to think that what I'd been jibing with wasn't her true personality—just the persona she'd been assigned to adopt.

"Until we find out different," Jacob was saying, "we chalk it up to the ventilation system and go forward with the plan we've all agreed on. Stay calm. Stay rational. And hang tight until the power comes up and we're able to get out of here."

Jibben and Alisha each gave a nod of agreement, though neither of them looked particularly pleased about it. Once that was settled, Jacob said to me, "A word?"

"Well, don't expect me to sit here in the dark while you two go out there and talk about us," Alisha said, and turned on her phone.

"That's not—" I said, and my flashlight flickered. I toed the gel pad out of the way and opened the door. "We'll make it quick."

The hallway looked twice as dark, twice as empty, and twice as ominous as it had before...but at least the floor was still dry. Urgently, Jacob whispered, "Did you see anything?" Meaning, did I see a ghost.

"No, nothing."

Normally, he'd be frustrated, even disappointed. But instead he seemed...pleased? "The papers—it was me."

"How'd you manage that?" It *had* been him holding my hand the whole time—right? I shuddered. "Have you mastered the art of silent blowing, or what?"

"I did it...with my mind."

The sigh that threatened to escape me was gusty enough to rearrange all those papers from the other side of the wall. "Jacob, since when d'you think you can all of a sudden—?"

"Hear me out. Base chakra energy. Underground. Stressful situation. It's the perfect storm—exactly the sort of thing that might spike latent ability into the next level. I've been focusing all my thoughts on grounding ever since we saw the electrical wires hanging down in the stairwell. The tension, the focus—it's the breakthrough I've been working toward all this time."

Here's the thing. I've seen Jacob in action. I've watched him bulge with red, veiny energy by the light of a GhosTV, and I've seen him rip a habit demon in half like he was getting ready to butter a dinner roll. But he couldn't *see* it himself. And though I tell him up and down 'till I'm blue in the face that his TK ability is plenty real, it's etheric, not physical—when it's all said and done, he still doesn't quite believe me.

"Okay, look," I said, "maybe you moved those papers, maybe you didn't—we haven't figured out the limits of your ability, so who's to say? Just don't go tooting your own horn in front of anyone but me. You know how the scientists border on fanatical around here. And Alisha...." I felt like a jerk for even thinking it, but if there was even a chance she was more than just a courier, I couldn't let Jacob flounder around in the dark. "She could very well be a plant from National—"

Now it was Jacob's turn to quell a sigh. "National doesn't have eyes everywhere. They can't. Think about the amount of resources it would take."

I *had* thought about it. I'd even considered the fact that I was being overly suspicious. But I'd seen how deep our own undercover team went—I'd done a stint undercover myself—and, frankly, I'd rather be paranoid than complacent. "Just do me a favor and watch what you say." I balled his polo shirt in my fist and tugged him up against me, pressing my forehead into his. "That's all I ask."

He nodded, which felt more like a gentle shove, and said, "You're right."

I could count the times Jacob's told me those two little words on one hand and still have enough fingers left over to poke someone in both eyes. So, I felt somewhat better by the time we rejoined the others.

But the two of them clearly felt no better at all. They seemed twice as exasperated, with Jibben lecturing, Alisha being lectured, and neither willing to concede their position. "True infrared would require a specialized sensor," Jibben was saying.

"It says *night mode* right on it!"

"The setting on your phone's camera is nothing more than a color correction with a catchy name."

"Hold on," I said, "back up. You're thinking we can video what's going on?"

Alisha said, "We could...only this guy here is awful quick to tell me it won't work, without even trying."

Exasperated, Jibben said, "I just think it's not wise to waste resources on a plan that has no chance to succeed."

But Jacob's wheels were already turning. "A regular phone wouldn't have infrared capability...but what about ours?"

The FPMP-issued smartphones were state-of-the-art everything. I'd always figured their main purpose was to spy on us by tracking our locations and dumping all our data on the agency servers. I hadn't explored the camera's features, other than to make sure I wasn't shooting up my own nose when I was attempting to document a scene.

I switched on my phone and called up the camera. Apparently, I had night mode, too—plus portrait, sports, telephoto, pano, macro, and....

Infra.

I considered saying we were shit outta luck and powering down the phone before anyone could see I was a big fat liar. On the off-chance that Jacob truly was capable of moving papers, would evidence of his ability show up on the infrared—and point directly at him?

I didn't think so. The "naked machine" out in the lobby scanned the same heat spectrum—yes, I did absorb something besides donuts from my tedious police in-service trainings—and Jacob had never raised any alarms walking through.

Then again, as far as I knew, Jacob hadn't been focused on moving things with his mind while he was being scanned.

"Well?" Alisha demanded. "Can your phone do it or not?"

"We'll give it a shot," I said, then caught Jacob's eye and added, "but keep in mind, if something nonphysical is at play, we don't know exactly how it'll show up."

He gave me a nod.

And, mollified, so did Alisha. "Now we're talking. At least someone around here takes me seriously."

Resisting the urge to like her was tough, but what choice did I have?

Since Jacob was the Stiff, he re-stacked the papers while Jibben showed me how to set my camera. We framed our shot, turned off the flashlight and lantern, and settled in to wait.

It was so quiet I could hear us all breathing. But judging by the lack of chair squeaks or clothing rustles, everyone was holding themselves very, very still.

Even Jibben wasn't twitching.

A few long minutes went by, and Alisha said, "How long has it been?"

Approximately forever.

She elbowed me. "Check and see if they moved."

I flicked on my flashlight. Everything was right where we'd left it. I flicked it back off.

Another uncomfortable stretch of silence, which Alisha broke again. "The poltergeist probably won't do it now that it knows we're watching. That's how it always is."

Jibben said, "Again, no scientific evidence of so-called poltergeists exists. Believe me, I've looked. It's much more likely that the HVAC system is working in fits and starts as repair crews work on getting the power back up."

There's only so long you can hold yourself still, and soon the small sounds of existence resumed. Jacob rubbed the back of his neck. Jibben twitched. Alisha shifted her weight in her seat, and I leaned into my backrest, unsuccessfully pretending I was anywhere but there.

After several tedious minutes of staring into the void, Alisha whispered, "Nothing's happening. We should just turn the light back on."

Jibben huffed. "The infrared spectrum is beyond the range of the human eye. Leaving the light off is necessary for any potential visualization."

"Then how much longer we gotta just sit here?"

I flicked on my flashlight and swept the beam over the papers. Still right where we'd left them.

"Well, we gave it a fair shot," I said...though we probably hadn't. Because if Jacob had been efforting the last time, but sitting on his hands now, all the infrared would have picked up on was a fine middle-aged man in cargo shorts.

"Well, that was stimulating," Jibben said dryly, squaring off the paper into an even more precise stack. "But in the end, what did it prove?"

My knees cracked as I stood up and stretched one way, then the other. "Look, it was worth a try but—"

A faint dripping sound cut me off. I went still, listening. It wasn't in this room. Out in the hall?

Jacob glanced toward the room where they kept the cadavers, then met my eyes, alarmed.

I held up a hand, signaling everyone to be quiet. The rhythmic drips echoed through the walls. Coming right from the spot we least wanted to hear them.

A chill ran down my spine that had nothing to do with HVAC. If cold storage was warming up...we were in serious trouble.

Chapter 19

Drip.

Drip.

Drip.

"I need to go check a temperature gauge," Jibben said.

Well, shit. Up until this point, I'd successfully avoided telling Jacob about Chance's body. But now my time was up. "Agent Marks and I will take care of it," I said.

"But—"

"It's not like you can climb up on that step stool anymore, now—can you?"

Alisha rose as if she was getting ready to come with us, but when I said, "And you stay put," in no uncertain terms, she settled back down. Not gladly, mind you. But she settled.

My light was thankfully steady when we stepped out into the hall, but my resolve wasn't. "I don't know how to tell you this," I said with no small amount of chagrin as I cocked my head toward cold storage, "...but we know one of the occupants in there. A little too well."

Jacob searched my eyes for meaning, hoping I wasn't saying

what he *thought* I was saying.

"I'm sorry," I said.

He turned away. "When did they send her back?" he asked.

"I don't know. Recently. I just found out today."

"Dr. Chance is here. And all this time, you'd just let me go along like nothing's wrong—?"

"Hey." I settled a hand on his shoulder. "Whatever's in that vault isn't her. It's just a shell."

Though I'll admit, even having that particular shell within spitting distance was bad enough. Our last physical encounter with Jennifer Chance had her jerking around in her corpse while poor Jacob held it down. And whenever he woke with a start in the middle of the night, I'm pretty sure the dead body flailing in a tank of antiseptic liquid was exactly the scenario he was trying to escape.

I caught Jacob's hand and gave it an earnest squeeze. "Power will be up again before you know it. Crews are hard at work even as we speak. Besides, think about how long it takes to thaw a freaking twenty-pound turkey." Not to mention the horror show you slice into if you leave the giblet bag inside the cavity. We may never eat turkey again. "We'll be fine. I promise."

With a tug, Jacob pulled me up against him and cupped my face, running his thumb along my jaw. "Somehow, I manage to forget how brave you are." Maybe brave, maybe stupid. "But then you remind me."

Between the research lab, the basement and the thawing cadaver, this fucked up scenario had plenty of nightmare fuel for both of us, but losing our heads wouldn't do anyone any good. "We both know Chance is beyond the veil—and we both know a dead body is just a dead body. Even on the off-chance her ghost should find her way back to her cadaver, I doubt she can take it very far—"

"Are you *shitting* me?"

We both whirled around, flashlight beam bouncing, to find Alisha lurking in the shadows. Then we caught the sound of Jibben desperately wheeling himself along behind her.

"Ma'am—" Jacob began....

Alisha was having none of it. "What in the hell do you people study in this lab? And if anyone says it's classified, I will make you sorry you were ever born—"

Jibben said, "It *is* highly classified, but there's protocol in place. You'd have to sign an extensive non-disclosure agreement...." He paused, out of breath from the one-legged scoot up the hall, then craned his neck around her to look to Jacob. "But it's not my decision."

No, it was the decision of the ranking agent.

Jacob wanted to keep her in the dark. I could tell by the set of his jaw. And, frankly, I understood. Big Brother doesn't like anyone catching him with his pants down, and sucking someone into the FPMP machine was not a thing to be taken lightly. Once you were in on the secret, you could kiss your normal life goodbye. And the day might very well come when a couple of black-suited agents show up on your doorstep and make you disappear for your own "protection."

But given the circumstances.... "Bring her in," I told Jacob. "She's stuck down here, same as us. She should know exactly what we're up against."

And if she was a fed, same as us...at least we could say we'd followed protocol.

"Okay, lemme get this straight," Alisha said, once she'd signed away her future and heard our spiel. "Y'all believe in ghosts, and Agent Blue Eyes here is some kind of expert—but you still think I made up that poltergeist?"

I said, "It's just that I've never—look, forget about your poltergeist for now. We have a real noise to worry about, and it's coming from cold storage. So we'd better check it out."

Alisha said, "So you got dead bodies in there—one of 'em you think might get up and walk its ass around—and your big plan is to open up the door and let the cold air out? Fool, you know the first rule when the electric goes off is to keep the fridge shut."

Well, when she put it that way.

"What you need to do," she went on, "is stuff a towel under that door to keep the cold air in, then put a chair under the doorknob so nothing gets out."

We all stared down the dark hallway for a moment, then Jacob said, "Sounds like a solid plan to me."

The door to cold storage, turns out, opened in—so, the chair idea wasn't happening. But we crammed a spill mat across the threshold, just to be safe.

Alisha said, "So one of the people in there is the evil Dr. Chance who's got y'all freaking out. Anyone else we need to worry about?"

"Evil is such a reductive—and inaccurate—term," Jibben muttered, then said, "The other subjects are documented psychics who've voluntarily donated their bodies to science to further the research."

"And what about the doctor?" Alisha asked. "Was her

'donation' voluntary?"

The awkward silence that followed her question was answer enough.

Alisha said, "And you're worried about the 'off-chance' her ghost can find its way back to her dead body and come kill us all."

"That's not gonna happen," I said.

Alisha looked at me, deadpan. "But it *could*." She waved me off like she was fanning away a really bad smell. "I knew it. I *knew* it. Folks don't hear even half the fucked-up shit the government's doing."

To be fair, I've only seen corpses move on a couple of occasions—so I'm pretty sure it hardly ever happens.

"So how do you keep a dead body from coming after you?" Alisha asked in all seriousness. "Like the movies? Shoot 'em in the head? Is that why you wanted your guns back?"

"It's just protocol," I said. "No one needs to shoot anyone." And frankly, now that I gave it some thought, I wasn't sure a head shot would even work. The last time Jennifer Chance reanimated, there was no blood in her veins, and she'd been dead so long that her nervous system couldn't possibly have been firing. She was literally a hunk of meat.

I wouldn't go so far as to say Alisha was a telepath...but she seemed to guess what I was thinking from nothing more than the look on my face.

She nodded once decisively, then said, "Well, if a shot in the head won't kill 'em, y'all can just cut off their legs and slow 'em down."

"No one is dismembering anything," Jacob said, sounding like he'd just cut into a big bag of turkey guts. "We keep the door shut, and that's that."

Since we were actually discussing tactics from zombie films…too bad there wasn't a handy armoire to drag in front of that door. Or maybe some random lumber to hammer haphazardly across the doorframe.

Then again, we'd all been stupid enough to go down in the basement. And everyone knows, those characters are the first ones to die.

Alisha nodded toward cold storage. "Are you sure those dead folks signed over their bodies on purpose?"

"Positive," Jibben said. "The test subjects were fully aware of what they were doing. They were proud to leave a legacy—and they signed a plethora of legal forms stating they wished to be studied."

I said, "At any rate, even if they did change their minds, I doubt they'd have the dexterity to…uh…" I registered the look of horror on everyone's faces. "Never mind. No one's coming back. And we all agree, the door stays shut."

Alisha recovered first. "What if these folks aren't the ones you gotta worry about, anyhow? Even if they soften up, they're trapped in their vaults, right? But the stuff from Argus Institute is just piled in the middle of the room."

Jacob said, "I thought Luther Hinman was your hero."

"I never said that—I said I knew who he was and what he was all about. That doesn't mean I think he was a saint. All those years people treated him like some kind of weirdo for studying telekinesis—and then once he's dead, someone comes along and proves it's all true. I don't know about you, but if that was me, I'd be pretty salty. And then there were those rumors about his lab assistant. The way the guy was all PTSD from Nam. The way he suddenly disappeared and no one would give a straight answer about what happened to him."

"Another episode of Psychic Mysteries?" Jibben asked.

Alisha narrowed her eyes. "No. YouTube."

Jibben scoffed. "Then it must be true."

Now, normally, I'd agree—with the lab manager's sarcastic tone, that is, not that the wild internet speculation about some lab assistant held any water. As far as I was concerned, YouTube was only good for looking up recipes I had no intention of ever making, or maybe a quick chuckle when I wanted to watch random people fall down. The so-called exposés were nothing more than clickbait.

But then Alisha said, "The video was gone less than an hour after it went up. And the usual page you see when a video is taken wasn't there. Just nothing. Nothing at all."

Which sounded exactly like the type of thing the FPMP would do.

Attempting to steer the conversation away from the agency censorship that most definitely did happen, Jacob said, "We're all on edge, but our original plan is still sound, and containment is the safest spot. Alisha, you and Dr. Jibben wait there. Agent Bayne and I will do another brief sweep of this level to assess the water situation and rejoin you in fifteen."

I could tell Jacob was less worried about the leak than he was about the dead bodies that might be floating around, but he did a fantastic job of getting everyone on the same page—and out of my hair so I could do a perimeter check of the metaphysical kind.

The whole time we'd been arguing in the hall, my flashlight beam was steady as can be, so I was on board with the idea of doing just one more sweep. It was my job, after all: a job that had gone to shit—spectacularly—when the delivery showed up, the storm bore down, and my old pal Darnell met the wrong end of a lightning bolt.

As Jibben struggled to make a U-turn in his office chair, Alisha clambered past him and strode back to containment. Maybe she was exactly who she claimed to be. She didn't seem to be fishing for classified information beyond what we'd volunteered. Though the tradecraft department taught me the best way to elicit information was by not pressing too hard, so....

A scream pierced the darkness—Alisha. Jacob shoved Jibben out of his way down a side hall, then took off to her rescue while Jibben spun around helplessly in his office chair. I was hot on Jacob's heels, sucking down white light for all I was worth. I might not put much stock in YouTube, but I'd seen more than enough spirit action in this facility to take any ghostly threat seriously.

We caught up with Alisha running towards us, away from containment. She shoved past Jacob—and latched onto me.

"What is it?" I demanded, but Alisha was making noises that bordered on hyperventilation. A few wild gestures were all I could get out of her as she used me for a makeshift human shield. I crept around the corner and found Jacob standing there in the containment doorway with his phone held high and the flashlight app aimed into the room.

He looked puzzled.

"What the hell—what the *hell*?" Alisha babbled as I scanned the hall for anything dead, but there was no one there but Jacob. He turned to look at me, face grim, and cocked his head for me to join him in the doorway. Alisha was holding my clean suit so hard I could feel her shaking...but she followed.

Jacob made room for me to come look without brushing up against him and losing my white light. He wasn't freaking out, but that didn't mean anything. After all, if Jennifer Chance's ghost had come back for a repeat performance, it's not as if he'd be able to see her.

Alisha, though? Who knows.

Anyway, I braced myself for something bad...and found that in our absence, the contents of the file folder—clippings, notes, photos—had been scattered from one end of the room to the other.

Gooseflesh prickled my forearms as I swept my flashlight beam toward all four corners, floor to ceiling, triple-checking to make sure there was no one dead lying in wait.

Thankfully, all clear.

As Jibben caught up to us and Jacob filled him in, Alisha pressed her forehead into my back and said in a small, scared voice, "I don't wanna split up—I wanna stay with you."

If something screwy was going on, that was probably for the best.

Although...it was also entirely possible that Alisha had strewn those papers around herself and started screaming, and this whole damsel in distress thing was all just an act to get deeper into the lab.

I felt like a grade-A jerk even as that thought occurred to me. She was still shaking, and I could feel her tears soaking through the clean suit. Yet, a small part of me was still thinking, *If our spies are good, National's must be even better....*

And then my flashlight flickered.

CHAPTER 20

The simplest explanation is usually correct.

Too bad secret governmental underground laboratories were anything but simple.

A few hours ago, if you'd asked me whether the joint was haunted—I would have said no, because I swept it regularly. Of all the places in this facility I'd run into something disembodied, the sub-basement was surprisingly low on the list. In fact, the only time we'd had a ghostly encounter in the lab—the Jennifer Chance incident—was the result of luring her spirit down here ourselves.

Now, though, I wasn't so sure we could chalk up the evidence to something as simple as air currents or sabotage.

"Let me take a look," I said. Once Alisha pried her hands off me, I slipped into containment, studiously avoiding stepping on the contents of the file folder. It would be awfully convenient if ghosts left fingerprints behind, but unfortunately, that's never been my experience. Without a ghost actively tossing things around, the papers were just papers. And the more I thought about it, the more I wondered if maybe the

HVAC system hadn't chugged on, just for a moment, and scattered the stuff. Because, seriously, I didn't see how a ghost could move anything in the physical plane.

Or maybe there was no energy blip, and the file folder had just teetered off the edge of a shelf as Jibben and Alisha hurried out of the room. Since everyone left in a rush, with Jibben last on his creaky office chair, it was a definite possibility that he'd simply knocked it over on his way out.

Unfortunately, since I couldn't be 100% certain it *wasn't* a ghost, I really couldn't write off any potential explanation... especially since my flashlight had been perfectly fine out in the hall, but now it was strobing like a pothead laser show.

Like cold spots and goosebumps, flickering lights actually were a ghost thing—though not because they had an etheric finger on the light switch. My theory was that certain things exist in more than one plane at a time, and some aspect of electricity might be one of them.

Still, if that were the case, then maybe a determined enough ghost could have caused the HVAC system to churn to life, if only for a brief burst of power.

Jacob eased into the room. "Well?" he asked.

"All clear as far as I can see."

He mirrored my pose with his hands on his hips and scanned the scattered documents. "This lab is a maze. There's no way of knowing where something might be hiding."

"There's nothing a ghost can do to any of you," I said. Me, on the other hand? I considered myself lucky my sidearm was locked in the safe. "Unless you're worried about death by a million paper cuts, there's no reason to panic."

I sounded pretty convincing...but then my flashlight cut out.

Fine. Jacob was right. I'd feel a lot better if I knew what we were dealing with—a confused security guard who didn't know he was dead, or the woman who kidnapped me, having clawed her way back from beyond the veil. He powered on his phone and cast the room in a different light, one with way too many shifting shadows.

The underground lab was a big place—and I didn't want to let the air out of cold storage unless there was absolutely no other choice. If only I had some hint as to where else to look. Jibben wheeled himself into the doorway and came to the same conclusion. "I'll check the manifest—I suspect there's something in the shipment we can use to narrow down our search."

I was doubtful that after all these years anything in those crates could still function, but we needed all the help we could get.

He grabbed the clipboard and ran a finger down the fine print, scanning. "Aha, here it is—the Telekometer. It runs on magnetics. Same principle as a compass."

I turned to the daunting pile of crates.

Jibben said, "Don't worry, everything's numbered—and luckily, the Telekometer is in one of the boxes that hasn't spilled." While Jacob and I got to work locating the device, Jibben tried to explain what it was supposed to do. "Dr. Hinman theorized that telekinetic activity could be measured by calculating the difference between the Earth's magnetic fields and ambient electric fields."

Alisha was watching from the doorway. "What are we trying to measure, then? Telekinesis—or ghosts?"

"Nonphysical entities," he corrected absently. "And the

answer is, neither. We're just looking for the source of the fluctuations. Coming to any conclusions about what the cause of those fluctuations might be is premature at best—"

I tuned him out. All the science made my head hurt—and besides, I was worried about more pressing concerns. Maybe Luther Hinman—with his crazy sideburns and his outdated tech—did come off as some kind of joke. But what if he'd been onto something?

And what if his gizmo pointed a big red flag at Jacob?

Too bad I couldn't be concerned enough for both of us. "Here it is," Jacob declared as he triumphantly plucked the numbered box from the shipment.

He handed it directly over to Jibben. And while the scientist carefully pried open the cardboard, the rest of us all held our breath. Reverently, he lifted the handheld device from its protective case and presented it to the rest of us with evident satisfaction.

"It's a compass," I said.

"It's a *modified* compass." Jibben said.

I managed to keep from rolling my eyes. I knew for a fact that compass readings didn't pick up on ghosts. I'd been using them since my Camp Hell days to find the cardinal points and plant my exorcism candles. And while I don't generally use candles nowadays—and my partner Carl handles those details for me if I do—it's like riding a bike. A *haunted* bike... but a bike nonetheless.

I was about to dismiss the whole thing when I saw the second needle—and figured I shouldn't be so quick to judge. As Jibben swung the device in a slow arc, one needle moved, while the other stayed put. "The differential would be significant," he said. "But without a chart, there's no way of knowing—"

He cut off abruptly as the second needle jumped—right as it passed by Jacob.

"I should really be the one to handle this." I plucked the thing out of Jibben's hand. "In fact, I've got a compass in my—" I almost said *exorcism kit*, which the FPMP management frowns upon even in the best of times. "In my toolkit. I'll go grab it."

Jibben nodded. "As a point of comparison. Good plan."

Jacob had *I'll go with you* written all over his face—but if he came along, everyone else would glom onto him. "The rest of you hang tight," I said firmly. "I'll just be a minute."

"Will you be going by the restroom?" Alisha asked.

I'd shed the thing back in the break room while I was moving around chairs, so the can was right on the way. And since all I cared about was keeping the compass needles off Jacob—especially in front of a psychic researcher and a potential spy from National—I said, "Yeah, we can make a pit stop. Let's go."

Out in the hall, my flashlight beam steadied as we headed for the can. Whether or not anyone else noticed, I wasn't sure, but I kept that observation to myself. Logically, I'd need to stay on my toes and make sure I didn't say anything that couldn't be un-heard. Because if someone from National was pumping me for information—

"How long you been working with Darnell?" Alisha asked.

Morbid topic. But at least it wasn't classified. "He and I didn't generally work the same shift."

"So you didn't know him."

"Not since we were kids."

Alisha's voice went wistful. "What was he like?"

What was anyone like when they were that age? "He didn't eat paste or lodge crayons up his nose."

"I only knew him through pictures and texts. He was all flirty at the beginning, Mr. Smooth. Until suddenly he was 'busy'... and then he totally disappeared. Maybe he met someone else."

"Maybe."

"Or maybe I mentioned Kelvin, and Darnell didn't want any part of being a father."

I could relate. But back in those early days with Jacob, if I'd found out he had a kid? I was so baffled—and, yeah, flattered—by his attentions that I doubt it would've stopped me. "Logically, at our age, most people are probably gonna be parents," I said.

"See? That's what I'm talking about. And in a few years, my son will be out the house. Anyway, that's what I tell myself whenever I get the urge to smack his lazy ass out of bed."

Clayton was practically in high school. No way could I see him being ready for college in a few short years—but it was reassuring to picture him guzzling wine coolers in some dorm room that stunk of teenage boys, and not rotting in a secret cell in Camp Hell.

While Alisha did her business, I stood there in the dark hall and pictured Clayton huddled on the couch in the cannery—and I was fully unprepared for the surge of emotions welling up in my chest. Fear for his safety. Guilt over my absence. And a staggering empathy towards him for having to weather this whole storm alone.

Alisha emerged from the can and handed me my flashlight.

"I don't wanna go back to containment," she said. "It's ugly and stuffy...and creepy as hell."

I was none too thrilled about it either, given its proximity to cold storage with all its disturbing dripping. "Maybe we can relocate to the break room."

Alisha brightened. "Dr. Twitch won't like it...but Cargo Shorts will listen to you."

"Let's go size it up." I pictured the room in my mind's eye as we approached. It would be just as dark as containment, and we'd already raided all the food. But at the very least, there'd be a couch. And a sink, too.

I was so eager to splash off my face that it took me half a second to register the sound of water and realize it wasn't just part of my overactive imagination. Alisha and I both stopped in our tracks, and I shone my flashlight beam into the break room's open door.

The sink I'd been so eager to use was now a waterfall, with its contents sheeting over the side and splashing onto the floor. "Who was dumb enough to leave the faucet on?" I snapped.

"Maybe it turned on itself."

"That only happens in the movies," I said...though I did suck down a volley of white light and check to make sure nothing ghostly had its hand on the tap.

The faucet was off, I realized...which meant the water was forcing its way past the trap and up the drain.

The fact that it had a perfectly physical explanation was only somewhat comforting. I could banish ghosts. But I couldn't do anything about the water table.

Speaking of ghosts—my exorcism gear was right where I'd

left it, perched on the countertop, just out of reach, with its shoulder strap dangling over the side.

"Is that your toolkit?" Alisha asked. "The purse?"

I sighed.

The water on the floor probably wasn't electrified water, I reminded myself, just sewage. But after I'd read Jacob the riot act for wanting to hop the stairwell puddle, could I really take that chance?

I leaned in to reach over and see if maybe the kit was closer than it looked, but no. I was still a good foot away— and I was none too eager to brace myself on the metal doorframe.

"Take my hand," Alisha told me. I hesitated, and she made a "gimme" gesture. "Don't worry. I got you."

Well, this was it. Either I trusted her, or I didn't. And while my paranoia was eager to rattle off everyone in my life who'd pretended to be someone they weren't—Roger Burke, Patrick Barley, Officer Andy, Jennifer Chance...hell, even *Stefan*—my rational side reminded me that I'd even been leery of Jacob at first.

And he'd turned out okay.

I took Alisha's hand, and as I did, she looked me in the eye and repeated, "I got you."

And I believed her.

I'd be lying if I said some small part of me wasn't aware of just how easy it would be for her to let me topple into the puddle. But Alisha's grip was strong and sure, and a moment later, that exorcism kit was back in my eager grasp, right where it belonged.

Though the break room had turned out to be a bust, we

were encouraged by our small victory as we headed back to containment.

"That purse doesn't look like it'll hold much," Alisha observed. "What d'you got in there that's so important?"

"Well...." How to explain? "The tools are pretty...specialized."

"You got something that'll open the lobby door?"

"Not really."

"Then what good is—?" Alisha stopped in her tracks with a gasp, grabbing me by the arm and jerking me to a halt right along with her. We were just up the hall from containment, though the door was shut tight, so it looked pretty much like every other closed door. But Alisha wasn't looking at the door.

"There—" she jabbed her finger emphatically toward the floor. "Shine your light there."

If water was creeping in all the way over here, we were truly shit outta luck.

But when I scanned the floor and something glistened in the flashlight's beam, it wasn't a puddle I saw...but a single, wet footprint.

CHAPTER 21

We barged back into containment and found the others sorting through one of the shipment boxes. Jacob glanced up at me and said, "There's a hand-crank emergency radio on the manifest."

Jibben added, "Keep in mind that there's still battery power involved, so after all this time, it may not be operational."

Maybe not—I've had remote control batteries go crusty after just a couple of months—but we owed it to ourselves to at least take a look. "Okay. Good. But where's the leak coming from?"

"What leak?" Jacob asked.

I gestured toward the hall with my flashlight. It dutifully flickered...and the hair on the back of my neck stood up. "Did either of you leave this room while we were gone?"

"No," Jacob said cautiously.

It was tempting to say, *Are you sure?* But I figured at least one of them would have remembered, given that Alisha and I were gone for all of ten minutes—fifteen, tops.

"Oh my god," she said under her breath.

Jacob and Jibben both stopped what they were doing and looked to me for an explanation.

I nodded toward the hall. "There's something out there you'd both better see."

Things had turned so weird, I half-expected it to be gone in the ten seconds it took to get back there. But when we trooped out to see it, there it was, in all its wet, shoe-shaped glory. "Male," Jacob said. "A plain, leather-soled dress shoe." As my shoe was the only one that matched, I put my foot down next to the print, figuring I'd somehow managed to track water in the opposite direction.

The sole was a smidge shorter than mine, and a lot wider.

"It's a ghost," Alisha said.

"It's not a ghost," I said...but I almost wished it was. Because I had a fully stocked exorcism kit on hand, but no sidearm. And if somebody was lurking around the basement lab with us—somebody in the physical plane—a spritz of Florida Water wouldn't do us a whole hell of a lot of good.

Maybe Jibben had *thought* he was the only one in the lab when I first showed up—but someone else could have very well been down here this whole time. It's not as if we'd asked Darnell to see the sign-in roster. I'm sure plenty of folks had lab clearance, not just the researchers or the important so-and-sos like Jacob, but the folks who sweep the floors and squeegee the glass.

The lab was a big place with plenty of nooks and crannies. So the thought of another person being down here with us was no big stretch.

It was the fact that they hadn't come forward yet that made it weird.

Then again, anyone who'd gotten past Darnell would've had to surrender their gun and go through the naked machine, just like the rest of us. That just left all the various chemicals and drugs that could be used as a potential weapon. At least the butter knives in the break room were off-limits now. Though who's to say the lurker didn't get there before the sink overflowed....

Jacob leaned in and murmured, "Are you thinking what I'm thinking?" Unless he was hoping that the butterknives around here were really dull, probably not. He said, "We should go check on Agent Thompson."

"Absolutely," Jibben agreed. "In case our initial assessment was wrong and he simply lost consciousness from that shock. A small possibility. But if so, he'd need medical attention."

That hadn't been what Jacob was thinking either—he knew damn well Darnell was dead—but it seemed a lot less panic-inducing than announcing we had to make sure Darnell's corpse wasn't making the rounds.

My flashlight beam danced ahead of us as we made our way down the dark hall toward the lobby. I tried to listen for any footsteps besides our own, but with three pairs of feet and one office chair struggling along, I couldn't hear squat.

As we drew closer to the lobby, I swept my flashlight across the scene. Darnell lay where we left him, face up on the floor on the other side of the glass. The divided room was so still and quiet, I could hear the blood rushing in my ears. And on his side of the door, Darnell's repeater flickered to life, came at the door, blew back and blinked out again.

Jibben wheeled forward to get a closer look through the glass at Darnell's body. "I truly thought he might be—" and then he cut his eyes to me, as if realizing that all this time, I'd known damn well the guard was dead. But at least Jibben wasn't tactless enough to blurt it out in front of Alisha.

We were all standing there staring out into the elevator bay when a crash rang through the hallway, echoing all around us. I spun, flashlight lashing through the dark. The beam caught a supply cabinet swinging on its hinges near the far wall.

"Vibrations from the storm must have worked it loose," Jacob said, but a muscle in his jaw leapt.

I nodded mutely, drinking down white light. Though if someone physical was down here with us, it wasn't as if the white balloon trick would stop them.

Alisha turned back to the safety glass, looking forlornly at Darnell's body. "Are y'all sure he's not just unconscious? Maybe he's in a coma. I think his arm wasn't in that exact same position before."

Unfortunately, she was probably right about his arm. With the ventilation down, it was stiflingly warm. The perfect atmosphere for bloat to set in early.

Hopefully she wouldn't see the worst of it in the dark.

A muted burst of static from Darnell's walkie made us all jump. Its screen lit up, casting a green glow in the dark elevator bay. Words came through, distorted and nearly inaudible through the barrier of the safety glass. We all strained our ears to listen, but the sounds remained frustratingly unintelligible.

Alisha plastered herself against the glass, thumping it with her fists. "Hey—help! You got hurt people down here!"

Gently, Jacob settled a hand on her shoulder and eased her away from the glass. "Alisha...they can't hear you. Not unless you press the button."

She jerked away. "I know how it works—but it can't hurt to try. It's more than anyone else is doing."

The last thing we needed was to piss each other off. Briskly changing the subject, I said, "Okay, what about that emergency radio on the manifest? Maybe we'll find out when we can expect the storm to blow over instead of just sitting here in the dark imagining the worst."

As we turned to go, I took one last look at Darnell's repeater, a flicker of motion as he came at the door, so damn determined to save us all—only to get blown back, dead before he even hit the ground. And I checked once more for his ghost, just in case there was something more than just the residue of a sudden death lurking in the shadows. But as far as I could tell, he'd left no spirit behind.

We all trooped back to containment. The dark hallways were just as long and forbidding as ever, only now with the added threat of a mysterious stowaway creeping around down there with us. The wet footprint was still there, mostly. Though it was smaller now thanks to evaporation, and a tire track led away from it where Jibben's chair wheel had caught the very edge of the print.

It bothered me. Not that Jibben had driven over it—he could hardly help it—but the whole fact of it being there to begin with. Who left it, where did it come from, and where did it lead? And why was there only one?

I supposed someone could have materialized out of the astral, taken a single step, changed their mind, and disappeared. (And I supposed I could also win the lottery on a snowy day in August. Chicago weather might be notoriously weird, but since certified psychs are disqualified from gambling, that wasn't gonna happen.)

Besides, if someone was shifting planes, it wouldn't be water they'd leave behind, but ectoplasm. And that would've evaporated the second our backs were turned.

I was none too fond of containment. With the big shipment of boxes in the middle and not much else, it felt both sparse and crowded at the same time. And with no ventilation, when we closed the door, it got stuffy, quick. But there was only one door in—and four of us to keep an eye on it. I liked those odds better than roaming up and down a warren of pitch black hallways where anything at all could jump out at any time.

Great, now I was feeling even more paranoid than before. Damn footprint.

Once we sealed ourselves back into the airless containment room, Jacob told Alisha, "As much as we all want to pitch in and help, the less you see of this shipment, the better."

Alisha's resulting eye-roll spoke volumes.

"I'm only trying to look out for you," Jacob said earnestly.

Alisha plunked down on one of the break room chairs, crossed her arms, and said, "I didn't wanna have to paw through that old pile of junk anyhow. You'll probably get stuck with a rusty nail."

Or, at the very least, pick up a hell of a splinter from all that sixties dark walnut veneer. Everything was covered in it, from the pencil holders to the waste paper baskets. The weather radio was all the way at the bottom of the pile—of course it was—and it, too, was wood veneer.

A very crusty wood veneer.

"I'd be surprised if the battery was still intact," Jibben said as he took the radio gingerly from Jacob's outstretched hand.

"But we're in luck—there's a servo bypass."

Whatever those last couple of words meant, I gathered they were encouraging.

A crank folded out from the veneered cube that would provide power, even with the battery juice long ago leaked away. But the radio didn't seem to be tuned to anything in particular. In other words, between cranking, tuning, and holding the thing steady, it was at least a three-handed operation. So I let Jacob and Jibben get to it and joined Alisha by the far wall.

"What about your purse?" she said. "The 'specialized equipment' you nearly got yourself electrocuted for?"

Good idea—I'd much rather futz with my compass without Jibben know-it-all-ing over my shoulder. But when I snapped open the kit, I realized that aside from the salt and Florida Water (which is typically all I use) there was a spare pocket flashlight, a charcoal puck and a small baggie of incense, a plastic lighter, and half a dozen votive candles.

By the stuttering light of my flashlight, Alisha and I both looked at the candles, then locked eyes.

"Flames use oxygen," I reminded her.

"But what if we opened the door a crack? Let in more air?"

I glanced at the door. If not for that damn footprint.... Though if we had a rescue ETA, maybe we could afford a bit more light. "Say, Jibben—exactly how long would it take for a flame to use up the air in here?"

Preoccupied with cranking, he spared me just a fraction of his attention. "Taking into account the volume of the room, the amount of oxygen consumed per hour, and of course, the size of the flame—"

That sounded like way more math than I was prepared

to deal with. But luckily Alisha didn't panic when someone whipped out a formula. "What would use up more air—a bunsen burner, or a candle?"

"Oh. Well, certainly, a gas burner exhibits a considerably higher rate of oxygen consumption than a standard candle flame. The magnitude of this difference would vary depending on several factors, of course—the specific design of the Bunsen burner, the type of fuel used, the flame settings."

My flashlight beam flickered. "Guesstimate," I said.

Jibben gave a frustrated huff. "Again, it depends—"

"How many hours 'till a candle burns through all the air?" Alisha asked.

"Ten thousand?" he said doubtfully.

We all frowned, and Jacob said, "More than a year."

So much math.

Jibben said, "But keep in mind, that doesn't even take into account four people breathing—"

I pulled out a match and struck it. "Worse comes to worse, we'll crack the door."

When the wick caught the flame, the shift in the room was palpable. My flashlight was still flickering away, but by the steady glow of the candle, it was nowhere near as strobey.

Funny how something as basic as a reliable light source can turn the whole mood around. The flickering LEDs had been making me tense up, but now I felt my shoulders unhitch. As Jacob and Jibben futzed with the radio, I did my best to just sit there and breathe. I might never consider myself an optimist. But it felt a lot better to believe that we were on the brink of getting back to our normal lives.

Static burst from the radio. It cut out when Jibben's crank

paused, then picked up again as soon as the cranking resumed.

 —*severe weather warning for the Chicago area.*

Tell us something we don't know.

CHAPTER 22

The weather alert voice was as robotic as ever. I'd always found it unsettling. Then again, no one tunes in to the weather band on a nice day just to verify the sun is high.

—*funnel cloud sighted in Wheaton, and residents should take cover*—

Alisha grabbed my knee so hard I nearly fell out of my chair. "Like a hurricane?"

Jibben was the one who answered. "We're too far inland for a hurricane." Alisha exhaled a shaky breath, and he went and added, "Funnel clouds are associated with tornadoes."

"Like in the Wizard of Oz," I added, with the intent of keeping her from tearing off my kneecap.

Jacob said, "Even if a funnel cloud were to touch down, the basement is the safest place to be."

"But not during a flood!" Alisha said.

She had him there.

—*has issued a tornado warning for the following counties: Cook, Lake, DuPage, McHenry*—

Jacob tried to tune in another band—likely with the hope

of dredging up some news that was a bit less harrowing—but all he could find was a distorted snatch of random pop music and some advertisements in Spanish. When it was obvious he wasn't going to find anything helpful, he said, "Tornadoes usually blow through fast. I've never spent more than a couple of hours in a shelter."

"And he's from Wisconsin," I added. "He should know."

Jibben said, "Tornado durations can vary widely depending on their intensity and size. It's possible for a tornado to persist for several hours under certain conditions. Each one is unique in its characteristics and lifespan."

"Good to know," I said testily. "But the point is, we're talking hours. Not days. We just need to hold out a little bit longer."

If there was ever a good time for Jacob to gloat, that time would be now. *I didn't like the look of the sky* had become the understatement of the year. The next time he had a feeling about the weather, I'd run out and grab some toilet paper, beef jerky and bottled water.

Jacob came over and sat on the floor beside me with his back to the wall. "I hope Clayton knows enough to go in the basement."

"Don't they have tornado drills at school?"

"Who knows?" Jacob draped his arms over his knees and pressed his forehead into them. "I'm not sure if it even matters. He's at that age where listening to authority figures is suddenly optional."

Alisha clutched even harder—that woman had one hell of a grip. "I hope Kelvin didn't do anything stupid. I shoulda called my sister to go get him when I had the chance."

"I've got an idea," Jibben said. While the rest of us had been wringing our hands over the various teenagers in our care, he'd been scouring the manifest. He pulled a piece of equipment out of the crate and set it on the tabletop.

The contraption was a tripod with foldable legs, but instead of a camera mount up top, there was a weight dangling from the center, and a plate on the bottom marked with concentric circles. "A pendulum," Jibben explained. "We can use it to observe ambient vibrations that are too subtle for us to sense ourselves." The weight swayed slightly. "Any minute tremors transmitted through the earth, structure, or atmosphere should cause the pendulum to move."

I had my doubts as to how effective that might turn out to be, but I figured that anything that could keep us busy was a good idea.

Jibben said, "The plate at the bottom measures the swing. The larger the swing, the greater the force." He levered up on his good leg, looked down from overhead and said, "Current distance, approximately 3.5 centimeters." And then he made note of the time and jotted his finding down on the back of the manifest. "If we track the motion in predetermined increments, we'll have some idea what's going on out there."

I had no idea if the tripod would do anything useful, but at least it distracted Jacob from his Clayton worries. He said, "How was this used to measure telekinesis?"

Jibben said, "The mechanics of the device make it possible for even a minute physical vibration to be measured and quantified. Telekinesis is notoriously subtle, and using an apparatus such as this will amplify the motion and make it much easier to detect, even without any costly sensors or electronics. An elegant solution."

Everyone's eyes went to the pendulum which was now just hanging there dead center, lifeless.

Though not for lack of trying. Because the way Jacob was staring at the pendulum, it was a wonder it didn't blow through the far wall like a .45 caliber bullet.

If the pendulum was etheric, maybe it would.

I supposed I should be glad for small favors. No clue if it was possible to put an etheric hole in the wall. But if it was, that hole would lead straight to cold storage.

A thunderclap rumbled through the foundation, and the pendulum began to swing. Alisha looked from the pendulum to me, and gave my knee another painful squeeze. "Reminds me of my cousin's gender reveal party. They hung a ring over her belly, so the way it moved—in a circle or a line—would tell if she was having a boy or a girl."

"Utterly unscientific," Jibben said without looking up from his notations. "Unless the point of motion is restricted in some way, a pendulum will swing back and forth. It's simple gravity."

"Oh yeah? Then why's it going in a circle now?"

"The conservation of angular momentum. A tremor could easily cause it to deviate from its straight-line path—"

Alisha huffed. "Whatever. The baby reveal pendulum might not be all scientific, but it was fun. Isn't that the whole point? And, by the way, it got the sex right."

Even Jibben couldn't be bothered to point out there'd been a fifty percent chance for that to happen. And if that pendulum were dangling from the grasp of a precog...maybe more

Back in Hinman's time, pendulums were commonly used

as divination tools. Something akin to Ouija boards or dowsing for water. And while I knew firsthand that Ouija boards could damn well channel the dead, they only worked in the hands of a medium. For anyone else, they were nothing more than a creepy toy.

Most people consider the Ganzfeld Reports incontrovertible proof that psychic abilities actually did exist, but in fact, they debunked even more common practices than they proved. Like a Ouija board, a pendulum was activated by unconscious micromotions from the hand that held it.

Looking at the pendulum now, suspended on its tripod, I couldn't help but wonder. The pendulum could pick up vibrations from a hand, and most definitely from a tornado. But an etheric force?

No. Wrong plane.

Which was why Jacob could stare at it all he wanted without changing a circle to a line...or whatever it was he'd been trying to do.

He must've come to the same conclusion. He scowled and turned his focus back to the radio.

After a few cranks, the radio crackled back to life, and the weather robot was talking.

—funnel cloud touched down in Elgin. All residents urged to seek shelter—

"No one did the pendulum at my shower," Alisha said. "I thought I was having a girl. I was sure of it. Everyone said, you carry high, that's a girl-baby. Plus, the cravings. Anything sweet—especially strawberry milk. Couldn't get enough of it. But chips? I could take 'em or leave 'em. Everyone knows, it's salty for a boy and sweet for a girl."

Jibben said, "And yet, clearly your 'evidence' turned out to be faulty."

Alisha sighed wistfully. "I was gonna name the baby Imara. It means *strong*."

I gently pried her hand from my knee, searching for something to distract her. "What about Kelvin—what's that mean?"

"It's a river in Scotland. I just liked the way it sounded."

Jibben cleared his throat. "While I understand the human tendency toward magical thinking, the fact remains that the world operates on scientific principles. Motion, gravity, entropy—these forces dictate the workings of the universe in quantifiable ways."

He leaned forward, eye twitching in emphasis. "Psychic powers are real, make no mistake. But even psi phenomena operate within certain boundaries. The human mind craves narratives to explain the unexplained. But the truth often lies in mathematics, measurement, replicable experiments—"

"Oh yeah?" Alisha grabbed my wrist and pointed my flashlight beam at the pendulum. "Explain *that* with your science."

Dangling there from its tripod, the pendulum quivered like a bee doing a communication dance with its hive buddy. But the thunder vibrations we'd periodically felt coming up through the floor were utterly still.

"I'm sure there's a logical reason," Jibben said.

And then my flashlight beam flickered.

CHAPTER 23

"Things happen for reasons!" Jibben twitched so hard he nearly toppled out of his chair. "Real reasons! And just because we don't know what they are shouldn't make us devolve into believing a bunch of fairy tales!"

Everyone stared at him blankly.

"What about the Telekometer?" Jacob suggested—and, unfortunately, there were too many boxes between us for me to shut him up with a subtle kick to the shin. "Hinman's equipment is acting up. Use Hinman's equipment to figure out what's wrong."

After Hinman's gizmo jumped when I ran it past Jacob, the last thing I wanted was to aim it there again while Jibben was looking. But refusing outright would seem suspicious. "I thought you said the Telekometer thing measured electromagnetic fields. The pendulum measures vibrations. Apples and oranges."

"Be that as it may, additional data points can only help us analyze the situation more accurately." Jibben's eye ticced expectantly.

"Vic should handle the Telekometer," Jacob announced. "The rest of us will watch the pendulum from three different angles. And Dr. Jibben will record our findings."

Thankfully, Jibben was a team player, so he didn't argue with Jacob's plan. As the rest of them stationed themselves around the pendulum, I slipped the compass out of my exorcism kit and compared it to Hinman's device. The compass needles matched, and when I turned my body one direction, then the other, they both stayed on magnetic north.

The spare needle on the Telekometer did nothing.

That was a relief.

I said, "I don't think this actually works."

"Let me see that." Jibben grabbed the Telekometer from my hands before I could react—and aimed it directly at Jacob.

The needles remained steady. I let out a breath I hadn't realized I was holding. Jibben's forehead creased in confusion as he swung the device toward the now-steady pendulum. Again, no reaction.

"Curious," he said. "I thought we might detect something in the electromagnetic field. Especially with the lights flickering."

"Maybe it's a different field," I offered vaguely.

Jibben's eye ticced again as he scrutinized the oscillating pendulum. "Clearly there are unknown factors at play."

And if that factor turned out to be Jacob's ability, it had better remain just that—unknown.

He began muttering about quantum entanglement as he took more notes. Our secrets, for now, were safe.

Alisha stood up with a sigh. "I gotta pee again."

Jibben said, "You should make sure you don't have a urinary tract infection, once we get out of here."

"*If* we ever do," she shot back.

"I've gotta go too this time," I said. "C'mon. Let's get it over with."

Alisha and I filed out for yet another bathroom break. Crisis averted. For now.

I had the spare flashlight from my exorcism kit in my pocket, but I didn't need to use it. Once we were out of containment, my regular flashlight beam steadied. I might not know jack about electromagnetic anything, but I knew how the FPMP operated...and electrical weirdness seemed like a logical enough explanation to me. And if some sort of experimental field had been constructed around that room—one that was currently wonky thanks to the storm—let's just say I wouldn't be surprised.

"Keep your eyes peeled," I told Alisha as I scanned the dark hall ahead with my light.

"For what?"

"For anything that shouldn't be here." We'd certainly made the trip enough times for her to get the lay of the land. Footprints don't just appear out of nowhere...but now I was second-guessing what I'd seen. Maybe Jibben's diatribe about scientific explanations had gotten to me. But now I was wondering if maybe there'd just been some kind of latent print there, maybe a residue of some sort that drew water up through the flooring when it was combined with whatever magnetic disturbance was going on.

Then again, Occam—whoever he was—would probably say that the most likely explanation for a footprint was a person with a wet shoe.

Given the long, empty expanse of the halls, if there was

a random guy down here with us...at least we'd hear him coming.

Once we made it to the can unscathed, I handed Alisha my spare flashlight, angled toward the bathroom door, and said, "Can you hold it? I'll be quick."

Her eyes went wide. "But you said this was the Ladies' Room!"

"That was before the break room sink started spewing water. Don't worry. I did a dozen years in homicide. I won't faint at the sight of a tampon."

"Well, I put 'em away. But hurry up, or else there's gonna be another puddle on the floor!"

Speaking of a dozen years in homicide...over that course of time, I'd learned a few things about human nature—and I found it pretty obvious that Alisha's behavior wasn't currently adding up. She hadn't rushed me down the dark hall with the urgency of someone on the brink of imminent embarrassment. But now, suddenly, I was supposed to hurry.

Which meant there was something in that bathroom she didn't want me to find.

And here I'd been so good at convincing myself she was someone I could trust.

I shut the door on Alisha's anxious face and slid the lock home. The bathroom was small. I could scan it with a single sweep of my flashlight.

Nothing obvious.

Though I didn't expect there to be.

Modern surveillance equipment is not only ridiculously small, but it's easy to disguise as something innocuous, like an air freshener...or a tampon. But when I scanned the counter, there was nary a tampon to be found.

As I relieved myself, I bounced my beam around the small enclosed room, noting all the places Alisha could've stashed a small piece of tech. Light fixture. Vent. Heck, she could even have stowed something in the core of a spare toilet paper roll.

The only thing I knew for sure was that she'd been doing something she didn't want me to hear while the water was running—and I didn't think it was a number two.

I glanced at the toilet tank.

When you search a scene, that's the first place to look. Why criminals think they're so clever for hiding stuff back there is anyone's guess, but I've found everything from a murder weapon to a stolen koi just by looking in the tank. So, if Alisha was a spy from National after all, reverse psychology would be the only reason she'd hide something in such an obvious place.

But in the spirit of leaving no toilet tank lid unturned, I zipped up and took a peek.

And floating there in the water was a plastic trash bag.

Alisha banged on the door. "I really gotta pee!"

I held my flashlight between my teeth and fished out the bag. It was small, about the size of a grocery bag, and it had been tied off with some air inside like a saggy balloon. But it wasn't full of murder weapons, or surveillance equipment, or drugs.

It was full of food.

String cheese. Peanuts. That Asian mystery snack. All of the granola bars—and not just the ones she'd talked me into giving her. Every time our backs were turned, Alisha must've palmed something from the piles Jibben had so diplomatically rationed, then asked for a bathroom break to stash her ill-gotten goods.

On one hand, I always feel sorry for hoarders—so long as I don't need to spend any time in their house. But right now, I just felt relieved that I hadn't uncovered a surveillance device.

When I opened the door, Alisha managed to look both guilty and defiant, daring me with her eyes to make a scene.

"Listen," I said calmly, "no one's gonna starve here. Even if it takes a while for the power to come back up, just as soon as the storm blows over, I'm sure Darnell's boss will sweep the building."

"You don't know that." Alisha's voice was strained.

"But I do. You saw how gung-ho this place is with security. Someone's gonna check just as soon as they can—"

"Which could be five minutes from now. Or five hours. Or five *days*."

"Probably not that long."

"New Orleans. 2005. At my grandmother's house down in Jefferson Parish. Me and Gramma got ourselves to the Superdome before the storm hit. I was so excited to see that big stadium—we never could afford to go see a game—but I had no idea we were walking straight into hell.

"Once we were inside, it was too late to change our minds. People struggling over food, getting sick from the bathrooms overflowing. The heat. The *smell*. National Guard giving out food, but pretty soon they ran low. I was so hungry I would've eaten anything. Gramma talked about Jesus the whole time to keep my spirits up...while she kept one eye on the men roaming through the crowd looking for anyone they could rape.

"We were trapped in there for a week," she said. "So, five days? It can happen."

I sure as hell hoped not—and not just because of the food. In five days, the lab would flood, the cadavers would thaw, and god-knows-what would happen to Clayton.

"Tornadoes aren't hurricanes," I said. "We'll make it through. And, don't worry. Your food stash is safe with me. Just...leave whatever's left in containment for the others."

Alisha's eyebrows twisted up and her chin quivered.

Cripes, the last thing I needed was *more* waterworks down here.

"And give me back my damn granola bar," I added sternly, though I'm pretty sure she saw right through it.

We ate, sitting there in the dark hallway with our backs against the wall, while Alisha talked. She told me about her grandmother losing everything and coming up here to stay with family in Chicago. Hating the winters—but never forgetting the brutally hot week she'd spent stewing in that reeking stadium.

There was a lull that I chalked up to the normal ebb and flow of conversation, and then Alisha cleared her throat. Once. Twice. Three times. And then she was slapping urgently at my leg.

She'd gone up on her knees, eyes huge, waving at her neck.

"You're choking?" I demanded.

She wheezed. And since there was air going in and out, the Heimlich maneuver wouldn't do her any good. Her knee crunched on a wrapper. I swung down my flashlight beam and saw it wasn't a granola bar she'd just eaten, but the Asian mystery snack.

And she'd told us all she was allergic to shellfish.

CHAPTER 24

Who knows what was in that snack—prawn crackers, shrimp paste, a whole host of things that could've set her off, and that's not even taking into account cross-contamination. I only knew I needed to help her, fast. The spare flashlight was on the floor where she'd dropped it. I pressed it into her hand and said, "Stay here—stay calm—I'll be right back."

Then I tore down that dark hallway for all I was worth, visualizing the first aid kit we'd scavenged, fervently hoping it was more than just alcohol wipes and Band-Aids. At the very last second, I remembered the footprint, vaulting the general area so as not to disturb whatever hadn't yet evaporated. I didn't know if it was evidence, per se, but old habits die hard.

As I cleared the print, a chill raged down my spine. The HVAC system chugging briefly to life as crews restored power—or a cold spot?

No time to think about that now.

"EpiPen," I gasped as I shoved my way into containment. "Alisha's airway—"

Jacob and Jibben had been talking fervently over a pile of

naugahyde and veneer, but they immediately snapped into action. Jibben grabbed the first aid kit—hallelujah, there was an injector—and handed the pen off to Jacob. I barely scrambled out of the way before Jacob barreled past me and took off toward the bathroom.

Jacob is fast, and even if he's not wearing gym shoes, he can run circles around me. By the time I caught up with him, he was already on his knees, jabbing Alisha in the thigh right through the clean room suit.

"You're going to be just fine, Alisha. Slow, deep breaths. This will only sting for a second—there you go, squeeze my hand, squeeze as hard as you need. I've got you, just stay with me. Focus on my voice."

As if anyone could hear that low, calm, velvety voice of his and think about anything else. *That's my husband*, I thought, and my heart swelled with pride—though, obviously, I'd never say as much aloud. We're trained to handle crises. Helping people is what we do.

And yet, I'd be lying if I said I didn't get all drippy inside watching him step into the role of the strong, solid protector like he was born to play it.

Even in cargo shorts.

Once Jibben finally caught up with the rest of us in his chair, he told us in no uncertain terms that crowding around him while he tried to stabilize her was only making things worse. A more tactful person would have suggested we go grab the couch cushions—and take our time. But if Jibben is tactful, then I'm the King of Extroverts. "This would be a lot easier without the two of you breathing down our necks!" he said. So, Jacob and I exchanged a glance, then headed off to containment to give him some space.

As we approached the room, I saw the wet footprint in the hall was now a smear on the floor, mostly dry. And when I felt for the cold spot again, I got nothing.

"Come look at this," Jacob whispered—not losing any sleep over the fact that we'd been given the brush-off. "I found it in the shipment while you and Alisha were gone."

I swung my flashlight beam in the direction he was pointing and saw another archaic device had joined the others on the worktable. This one looked more like a desk toy of some sort—like those clacking metal ball pendulums you'd always see on douchebags' desks back in the day—except it involved a wooden track marked with measurements and a ping pong ball.

"It's another TK test," Jacob said. "And I made it move."

Jacob was already a hero. He didn't need to keep trying to prove himself...but something in his nature just wouldn't give it a rest. I didn't groan, or sigh, or roll my eyes—but make no mistake, on the inside, I was doing all of that and more. "Great," I said. "We can set something up just like it at home—where it's *safe*—and test it for ourselves—"

"But you won't have access to a Telekometer at home."

"We don't even know how to read the thing."

"It did something, though, back when you were comparing it to your compass. I could tell by the look in your eyes."

Then my resting scowl face needed some serious work. "Jacob, Alisha's out there—"

"With *Doctor* Jibben, who made it pretty clear we weren't helping anything by hovering around. Two minutes. That's all I ask."

"Fine." It was easier to get it over with than to argue, though I sensed that in either case, Jacob would end up disappointed. "What do you want me to do?"

"I'll focus on the ping pong ball, you see if you can pick up any readings."

Naturally, I considered lying and telling him, *Yes, wow, you were totally right, your talent is off the charts...now let's shelve this discussion until it's safe to talk.* But no matter what I said—yea or nay—Jacob would only want to dig deeper.

I parked my flashlight on the table and took up the compass and Telekometer. The compass needles both stayed at magnetic north. The second needle on the Telekometer wobbled as I moved. But once I trained it on Jacob it settled into place, doing nothing at all.

"Anything?" he asked tightly.

"For crying out loud, we don't know if it even works. This Hinman guy was working with tech he cobbled together from paperclips and rubber bands. What makes you so sure this thing is good for anything but finding your way out of a paper bag?"

I grabbed my flashlight, trooped over to the door and looked for the smeared footprint. The beam was steady, but the footprint was gone, dried in the stifling heat of the stuffy basement.

"What are you doing?" Jacob asked, genuinely curious.

"Seeing if what I felt out here was a cold spot or just wishful thinking."

"You felt a cold spot?" He hurried over to get a look for himself.

"It could've been a vent."

"Without power?"

"Just because we don't have power down here doesn't mean there's no power somewhere else in the building—wherever it is they keep the air conditioning. And you remember how it was back at the cannery the last time a water main blew. While the crews on the street patched it up, there was no water, then sputtering water, then brown water, then a bunch of crazy gurgling sounds—"

"All right. It *could* have been a vent." Jacob was just humoring me, obviously. But if he was willing to stop trying to prove his telekinesis for the time being, fine. "Keep in mind, though, Agent Thompson just died."

"Nothing but a repeater."

Jacob cut his eyes to cold storage. "And the cadavers."

I'd be lying if I said I wasn't concerned about the thawing bodies myself...particularly my ex-fake-doctor's. Since I was running on adrenaline right now instead of white light, I slipped my hand into Jacob's and threaded them together, getting a little jolly from the feel of his wedding band warm and hard between my fingers. I pulled him close and said, "Remember, mister—you're a Superstiff. You'll be fine."

His eyebrows twisted. "But...we can't say the same for you."

I tugged Jacob closer, dropping the flashlight beam to my side, and settled my lips against his. It was a shallow kiss. Chaste. Barely even there. And I felt it from the soles of my feet to the top of my crown chakra.

Jacob thinks he's a man of steel, and he's always the first to leap into the path of danger—whether that's relocating a shower spider or rappelling up an electrified elevator shaft. He may not appreciate his own talent, but I sure did. At least I didn't have to worry about him when he insisted on stepping in front of an oncoming ghost. I took some small comfort in that.

But comforting as it might be, we couldn't stay in that moment forever. I stepped back and released Jacob's hand, our fingers slipping apart with a reluctant brush of skin on skin. I instantly missed the connection, and busied myself with gathering up couch cushions so I could occupy my mind with something useful—something other than the fact that I almost couldn't recall what it felt like to do something normal like sit on the couch and walk my fingers through his hair.

Thankfully, the flashlight was on its best behavior. Though when we headed back to Jibben and Alisha, we saw theirs was twinkling like a string of Christmas lights. Jibben had his fingers on Alisha's wrist, looking surprisingly competent for a guy riding around on an office chair. Alisha was dozing. "She's improving," he said. "But we'll need some supplies from the medical bay. It's likely her blood pressure is low. She'll need fluids. Possibly a corticosteroid."

The last thing I wanted to do was kill Alisha and have yet another potential ghost wandering around with us. Jibben led me down a dark corridor to a room with a physical lock—not just a keycard—to which, thankfully, he had a key. As much as his heebie-jeebies made me a bit twitchy myself, it was a comfort to have someone with us who at least knew the lay of the land.

The room was small, more of a glorified closet, dark and very still, and cool as though it had been under temperature control, at least until we broke the seal and let all the good air out. "The blood pressure cuff should be in that cabinet.

Check the shelf for another first aid kit. Alisha might very well have a secondary reaction."

IV saline, antihistamines, and some steroids. As I piled it into a bin to bring it all back to Alisha, Jibben said, "This is why you don't drag civilians into a potentially hazardous situation. If anything happens to Alisha, it's on our heads."

Frankly, I thought Darnell could take at least some of the blame, since we would have been long gone if he'd only handed us back our guns. But I did my best not to think ill of the dead. As far as I knew, Darnell was no telepath, nor did ghosts retain their psychic abilities...but why take chances?

I thought Jibben would keep chewing me out over my failure to protect the civilian, so it surprised me when he switched gears and said, "You've been a psychic investigator as long as anyone. Tell me, Agent, do you think it's possible the things from Argus Institute could be cursed?"

My knee-jerk reaction was that curses were what came out of your mouth when you stubbed your toe on the dresser for the fourth night in a row. But shaman charms were legit, if incredibly rare. Why not a curse? "Why do you ask?"

"Ever since that shipment came into the building, everything that could have possibly gone wrong, has."

"That's what happens in emergency situations."

"But accident after accident, it hardly seems random—and you already know how I feel about accidents. The curse could operate on a quantum level. Quantum entanglement allows for a connection between particles, so if a 'curse' could somehow alter or manipulate this entanglement, it could theoretically influence events in a cascading sequence."

And now there might be a scientific basis for curses? This

day just kept getting better and better. "Why would anyone want to curse Luther Hinman? That's like giving the finger to Bozo the Clown."

"Hinman might seem ludicrous by today's standards, but he was utterly dedicated to his research. And to this day, several of his theories are still considered viable avenues of research." He dug out another first aid kit and piled it into my bin. "And then there were the rumors...."

"Is this the part where you tell me he built his institute on an old Indian burial ground?"

"There was a very public fallout with his first assistant, Gordon Tertz—the man Alisha mentioned learning about on YouTube. But since Tertz had come back from Vietnam with numerous issues, no one was surprised when he eventually dropped off the radar." As he finished his thought, Jibben twitched so hard he jabbed me in the ribs. His elbow was incredibly sharp. "His brother called foul play. But his brother was a morphine addict, so the investigation didn't exactly receive top priority."

"And so you think this Tertz guy cursed something in the shipment?"

"I just don't want to rule anything out. You're the PsyCop—you tell me. Is this something we should be worried about?"

Quantum entanglement theories aside, in all my years of dealing with things that go bump in the night, I'd seen a whole hell of a lot of ghosts—but to my knowledge, not a single curse. And ghosts tended to stick where they'd died. "I'm not ruling anything out, but Occam would probably tell you we're under a hell of a lot of stress and we're making a shit-ton of bad decisions. If anything...." I trailed off, disturbed.

Jibben leaned in. "Tell me."

I waved my hand in the general direction of cold storage. "I'd just be a lot more comfortable knowing I wasn't within spitting distance of a bunch of cadavers. The bodies themselves might be sealed in their vaults—but that won't keep a pissed-off spirit inside."

Jibben fidgeted for a long moment, then quietly said, "If you didn't have an extensive history with one of those bodies... would it still worry you?"

I shouldn't be surprised that Jibben knew about the kidnapping fiasco. Everyone over a certain clearance level probably did.

He added, "According to your report, you achieved the spirit's transition."

True. I frowned.

"Have you known any other spirit to return to the physical plane?"

Only the really evolved ones like Miss Mattie, who'd told me she'd seen God. And I had the sense that her return trip wasn't something you could finagle without the proper clearance. "No," I grudgingly admitted. "Once they're beyond the veil, that's that."

"If that's the case, then why are you concerned about the body?"

"It's like food poisoning. You'll never have a taste again for the last thing you ate."

"We're hardwired that way—to associate negativity with its sources. It's an evolutionary tactic, the main reason we've survived as a species. But if you say it's unlikely we're dealing with a curse, then I bow to your experience and will attribute

our problems to a run of crises exacerbated by hasty decisions. It just means we'll need to start being more deliberate
and methodical."

"Fine. No curses. No ghosts."

But even as I said it, the flashlight started strobing like crazy.

Jibben reflexively shoved his office chair back with his good
foot, but the casters locked. He dipped back alarmingly, then
snapped upright again—just as the height adjustment lever let
go and ratcheted down three cranks. He flailed, rocking back
so hard that the momentum nearly launched him out the
door on the return swing. And then an empty beaker tipped
off the top shelf, missing him by a hair, and shattered on the
floor in an explosion of glass.

CHAPTER 25

"What was that?" Jacob demanded from down the hall.

"Nothing," I said, not wanting to start shouting back and forth about all the fucked up things that might be going on "Nothing...important." Lowering my voice, I told Jibben, "First, we take care of Alisha. Then figure out our next step."

Jibben was right about one thing. The accidents were starting to feel anything but accidental. As we headed back toward Jacob and Alisha, I passed the spot where the wet footprint had been taunting me, and wondered if maybe a lurker had been responsible for all the craptastic turns of event we'd endured.

And I'd spent so much time being suspicious of poor Alisha that I'd let him get away.

"Are there any disgruntled employees in the lab?" I asked Jibben. "Maybe someone who got passed over for a promotion—or, hell, even for that dumb trip to Nantucket?"

Jibben jerked his head side to side. "We're a solid team. Everyone's contribution is valued, everyone's ideas are heard. Plus, the random polygraphs do weed out the bad apples before they have a chance to fester."

I suppressed a twitch of my own over the thought of being hooked up to a machine. "Fine, the lab's all one big happy family. But what about the maintenance crew?"

"I would imagine they're under just as much scrutiny as any other employee, if not more."

I pondered this as we rejoined the others. Alisha was laid out on the couch cushions with Jacob kneeling beside her. I set up the IV pole while Jacob helped Jibben down from his chair. Alisha was only somewhat aware of her surroundings.

And for that, I envied her. The halls were dark. The flashlights were both flickering. And the sound of water bubbling up from the break room sink was inordinately loud in the stifling silence.

Once Jibben took Alisha's blood pressure, he swabbed her arm and tied on a tourniquet. But before he stuck her with the needle, I said, "Wait! Triple-check that it's saline." With the way our day had been going, it was probably full of lobster juice.

Not only did Jibben re-read the bag, but he squeezed out a drop and tasted it. "Saline. Nothing more."

Voice low, Jacob asked, "What were you expecting?"

I didn't know. Just that the less we took for granted, the more likely we'd come out of this whole thing alive.

I personally wouldn't have wanted a guy known as Heebie Jeebie to set my IV, but he slipped the needle in on the first jab. Alisha didn't even flinch. Then Jibben got busy monitoring her pulse, brow furrowed in concentration. "The fluids should help her BP. Heartbeat's steady."

It wasn't quite as stifling out in the hall as it was back

in containment, but it was still uncomfortably warm, and Alisha's brow was sheened with sweat. I found a cold pack in the first aid kit and squished it to release the chemicals. While it cooled down, I grabbed a handful of paper towels from the restroom to make a half-assed cold compress and balanced it on her forehead.

Her lips curved into a faint smile. "My heroes."

Jibben crawled back into his chair to keep an eye on the IV bag. I settled on the floor beside Jacob, who kept a steadying hand on Alisha's shoulder as her eyelids fluttered shut.

Jacob murmured, "The situation's under control...for now. But something's not right here."

"Agreed." My mind went immediately to the footprint. "It's probably sabotage."

But instead of wholeheartedly agreeing with me and coming up with a plan to make sure no one could sneak up on us, Jacob said, "What you mean, sabotage?"

"Well...things don't just fall by themselves."

"There's torrential rain outside. Water seeping in. Funnel clouds. The building is shifting—"

"We feel bigger vibrations in the cannery when the neighbor's kid cranks up his car stereo—and you don't see our cabinets falling off the walls. Besides, what about the footprint?"

"It must've belonged to one of us."

"It didn't match—"

"It was water, Vic, not concrete. It's not a stable medium. Maybe there were treads, and maybe they filled in. Maybe it evaporated, or maybe it spread. All I'm saying is, if there were anyone down here besides us, we would have heard them by now."

Given all the arguing he was doing, probably not. "Fine. You don't think we've got a stowaway? Then what's your idea?"

Jacob squared his shoulders like he does when we're about to accuse each other of forgetting to take out the trash, and said, "Residual telekinetic energy."

Was that an actual thing...or had he just made it up? I cut my eyes to Jibben, hoping he'd call bullshit if Jacob was just railroading us all.

Jacob said, "If trapped etheric energy can exist as repeaters, then why not other types of psychic energy? It could account for things like deja vu—"

Jibben cut him off. "Interesting premise. But deja vu has already been proven to have a thoroughly mundane neurological cause."

Nostrils flaring in indignation, Jacob countered, "Then how do you account for the scattered papers?" and turned and stalked down the hall toward containment.

"Stay with Alisha," I told Jibben, and hurried along after my infuriating husband.

I caught up with him near the site of the footprint, just outside containment. "What gives, Jacob? Now suddenly you're an expert in psychic theory?"

Jacob held a finger to his lips, then dropped his voice low. "I just wanted an excuse to talk alone." And I'd bought every minute of it. He was a scary good liar now that Carolyn wasn't around to keep him in check. "I've been focusing so hard on grounding myself and getting something to move, I really think I might have—Vic, don't make that face."

"What face? This is how I always look."

"Stop trying to make me wrong for half a second—"

"Hey, that's so not fair—"

"—and consider what would happen if I *did* manifest a surge of TK energy—and one of Hinman's devices recorded that surge while Dr. Jibben was looking. Introducing the 'residual telekinetic energy' idea takes the focus off me and puts it on something that will probably never be proven."

I planted my free hand on my hip. "Fine. That makes sense. But you know what also makes sense? *You not trying to move things with your mind if you don't wanna get caught.* And why is it so crazy to think that there might be someone else down here with us? It's not like we conducted a room-to-room search."

"But isn't that exactly what you were doing before I got here? Checking every part of the lab?"

"For *ghosts*."

"And how many people did you come across inside the security check?"

"Just one," I admitted. "Jibben. But when the lights went out and everything was in chaos, someone could've easily slipped inside."

Jacob stroked his beard. "I'm sure the research here is worth a fortune. But if anyone had this facility under surveillance— one of our experts would have noticed."

"What if our infiltrator wasn't scoping out the FPMP building?" I suggested. "What if they were following that shipment?" I warmed to my own idea. "What if the motives weren't financial—but personal? There was a lab assistant named Tertz who dropped off the radar, and the whole thing was covered up. Maybe it was him."

"If he was in his twenties then, he'd be in his eighties now."

True. Vietnam vets were hardly spring chickens. Tertz

could've had a kid who was trying to pin his disappearance on Hinman, I supposed. Or maybe his addict brother did. But the more I thought about it, the more it seemed like I was grasping at straws. "Okay, look. Let's just grab anything that might be useful and get back to the others. They're sitting ducks without us."

The votive candle in containment was still lit, so I blew it out so as not to burn the whole place down, then tucked the weather radio under my arm. We took the long way back, but there were no more telltale footprints. The doors were all locked. And there was no one clinging freakishly to the ceiling in the dark.

Though that was now a thought I couldn't unthink.

Alisha was still resting in the hall, the bathroom door was open, and light was strobing inside the can. We found Jibben leaning over the sink from his office chair, lantern flickering away on the counter while he dug at his hand with a pair of tweezers and the water running. "Bring your flashlight over, would you? There's a shard of glass under my skin that would be hard enough to see even in good conditions."

There must've been enough water left in the hot water tank for it to still come out hot, likely because there'd been no one around to use it up, and the bottom of the mirror above the sink was hazing over. I aimed my flashlight so Jibben could see where he was digging without casting a shadow on himself, and my previously steady beam gave a flicker.

Hard not to notice that my flashlight was only acting up intermittently. I'd figured there was something in containment making it wonky—some kind of mad scientist magnetic field. But it had been fine back there just a minute ago.

So, what if the common denominator in the wonkiness was Jibben?

Maybe all that jerking and twitching wasn't just some unfortunate bodily affliction. He could be responding to something outside the physical plane. Jacob sometimes felt a little twinge from the etheric. Why not Jibben?

And if that were the case, adolescent Jibben might've very well had a run-in with a poltergeist all those years ago. Only the poltergeist was no ghost—it was his own undocumented telekinetic talent.

I glanced up at the mirror to see if Jacob, out there in the hallway, happened to be chafing the back of his neck, but he was outside my line of sight. There was movement in the mirror, though—but even as I sucked down white light, I realized it was nothing but the steam fogging up the mirror distorted by the flickering beams of the flashlights. Most people have a fight or flight response—but mine's more like fight, flight or white light. Apparently, it's hell on my adrenal system. But I'd rather overreact to a false alarm than get caught with my pants—

Something moved.

In the mirror.

I was focused so hard on finding an apparition there beside me—Dr. Chance appearing in the glass like Bloody Mary because we'd said her name one too many times—that I didn't comprehend what was actually happening...until I heard the creak.

Years of responding to half-seen threats meant I reacted first, questioned myself later. I'd already grabbed Jibben's chair and started backpedaling when I registered what the motion was: a hairline crack that had appeared at the top of the mirror.

And then it zigzagged its way down, widening as it went... and the entire thing shattered in a rain of razor shards.

CHAPTER 26

Jesus Christ.

As white light thundered down through my crown chakra, I yanked Jibben's chair back so hard it whirled around a couple of times in the hallway once I let go of it. A spritz of his blood flew out and painted the walls like spin-art.

"My arm!" he grunted.

Thank God it wasn't his freaking jugular.

I reached into my clean suit and yanked off my tie, but Jacob had already grabbed the first aid kit tourniquet and was looping it around Jibben's bicep. I scooped up the emergency lamp and aimed the beam. "Any glass in the wound?"

"No big pieces," Jacob said.

Jibben nodded grimly. "Then we need to get the bleeding under control and worry about the smaller shards later. Wrap it tight. Use the gauze. And Alisha—stay put!"

Alisha was a good couple of yards away from the shatter zone—but since she was half-delirious, she didn't know that. She'd been trying to burrow behind the couch cushions and use them as a shield. I handed off the lantern to Jacob, being careful not to touch him since I was hopped up on light. Jacob and I can flow the energy deliberately, but it takes a lot of concentration, like trying to fill a thimble from a gallon of milk without christening your entire kitchen. Now—hungry, fatigued, and all around stressed out—I might very well blast him to the end of the hallway.

He took the lantern without incident and balanced it on Jibben's lap, while I hurried over to help Alisha before she pulled out her own IV. "It's okay, Alisha—you're okay—"

"We're gonna die," she sobbed.

"We're okay," I said firmly. "It was just a freak accident. That's all."

Obviously, it was no accident—but she didn't need to know that. In a situation like this, our main concern would be keeping everyone calm enough to survive 'till the power grid came up.

Jacob rummaged the gauze roll out of a first aid kit and turned back to Jibben. Despite the fact that the lab manager had been beaten up by more inanimate objects in the past few hours than most people had in a lifetime, he'd kept a cool head. He'd torn his sleeve away from the wound and was holding one of the flashlights steady.

Jacob fiddled the gauze out of its plastic. "What happened in there?"

Through grit teeth, Jibben said, "I have absolutely no idea."

And though I didn't believe in poltergeists—or at least I hadn't, as of a few hours ago—I was starting to wonder if maybe I simply hadn't encountered one yet. Because no one's luck was as bad as Jibben's...and that was *before* the broken mirror.

But as much as Alisha would feel vindicated if I told her I was reconsidering my stance, now was not the time. Not when she was sprawled on the floor in the dark with an IV in her arm.

"We haven't known each other long," I said as I crouched beside her, "but you're strong. That much is obvious. You'll get through this. You're a survivor."

I flinched when Alisha grabbed my hand and squeezed it tight, but there were no white light fireworks at all. Just a couple of people muddling through an incredibly fucked up situation the best we could. I settled her back onto the cushions and said, "Look at me."

She met my eyes, chest heaving.

"I won't let anything happen to you. Got it?"

She nodded once, and the tension went out of her—probably due to sheer exhaustion more than anything else. I double-checked her IV was running and her pulse was still strong. I was about to go help Jacob finish wrapping up Jibben when she whispered, "What if it's Darnell?"

A shiver crawled down my spine. "It's not."

"Hear me out, though. What if that lightning didn't kill him right away? We could've helped him, but we just left him there to die. What if his spirit's trapped and he's pissed we didn't try to save him. He's making all this stuff happen to get back at us—"

"Alisha—ghosts aren't physical. They can't knock over beakers or break mirrors."

"What if he was telekinetic?"

Thanks a lot for planting that idea in her head, Luther Hinman. "Darnell wasn't telekinetic," I reassured her.

"Everyone who works here gets tested out the wazoo for every flavor of psychic ability there is. But his badge read NP—non-psychic. If he had telekinetic ability, someone would've picked up on it—" even as the words left my mouth, I caught sight of Jacob's profile in the light of the emergency lantern. He'd skated past with no one the wiser. Why not Darnell?

Huh.

Did psychic abilities stick with us after we died? I presumed I'd be pretty much the same after I croaked, maybe with a bit more clarity. But the empaths, the telepaths, the precogs—would they retain their powers?

I couldn't see why not.

And if that were the case, why *not* TKs?

Still, Darnell hadn't left a vengeful spirit behind—I would have noticed. But there *was* a repeater.

Could repeaters have telekinetic power?

Weirder things had happened.

So, what were we looking at: a mindless loop of etheric energy with the ability to make lights flicker and glass break in the physical plane? If so, then what we were dealing with was more like a force of nature than a haunting. In Darnell's last moment, he'd been throwing himself at the door with a tire iron in a time of extreme stress. An undocumented TK would probably be swinging more than just a crowbar. Especially if a TK's automatic response to a tense situation was to power up his most useful chakra.

"Whether or not Darnell was telekinetic," I finally said, "a little send-off ritual wouldn't hurt."

And while it was clear from the look on her face that Alisha thought I was about the last guy capable of laying someone to rest...I was all she had. So I'd have to suffice.

If Alisha hadn't been flat on her back, she would have insisted on coming. But I told her Darnell would hear her prayers just fine from where she was—and since she didn't fight me on it, it was clear she was still way too weak to drum up any pushback.

With Jibben all wrapped up and parked out of the range of any potentially hazardous objects, Jacob and I headed toward the lobby to deal with Darnell's repeater. Normally, I would have gone myself and left Jacob to make sure no one did anything dumb while we were gone. But the more I thought about it.... If there was a telekinetic repeater spewing out random waves, did I really want to face it without Jacob?

When I told him my theory, he said, "You think Darnell has been attacking Jibben?"

"Not intentionally, no. Even if Jibben was a real prick to work with, Darnell didn't strike me as the type of guy who'd take it personally." Revenge was absolutely a powerful motivator, don't get me wrong. But you'd be talking the type of self-righteous rage you feel when someone destroys your life's work—not just noses into your parking spot.

I cut a glance to cold storage as that particular thought crossed my mind...but kept my mouth shut about that. "I think that energy's energy. And if there is some kind of TK shockwave rolling through the lab, we need to try and neutralize it before anyone else gets hurt."

Flashlights were steady as I grabbed my kit, but I couldn't presume the tempest had played itself out just yet. Ghosts are persistent, and their expiration dates are measured in decades, not hours.

The lobby and elevator bay were just as we'd left it. Darnell's body was starting to look puffy. On the other side of the doorframe, his repeater flickered.

Jacob followed my gaze. "Will the safety glass be a problem?"

I rolled my shoulders. "I guess we're gonna find out."

Normally, I can make do with a spritz of Florida Water and a handful of salt. But given the seriousness of the situation, I couldn't afford to cut any corners. Chicago is a big grid, and the hallways of the FPMP run along predictable axes. Still, repeaters were a lot tougher to send packing than actual ghosts, because you couldn't reason with them. Bad enough I couldn't set the candles around the repeater, thanks to the wall of glass between us. I wanted to make sure I at least knew which way was north.

But when I pulled my compass out of my pocket, I came up with Hinman's goofy Telekometer instead.

Well, the compass pointer was calibrated the same as mine, and it found north exactly where I'd expected it to be. I set the votives on the floor and lit them in sequence, then readied my Florida Water.

On the other side of the glass, the repeater flickered. His cycle was a couple of minutes in between resets. I paused with one eye on the spot where Darnell died and the other on the Telekometer. I counted to a hundred and ninety-one when the flicker came again. I thought the additional pointer on the device might jump.

It did nothing.

I should probably consider myself lucky that the compass needle still worked.

I'm not generally afraid of repeaters, since they're nothing

but trapped energy, but death moments do tend to be discon-
certing. Add to that the fact that I'd witnessed this particular
death—with me feeling a bit guilty that I was someone Darnell
had thought he was rescuing—and it was no fun to watch.

I centered myself and opened up to the white light, focusing hard on my crown chakra. It's easier to load up reflexively in a moment of panic, but the one-eyed hangover was
a lot less punishing when I did it deliberately. There's never
any guarantee that I'm at full charge. Just a gut feeling I've
developed over the years. Sometimes I feel a bit loopy, and
sometimes my vision gets a bit weird. But I was working
by the light of a flashlight and a few votive candles and I'd
eaten nothing in the past twelve hours but a granola bar and
a couple of pickles, so I just made my best guess as to when
I was actually topped off.

The scent of Florida Water greeted me—alcohol and
cloves—and I relaxed into its familiar smell. And when I
spoke the normal words I used to send spirits where they're
supposed to go, it was more for me than for Darnell, since I
figured his repeater didn't much care.

"You're dead—you died trying to save us. You might not
have known it was a sacrifice, but you died trying to help
others. And in the end, maybe that's the best any of us can
hope for."

I tipped a handful of salt into my palm and imagined my
white light flowing into all those little grains.

"The physical plane isn't a good fit anymore. You shouldn't
be here. Most of you is probably off beyond the veil doing
whatever it is spirits do, and this part of you needs to move
along, too."

I scattered the salt, visualizing a refraction of light coming from each crystal and bathing the repeater in light.

"Feels good, right? It can be all this, all the time. Just cross over so you can be where you...belong."

My white light fluttered like an incandescent lightbulb in a brownout, and I turned to see Jacob looking directly at the spot where Darnell's repeater should be. And as I faced him, the Telekometer in my pocket clicked.

CHAPTER 27

"What?" Jacob asked when he saw me looking at him. "I'm all the way over here—I'm not stealing your light."

I pulled out the Telekometer. The additional pointer was at one o'clock now instead of noon. "What were you just doing?"

"Nothing."

"Nothing," I repeated as I swept the device back and forth across Jacob. The compass needle wobbled, but the other needle didn't budge. "Nothing at all? Even in your mind?"

"Well, I...." Now he wasn't so sure. "If I did, it wasn't deliberate. You just always tell me repeaters are hard to scrub out and..." he shrugged helplessly. "Maybe I focused."

"Shit." I clipped off the end of the word more forcefully than I needed to. "Lucky for you, the only one who knows how this happened is me. I don't care if the only scientist down here is busy rolling around on an office chair and spurting blood. You've gotta watch yourself in front of the researchers. They're smarter than either of us and they're dying to unlock a new psychic secret. You can't afford to set off his warning bells. Not even a little."

Smoothly, Jacob said, "Everything's fine. It's just me and you." He cut his eyes to the elevator bay. "Or is it?"

I turned and looked at the spot where I expected Darnell's repeater to appear...and waited, and waited....

And waited.

Nothing.

"Look, I appreciate the help," I finally admitted. Repeaters hardly ever got gone on the first go-around. "But you've gotta start being more careful."

"I will," Jacob said. He even managed to sound contrite.

"Because once you're on the radar—"

"I know," he said gently. "I get it. It's just...not being able to actually see what's going on—especially after all these years being told I'm just a Stiff—well, old habits die hard."

"*Just* a Stiff? The fact that ghosts bounce right off you is huge. I can focus on what I'm doing because I don't have to worry about you—" other than the fear that he'd TK in front of the wrong person and be spirited away by National...or someone even worse.

"I know I shouldn't need to keep proving to myself that my abilities are real. I get caught up in the moment. That's all." Jacob took a step toward me, then paused. "I really wish I could touch you right now."

I considered the queasy white light buzz I was currently experiencing. "Best let me simmer down, first."

Jacob nodded regretfully, and I turned back to the spot where I'd last seen the repeater, and though I counted to a hundred and ninety—twice—he didn't reappear. I made an effort to stop clenching my mojo as I crouched down to snuff the candles. Even so, Jacob got a little jolt when we both reached for a candle and our fingertips brushed.

Our exorcism was cleaned up, except for the salt...though the FPMP janitors were accustomed to finding random patches of salt on days when Carl wasn't there to sweep up after me. I straightened up and gave the area one final sweep with the Telekometer, taking care to go nice and slow on Jacob.

Nothing.

"C'mon, mister." I slung an arm around him and gave him a squeeze. "We'd better get back to the others before anything else goes wrong."

We headed back and found Alisha dozing while Jibben pushed the shards of mirror he could reach from his chair out of the way with a piece of the mirror frame. I said, "Nothing else has fallen on you yet—I'll take that as a good sign."

Jibben shook his head ruefully. "And your efforts—were they a success?"

"All clear."

Jibben looked back at Alisha. "I'd hate to move her, but the water in the break room is spreading toward the threshold."

I missed the times when all we had to worry about were ghosts.

Jibben said, "It'll be safer to do it without the I.V. Let me just get a blood pressure reading to see if it's advisable to stop fluids."

I stepped aside to let him wheel past me...and as I did, the Telekometer in the pocket of my clean suit clicked.

I stood very still and held my breath. Jibben hadn't noticed. Jacob either. What with all the glass crunching underfoot, it was easy for a little click to go unheard.

Angling away from Jibben, I eased the Telekometer out of

my pocket and checked the dial. Now it was on two o'clock. If I palmed the device and kept it behind the beam of my flashlight, I didn't think anyone would see—especially with the focus on Alisha. I did a slow and careful sweep, hoping to target Jibben and not Jacob....

Nothing.

Suddenly, I felt like an idiot. This stupid device, whatever it was...what on earth led me to think it was the real deal? Look where it came from—a shipment of random crap. I stuck it back in my pocket. Of course it didn't respond to telekinesis. In all likelihood, it was just picking up some random jostling. This notion that a freaking compass could tell me where telekinetic waves were coming from was patently ridiculous.

Jibben wheeled past me again. The device clicked.

Random. Probably.

So, why was I holding my breath?

The simplest solution is probably correct. Those micro-motions that powered pendulums and dowsing rods were most likely the same thing causing the clicks. I was holding the compass. I was reacting to something. Simple as that.

"Alisha's BP is much better," Jibben began—

And then a tiny ping sounded by the ceiling, and a fish-eye security camera directly over him shattered in a shower of glass.

—and as I turned to avoid the fallout, I swung past the cold storage door, and the clicker in my pocket went crazy.

CHAPTER 28

"You're lucky it didn't hit your eye," Jacob said as he carefully de-glassed Jibben's hair with a piece of duct tape.

"Somehow, I don't feel so lucky."

Jibben's hazmat suit had protected him from the majority of the shards, though one of them had worked its way into his collar, and now his neck was smeared with blood.

While they worked, I was holding the flashlight in one hand, surreptitiously checking out the Telekometer in the other.

It had clicked all the way around to 11.

I pictured the hallway like a crime scene. Where I'd been standing with the clicker. Where Jacob had been, off to the side with Alisha. As for Jibben, well...hard to forget his position, directly beneath the jagged remains of the fish eye lens.

Maybe it was sabotage. Maybe it was the stress of the storm shaking the building. I couldn't say for sure, but between the Telekometer having a party in my pocket and the lab crashing down around us, I was willing to call it telekinesis.

Even if Movie Mike, the strongest TK I'd ever encountered, could barely flutter a sticky note.

The malfunctions in the lab weren't Jacob's doing, though. True, during the exorcism of Darnell's repeater, Jacob had earned a click. At the time he'd been focused on the etheric, though, which was where his abilities functioned.

But the glass breaking all around us was most definitely physical.

Thinking back, the problems had started small. Flickering flashlights. Moving papers. A falling pen. And one by one, they escalated.

I cut my eyes to Alisha—sitting up against the wall, propped by couch cushions—and considered her for a moment. What if her childhood poltergeist hadn't been some vagrant walking through the upstairs apartment? What if it was her own latent TK talent creaking something in the floorboards? It made sense, if the anecdotal evidence of poltergeists haunting adolescents could be chalked up to the pubescent onset of telekinetic ability. My light hadn't jumped into her before, but maybe that's just because she wasn't focused in the etheric.

And if Alisha *did* turn out to be a TK—and her hold on her self-control was getting worse and worse as the storm wore on....

I swept the Telekometer past Alisha.

Nothing.

To earn a click, the subject probably had to be actively doing their thing. I patted myself down and felt a familiar plastic crinkle in my breast pocket. I reached under the clean suit and pulled out a granola bar. "Hey, Alisha, look what I found." I crinkled the granola bar for emphasis, then lobbed it in her direction. It landed on her lap.

The Telekometer didn't budge.

"Thanks, Blue Eyes," she said softly as she opened the wrapper and tipped granola crumbs into her palm. "You're all right."

Hardly an exhaustive test, but it did help me narrow down my focus. Jacob's TK wasn't physically directed. Alisha didn't register. I turned back to Jibben. He might have scored a click earlier, but I couldn't seem to replicate the finding. And there were only four of us down here.

Unless you counted the cadavers.

We knew one of them, all right—far too well. But who else was in cold storage?

To Jibben, I said, "What information have you got on Dr. Chance's frozen roommates?"

"That data is on an encrypted server." He shook bits of glass from the fold of his sleeve. "Though I know where we might find a backup."

I followed as Jibben wheeled over to a door marked Copy Room. He told me, "We went digital several years ago, but Director Kim said it's not a priority to re-outfit this room as something else. Personally, I think she's keeping it around in case we need it again someday." He lowered his voice. "Or maybe she knows it's where Dr. K keeps anything he thinks should stay on paper."

Walking into the Copy Room was like stepping back into the 90s. Outdated copiers stood dormant, though the peculiar smell of toner still lingered. The entire far wall was dominated by boxes of paper reams that would never see any use, so old that the labels were starting to curl and fade.

Jibben wheeled over and pulled out a box, wincing as the corner dropped onto his wounded leg, and pulled out the top two reams of paper. "Check around. He moves it every so often so as not to leave an obvious trail."

Given all the Spy vs. Spy stuff I'd seen at the FPMP, hiding files in a box of paper was hardly a high tech solution—but it turned out to be a lot less obvious than a toilet tank. The boxes were heavy, and there were a lot of them. And even knowing there was something there to find, it still took us several tries before Jibben finally hit pay dirt.

"Here you are. Cold storage." He handed me a file.

The first corpse belonged to a precog who predicted the date of her own death, though not the manner. (Turned out to be a brain aneurysm.) She was found in her bed, neatly dressed, lying atop a plastic tarp covering the bedspread. Grim...but considerate. Her finances were in order. Her pet parakeet was rehomed. Her bank account was divvied up among her kids, and extensive instructions were left as to what should become of her body.

A photocopy of a handwritten note was attached to the paperwork. It read, *I want my death to have meaning. As my final act, I wish to contribute to the advancement of psych research, so all future precogs can benefit.*

Not exactly the type of person to leave a pissy ghost behind.

The second body was once a human rights activist, and a pretty high empath, who died of natural causes at the ripe old age of 82. No lofty bequeathals here. But there were several newspaper clippings showing him doing sit-ins and peaceful protests, going back decades.

Again...not the type of person who'd typically haunt someone.

Let alone spray them with broken glass.

Even so. If I was going around exorcizing threats—even distant ones—I'd be an idiot not to take care of those cadavers. For all I knew, the old guy had a bone to pick with Jibben, or the precog had experienced a last-minute change of heart. And so, I gathered up my exorcism kit and Jibben's keys, and did my best not to think about what I was actually getting into. I cocked my head for Jacob to follow, and together, we headed off toward cold storage.

Whenever Jacob jerks awake in the middle of the night, he might tell me it's just one of those dumb thrillers he reads at bedtime catching with him, but I don't buy it. The room beyond that insulated door was what figured in all his nightmares.

And now Chance's dead body was back.

"You don't need to do this," I told Jacob as we approached the door.

"The hell I don't."

So much for hoping he'd take the gracious "out" I'd been offering. I longed to slip my hand into his and give him what reassurance I could, but my head was already buzzing in anticipation of the work to come.

I approached the door of cold storage, picked up the gel mat across the threshold, and used it to give the metal bar on the door a shove. A rubber seal offered token resistance... then broke with a gentle suction.

Darkness. Followed by a rush of cold air. It would have been refreshing...if not for the contents it was designed to keep frozen.

While the power grid might've been down, my internal circuit breakers were working just fine. I flipped the psychic switch and mojo flowed in. I tried to pace myself, but as Jacob swept the room with his flashlight revealing one horror after the next, psychic energy blew through my etheric pathways like a fork of lightning.

To the untrained eye, cold storage wouldn't have looked like much—stainless steel worktables, a dozen square doors set into the wall, a warming room hung with plastic—but looks were deceiving. Every one of those innocuous things held a scarring memory for me.

A chatter behind me. I glanced over my shoulder. Jacob was shivering, and given where he was born and raised, it wasn't from the cold. "Let's get this over with," I said, and pulled out the wonky compass.

The regular needle found north. The other one didn't budge.

Jacob cleared his throat. "Do we need to pull out the... bodies? Set the candles around them?"

"We got rid of Darnell's repeater without him being in the center of the circle. We don't need to start screwing around with the vaults."

"Thank God," Jacob said under his breath.

But in the spirit of being thorough, I dug a charcoal puck out of the bottom of my kit and got some incense sparking. On one hand, I was in my element, and it felt good to have purpose—to have a task in front of me I'd done so many times before it was practically muscle memory.

On the other, if there was a worse place to do an exorcism than a morgue of a psychic lab, during a thunderstorm, in a *basement*, I sure as hell couldn't think where that might be... even though I scanned the room for ghostly presence and found none.

Once the candles were lit and the incense was smoking, I faced the vaults. A cloud of condensation was forming on each square, like frost settling around the edges of small window-panes during a cold snap. I swallowed hard and pulled out my Florida water. The smell was particularly obtrusive combined with frankincense and myrrh. It would cling to my nose hairs for a week. I gave the area a good dousing, and followed up with the salt, flowing white light all the while.

And once I was done, everything felt pretty much the way it had when we'd first walked in.

Except maybe a few degrees warmer.

I pulled out the Telekometer and checked the second dial. It was still at 11.

"What's wrong?" Jacob asked. "Did we set the candles wrong—do we need to start over?"

"No, it's fine—"

Just as the all-clear was about to leave my mouth, a violent hiss filled the room, and the thick plastic wall that divided us from the warming chamber shuddered wildly. The Telekometer dial spun like the Wheel of Fortune as Jacob dove between me and the plastic, and I danced back just in time to keep from shooting my psychic load all over him.

I scrambled, flashlight flailing, as I searched for a ghostly silhouette somewhere in the flapping plastic—and Jacob matched me step for step, always keeping himself squarely between the threat and me.

I knocked the hallway door open with my elbow and nearly landed in Jibben's lap, dropping my flashlight. "What's wrong?" he demanded. "We heard yelling!"

I couldn't have even told you if that was Jacob or

me—probably both.

I grabbed for the back of Jibben's chair to keep from tripping over a caster, but ended up grabbing Jacob instead. My white light surged into him so fast it left me crispy inside.

"Dammit," I snapped—he knew better. And even though he'd been Johnny-on-the-Spot when it came to putting himself between the apparition and me, he knew we couldn't afford to—

"Vic?" Jacob said urgently—and I realized he was still several steps away, in the doorway.

He hadn't stolen my mojo after all....

My light had jumped to *Jibben*.

CHAPTER 29

"Of course I'm not telekinetic," Jibben said. "There must be another explanation."

I said, "You're a scientist. Are you gonna trust your assumption, or my tangible experience...of something that happened to me with a TK I *used* to know...a long, long time ago."

Once we'd been informed that the ruckus in cold storage was nothing weirder than a safety valve activated by the rising temperature to let off a blast of pressurized gas, we could focus on something more important. Namely, the fact that my energy had leapt into Jibben. But, like most folks who've scored nil on umpteen psych tests, he figured that I was the one barking up the wrong tree.

"The simplest explanation is the most likely," I reminded him. "My etheric power-ups don't jump into NPs."

"If I were telekinetic—theoretically—then all of the malfunctions could technically be my own reaction to the stress of everything that's happened. But that's a big *if*."

Jacob said, "The stress could be forming a sort of feedback loop, with every instance cranking up the levels."

"There are tests." Jibben wheeled back until his chair bumped the wall and glanced down the dark hallway. "Two TKs are with the Program—a rarer talent than even mediums. We're currently working toward development of their abilities, though since they're so subtle, their application is more theoretical than practical. But all the equipment is computerized, so results can be measured to a high degree of accuracy. In other words, it's all electronic. Useless without power to run it."

Alisha was up and around now. She looked like hell, but the fluids had done their job and she was no longer on the verge of passing out. She crossed her arms and said, "Are y'all seriously gonna ignore the fact that you got a whole entire shipment of stuff from the Argus Institute on your hands?"

Jibben said, "Some of Dr. Hinman's theories might have turned out to be correct, but his equipment is entirely unproven."

The clicker hung heavy in my pocket. In the spirit of finding answers, I almost said something—but then quickly thought better of it, since its presence would expose Jacob.

"Still," Jibben added, "if something from Argus can help us find answers, we should take a look, if only to put our minds at ease. But keep in mind, these are relics. Even if they worked at one time, they may not be functional now. What do you think, Agent Marks?"

Jacob cut his eyes to me and I gave him a subtle nod. He said, "It's your area of expertise, Doctor. We'll follow your lead."

As Jibben wheeled into containment with Alisha following, I hung back, plucking at Jacob's sleeve to get his attention. He paused, and I brushed the back of his hand with my fingertips. No zap. Every last bit of juice had either poured into Jibben or discharged into the atmosphere. "Whatever you do in there, Jacob, don't flex."

"Of course I won't."

Jacob was no dummy—but that wasn't the point. "Not on purpose, maybe. But I mean the impulse stuff that happens before we even know we're doing it. I'm talking about reflex." Which, by definition, none of us could control…but he had to try. I grazed my knuckles down his jaw, and the two of us shared a look that encompassed everything we'd done, everything we were, everything we meant to each other. "Whatever your zen place is…you need to go there."

"I will," he said thickly. "I promise."

And if anything registered that shouldn't be public knowledge, I could always claim I'd somehow zapped it. Without a telepath present to call foul when I lied, it wasn't like anyone there could confirm or deny my allegation. I gave Jacob's shoulder a parting caress, and together, we headed into containment to face the telekinetic music.

With Jibben at the manifest, Alisha was working her way through another crate. "What are we looking for now?" I asked.

Jibben said, "It's called the Galvanic Conductor."

Alisha pulled out an object swaddled in umpteen layers of bubble wrap. "And here it is."

Unwrapped, the Galvanic Conductor resembled the offspring of a cordless lava lamp and a gumball machine. The top was capped by a metallic sphere that might've been shiny once, but was now tarnished with age. Glass tubes spiraled down the center like a couple of silly-straws, and the heavy wooden base was dinged and scuffed. Frankly, it looked like it was destined for a stoner's yard sale, not a lab.

But given that Hinman's clicker did apparently work, I wasn't gonna write it off just yet.

Jibben said, "The Galvanic Conductor was designed to respond to telekinetic energy. The idea was that a TK could focus their mental energy onto the device and excite the gas particles inside those tubes, without any need for electrical charge. But remember, it's based on theory, not fact."

Jibben set up the tube on the worktable and positioned himself in front of it. He placed a hand on either side of the sphere and focused.

Nothing happened.

"Come on, Doc, you got this," Alisha urged.

Seconds ticked by. One minute. Two. Jibben's brow furrowed deeply, his entire body tensed with effort.

Still nothing.

With a sigh, Jibben dropped his hands. "I'm no telekinetic. Surely you can't expect anything to happen."

"Not with that attitude," Alisha said. "Think of all the folks who struggled and searched, dedicating their lives to proving psych was real, even when the rest of the scientific world was calling 'em a bunch of frauds. I'll bet they spent more than a few minutes trying to get results. How many spent their whole lives trying to prove something they believed in? Y'all wouldn't even be here, fooling around in your fancy top-secret lab, if it weren't for the visionaries like Luther Hinman—"

A crash made us all jump—but it was just the lid of a shipping crate falling over.

Or was it? My flashlight flickered...and suddenly I wasn't so sure.

Alisha swung around and looked at me. "You *know* what we need," she said.

"Yeah? What's that?" I asked.

"A seance."

"That's not really...a thing I...do."

"Then what in the hell kind of medium are you?"

"Ma'am," Jacob said sternly—and his tone said *watch your step*.

Alisha threw her hands up in surrender. "If Luther Hinman's mad at you for going through his stuff, maybe you need to apologize. All I'm sayin'."

"If Luther Hinman were here," I said, "then all we'd have to do was say the words, 'I'm sorry.' We wouldn't need a bunch of silly incantations or hand-holding around a table. But he's not here. And besides, *ghosts can't move things*."

Though most telekinetics couldn't, either—at least, nothing any bigger than a bottle cap.

It must've said something about me that I wasn't afraid of Luther Hinman's ghost. Maybe it was the sideburns. Or, more likely, the fact that he'd appeared on so many dumb TV shows. And while it was entirely possible there was something dark lurking behind his public façade, people like Luther Hinman would actually *want* their inventions to keep going long after they were gone. I'd learned the hard way how obsessive researchers could be about getting credit for their contributions. But having his work validated by the FPMP would only enhance Hinman's legacy.

"You know," Jibben said, "the Galvanic Conductor may

not even be functional any longer. It relies on sealed argon. It's quite possible that after all these years, the gasses have escaped. But the metallic amplifiers in the device don't require any power or gas. Maybe infrared will reveal something the device itself can't."

"Might as well try." I pulled out my phone, and Jacob shut off the lantern. Darkness enveloped the room, save for the pale glow of my phone screen, which showed the room in shades of gray. "Okay, go."

I pressed the record button and the counter began ticking off seconds. Jibben, a specter of ghostly white on my screen, placed his hands back onto the Galvanic Conductor. His body tensed, the blobs of gray on my screen moving around, yet the Conductor remained dark, completely unaffected.

The room was dead silent, save for the sound of four people trying not to breathe too loud. After several long minutes, Jibben's hands fell to his sides and he sat back in the office chair with a creak. His body heat had risen a bit, probably just from the effort, but the Conductor remained a lifeless monochromatic prop.

"Sorry, guys," I said. "That proved nothing."

As we all flicked on our flashlights, Jibben said, "I beg to differ. While not exhaustive by any means, it does support the fact that I've tested NP many times over. And also that thermal energy isn't necessarily tied to telekinesis."

While Jibben reviewed my recording, Jacob looked like he was hoping for a lava lamp for his birthday. I was just relieved he'd kept out of the frame.

Jibben finished watching and handed my phone back to

me. "Your battery is very low, Agent. I recommend you shut down your phone."

I glanced at the battery icon. It had definitely seen worse, after a marathon session of Mood Blaster followed by a bunch of mindless YouTube. But that was within spitting distance of a charger, so I hadn't been too concerned.

When I flicked up the screen to get to my settings and shut it down, I accidentally jumped back to the previous video: a bunch of gray-looking papers on a gray-looking work table. Hardly riveting entertainment.

Then I noticed something I hadn't spotted before because I'd been watching those papers so hard: the weird fan in the background (a.k.a. the Rotational Indicator) was moving. Slowly—so slowly that when I blinked, I wondered if I was imagining the whole thing.

But when I put the playback on 4x, it most definitely spun.

The question being...was Jibben doing the spinning? Or someone—some*thing*—else?

CHAPTER 30

"I told you," Alisha said. "I told you Dr. Hinman was still around. Ain't none of us even looking at that fan on the video. We're all watching the papers. And yet, there you go. Plain as day. The fan's *moving*."

Jibben said, "That's quite the leap of logic. Why would Dr. Hinman be behind any of this?"

"Seriously?" Alisha shook her head. "We just brought in all his stuff. Who else would it be, Mickey Mouse?"

Jacob said, "It would make sense for Dr. Hinman to dedicate his life to researching telekinesis if he thought he might possess the ability himself."

Alisha cut her eyes to me. "Too bad we can't just ask him."

"It doesn't work that way," I said, taking no pains to hide the annoyance in my voice. "Because Hinman's ghost is not here."

Jibben said, "This is certainly interesting, but let's not jump to conclusions. After all, Dr. Hinman was working with very limited resources and technology." He gestured dismissively at the homemade devices scattered around the room: a pendulum, a lava lamp, a fan. "Just because telekinesis was eventually proven, that doesn't mean his methodology was sound."

Alisha said, "But something's got it in for you, Doc. You're a walking target, and I don't know it's even safe to be in the same room with you. Would it really kill you to say you're sorry?"

"For what?" Jibben asked, exasperated.

"You just *said* his methods weren't sound. Would you like it if someone said that about you?"

Jacob, being Jacob, felt the need to get the squabbling under control. "The fact remains that Agent Bayne—whose ability *is* extensively documented—noted a transfer of energy between himself and Dr. Jibben. Whether it bears any relationship to the accidents, we don't know. But if there is some sort of telekinetic backlash in play, it's in our best interest to find out. Especially since we don't know how much longer we'll be trapped down here."

I'd be glad enough to just cover Jibben in bubble wrap and let sleeping dogs lie. Any pushback on my part would undermine Jacob's authority, though, so I kept that thought to myself.

Alisha chose a chair as far away from Jibben as possible, sat herself down, folded her hands, and began to pray. "Dear Dr. Hinman. If you can hear me, know that if we did anything to offend you, we're truly sorry—"

Her Act of Contrition wouldn't do us any good unless Hinman's ghost was in the room, but I supposed it couldn't hurt, either. And at least it might make her feel better.

But Jibben was apparently none too keen on Alisha's lack of scientific method. He interrupted her with, "We need to do a proper experiment on the Rotation Indicator. As much as our circumstances allow. First, we eliminate the possibility of air currents influencing the Indicator. For that, I propose we create a shield with the Saline Transference Environment."

Oh, right. The fish tank.

"Then, we need a control group. Each of us taking a turn at influencing the rotation should suffice."

Which would put Jacob right in the line of fire. I kept my expression as blank as possible. I'd told him not to flex—he'd promised me he wouldn't—but I wasn't so sure he could control the impulse. The desk fan was physical and Jacob's talent was etheric...but what about the things that straddled both planes? The floors that prevent ghosts from falling through to the center of the earth—or the clothes they're wearing while they wander through their afterlives?

What about GhosTVs?

"I don't see the point in testing Agent Marks—" I began.

And Jibben immediately disagreed. "He's the most valuable control subject here. A verified Agency NP, and a certified PsyCop Stiff."

"It's not like we got something better to do," Alisha said, and I knew that if I pushed any harder, I'd only make us look like we had something to hide.

"It's fine," Jacob said decisively, all calm deliberation. "I'm happy to do it. For science."

We'd bagged up the Saline Transference Environment and its contents earlier in our haste to stop the fluid from evaporating. Jacob and I unbagged it carefully. Though all the saline had leaked out, it was heavier than it looked, due in no small part to the metal frame, which held the glass in with crumbling putty. "We got this," I told Jacob—while with my eyes, I said, *Please tell me we do*.

"Don't worry," Jacob said softly as we sidled over to the work table. "It'll be fine."

Nothing about the last twenty-four hours had been fine. But at least we had an understanding.

Following Jibben's instructions, we set the tank on its shortest side with the bottom facing us and the open side against the wall, enclosing the fan on all sides and making sure it was draft-free. We set up one of the office chairs in front of it, locked the casters, and marked the floor with duct tape to ensure the chair didn't budge. It was a good two yards away from the fan—and I very nearly mentioned that when Movie Mike was sliding his pennies around, he'd always done so from close range, close enough to reach out and physically touch them.

Since I didn't actually want Jibben's experiment to pan out, I opted not to mention it.

"We'll start with shorter sessions," Jibben said, "and increase if needed. Ninety seconds should do it. Agent Marks, you focus on moving the Rotational Indicator while the rest of us observe from different angles."

With Jacob in the hot seat, everyone faced the tank. My flashlight beam was steady. So was the emergency lantern. I'd prepared an argument that any motion in the fan blade was meaningless if all four of us were watching it—but it wasn't necessary.

The fan did nothing.

I took my turn—more nothing—and so did Alisha. And when Jibben finally took a stab at it....

Anticlimactic. Even for me.

Jibben said, "Well, I wouldn't take these results as definitive proof one way or the other regarding telekinetic abilities. Hinman's methods were primitive even for his time. Without proper controls or accurate measurement tools, it's impossible to draw conclusions from this exercise."

I suppressed a relieved exhale.

Alisha still looked miffed on the late researcher's behalf. "Maybe you just didn't try hard enough."

Jibben said, "I gave it my best effort. But you need to keep in mind that while Luther Hinman had many interesting theories, his methods left something to be desired."

"Oh yeah? Then why were you so bossy about getting all his stuff into containment? You must've thought it was worth something."

Jibben took in the scattered paraphernalia by the light of the emergency lantern on his lap and sighed. "That was before I saw the equipment. Don't worry, we'll still subject it to a thorough assessment, but I'd be shocked if we found anything useful. Hinman strikes me as a well-meaning man who unfortunately lacked the proper resources to realize his ideas. Earnest...but harmless."

The last word was barely out of Jibben's mouth when the lantern bulb popped with a sound like a gunshot, and our best light source winked out.

"Get him away from the fish tank," I snapped, and Jacob hauled Jibben's chair backwards. Alisha was already halfway across the room, crouching like she was under fire. The room was mostly dark again, lit only by my flickering flashlight.

And inside the fish tank, the fan blade was spinning so fast the blades were a blur. Whatever sound it might've made was blunted by the glass, just like any breeze it might've kicked up. The soundless, windless aspect just made the sight of it that much weirder.

Jibben pointed a twitching hand at the fan. "That's not my doing. I wasn't even thinking about the device."

"But you *were* reacting to the light bulb," Jacob pointed out.

I said, "That's the thing about psychic abilities. They can be a lot like breathing. The more you think about it, the more complicated it all gets."

Jibben shook glass out of his sleeves, though whether or not it helped at this point was anyone's guess. "That might explain the Rotational Indicator. But what about the bulb?"

Before anyone could float a theory on that, Alisha spooked us all with a startled yelp. "We got water coming in!"

I found her with my flashlight beam, then swung immediately to where she was pointing at the floor. Wet footprints crisscrossed the room—*our* footprints—along with tracks from the casters of Jibben's office chair.

"Find the leak," Jacob said urgently. "But don't panic. We've got plenty of gel pads to stop it from spreading."

The flashlight flickers were definitely not helping, though if Jibben's untrained TK ability was at fault, yelling at the guy to quit it wouldn't do us any good.

I scanned every wall—but the floor at the baseboards was dry. Even by the door. I thought back to the water bubbling up from the break room sink. "Is there a drain in here?"

"I don't recall," Jibben said nervously. "That's something I should know. But I can't picture it now."

"Start shifting crates," Jacob said, and I handed Alisha my

flashlight, which kept right on flickering.

Working fast, Jacob and I started in the center of the room and worked our way out, sliding crates away from the middle of the room, but not all the way against the walls, so we could keep an eye on the seams where the walls met the floor.

A few minutes later, we were left with a ring of jumbled shipping crates...and no floor drain.

Jibben said, "In all likelihood, it was dark, someone tipped over a water bottle, and everyone tracked through it before we realized the floor was wet."

Under normal circumstances, I'd have to agree. Back in the cannery, when a random wet spot on the kitchen floor freaked both of us out—more the hassle of getting a plumber out there than the fear of a walking corpse—and the culprit turned out to be nothing scarier than a dropped ice cube.

This circumstance, however, was anything but normal.

I took my flashlight from Alisha and gave the room another once-over, keeping an eye out this time for water bottles. But the only bottles to be found were lined up on one of the work tables with caps firmly in place.

I turned the beam to the floor again, searching the perimeter again for any seeping water we might have missed. Nothing, nothing and nothing. But when my light fell on one of my own footprints, I noticed an odd glint. It was already evaporating—nothing so strange about that in this heat—but the edges of the print had the telltale whitish rim you get in winter from tracking sidewalk salt into the house.

The center of the print was still damp. I knelt and prodded a fingertip into the moisture, then gingerly touched my tongue.

Salt.

These prints weren't water. They were saline.

And the bags from the transference environment were still sealed up tight.

CHAPTER 31

"Hold on," Jibben said. "Before we let our imaginations run away with us, bear in mind that when I removed Alisha's saline drip, it was still half full, and these are likely our own footprints."

Occam might have agreed that Jibben's idea was a sensible one...had the IV bag not been over by the bathroom.

Jacob, meanwhile, was looking intently at the rotational fan gizmo. Tell the guy not to do something, and sure enough, it's the very next thing he does. Lucky for him no one else was paying attention to him trying to move something with his mind. I flashed a hand through his line of sight to get his attention, and he looked at me, startled. Though not chagrined.

Of course not.

But then he exonerated himself by saying, "What if there was more saline somewhere in the shipment and we didn't get it all the first time around?"

They'd packed up everything, right down to the welcome mat, so why not *additional* saline?

We sifted through the junk, and eventually we came upon a bunch of plastic two-gallon containers—all of them crusty and long-ago dried up.

Alisha crossed her arms and let out a dramatic sigh. "Do I really gotta be the one to say it?" All eyes turned to her. "Fine. It's Dr. Hinman. Y'all threw shade on him and he blew up the damn light. And you're not using any of his stuff for real, like you're supposed to. You're just screwing around with it like a bunch of kids playing with toys."

If Luther Hinman *was* haunting his gear, he could save us all a lot of trouble by showing himself and telling me what the hell he was hoping to accomplish. Then again, being dead never made anyone rational if they weren't that way to begin with.

Plus, if Hinman's whole focus was proving telekinesis, maybe he'd never given much thought to ghosts. Back in his time, the whole talents-and-levels framework didn't exist—and mediums were just as likely as not to be charlatans looking to scam a quick buck from a grieving relative.

Maybe this whole time he'd been trying to communicate in the only way he knew how.

By moving stuff.

"We weren't screwing around," I said—partly to Alisha, partly to anyone else who might be listening. "We were trying out the equipment with an open mind."

"Do I keep an open mind when I come home and find Kelvin using my good plates like a Frisbee? Hell, no. If you want to try it all out, then use it the way it was supposed to be used."

"A valid point," Jibben agreed. "However, we don't know the

particulars of the experiments."

Alisha groaned. "You got Dr. Hinman's whole damn office, all the way down to his paper clips. You mean to say nothing here's gonna tell you how it was all done?"

We got to work combing through the shipment. It was a lot of stuff, and without the emergency lantern, it was slow going. Whereas before we were looking for gear, this time we were looking for paperwork. And since Hinman's whole operation was pre-digital, there were reams to go through. Most of it was unremarkable—financials, inventories, tedious blue-bar reports—but then Jacob turned up a series of heavy, cloth-bound registers that were specifically used for recording the experiments.

We pored over them as best we could in the flickering light. Alisha and Jibben scanned random registers for the saline tank. Jacob and I went chronological and started at the beginning.

Luther Hinman's telekinesis journey began with a ping pong ball. According to his notes, it was the perfect ratio of mass to weight to make "psychic energy transference" visible to the naked eye.

Unfortunately, they also tended to roll away for normal physical reasons too, so he started building environments to constrain the motion.

Critics might've called it pseudoscience, but seeing how he controlled for every possible detail—heck, seeing the experiments themselves—I thought his methods were a lot better than locking a shivering, exhausted kid in a room all night with a dead woman's wig.

"It's pretty benign," Jacob said, and I realized that while I was casting myself in the role of the lab rat, he'd steeled himself to bear witness to some horrible experiments that could have been inflicted on his grandmother—things she did in the spirit of "patriotism" that she took with her to the grave.

It was a relief not to find anything like that here. Our situation was psychologically damaging enough as it was.

According to the records, things really picked up when Gordon Tertz joined the Argus team. With limited funds to entice potential subjects, he and Hinman did most of their experimenting on each other. Tertz seemed to have potential—though his big claim to fame was making the ping pong ball that was dropped by an automated claw bounce in a specific direction. They tried rolling the ball in patterns and coaxing it through a maze, without any luck.

Maybe TKs were better at redirecting force than creating it?

Anyway, one of their experiments involved floating the ball on the surface of water instead of rolling it. That yielded nothing—nothing except the idea of putting salt in the water.

"We found something," Jacob said, and Jibben and Alisha crowded around.

We paged through, finding iteration after iteration of the Saline Transference Environment. They tried ping pong balls. They tried feathers. They tried balsa wood and sponges and ball bearings. They even tried fish—though those were quickly abandoned as having too many variables to control for.

Eventually, they tried lots of test subjects, too—college kids and minimum wage workers who were willing to trade their evenings for five bucks and a couple of slices of pizza. But Gordon Tertz was the only one who showed any promise.

In the end, Hinman theorized that the motion itself wouldn't necessarily take place in the solution—the saline was just a vehicle to amplify the telekinetic force.

That's when they came up with the Rotational Indicator. It hadn't been made to just sit on a table—it was supposed to be used in the saline. The weighted base would anchor the device, while the long stem kept the propeller out of the water.

Jibben said, "We have access to everything we need to recreate the experiment."

Whether or not that would appease the late Hinman was anyone's guess. But it beat just sitting in containment and waiting for our flashlight bulbs to explode.

We had ample amounts of fresh saline, thanks to the sensory deprivation tank down the hall. Once upon a time, Dr. K had offered to let me take it for a spin. At the thought of being sealed into a freaking coffin full of saltwater, I'd refused—so colorfully, he'd never offered again.

While Jibben and Jacob figured out how to transport the fluid, Alisha and I assembled the rest of the gear, following the diagram to the millimeter. (Good thing Alisha knew what all those little ticks and lines on the ruler meant.) The room was silent, filled only with the soft sound of our focused work, though once the fish tank was on its usual folding table, the mechanical stopwatch was wound up, and the Rotational Indicator was in place, there wasn't a whole lot else for us to do.

Alisha nudged the fan with her fingertip and gave it a little spin. "I wish I could see Kelvin throwing my good plates across the backyard right now. I might not even whoop his ass."

And I wished I could watch Clayton roll his eyes as if

whatever I'd just said was the dumbest thing ever known to man.

I'd always thought of putting up with Clayton as the cost of marrying a man with a family. Frankly, I'd considered myself lucky I was just gaining a nephew and not a stepson. Especially now that he'd given up soccer to pursue the trumpet—though while the instrument was way more obnoxious, the amount of times I'd need to travel to Wisconsin to watch the kid perform were blessedly few.

I swallowed past a lump in my throat, wishing I was in my car, cruising up the 90 with Jacob at my side.

The sound of many wheels coming down the hall brought me back to the present—Jibben on his office chair, and Jacob pushing a handcart holding a bunch of five-gallon buckets. Jibben used something called a hydrometer—even more convoluted than a ruler—and futzed with the dilution of the saline until he was happy with the numbers.

Soon, even by the paltry light of a couple of flashlight beams, we had Hinman's experiment set up to the T.

We all fell silent, watching.

The propeller did nothing.

Jibben said, "I suppose it's not enough to just set up the experiment. We need to run it. And since Agent Bayne theorizes that I'm the one who needs to be tested..." he rolled up the sleeve of his unbandaged arm. A bit of broken glass clinked out. "Let's begin."

Standing gingerly on one leg, he stuck his arm into the saline—and hissed. "Apparently I've got some cuts I wasn't aware of."

I'd wager he was plenty aware now.

So as not to potentially contaminate the experiment, Jacob and Alisha headed for the hall. I stood by with the stopwatch.

The propeller did more nothing.

"Time," I said.

As Jacob and Alisha filed back into the room, Jibben pulled his arm out of the solution and dunked it into a bucket of clear water. "Don't be so surprised at the results," he told me. "I've never scored anything other than average on a psych test—and our current methods are a lot more sophisticated than this."

I'd felt the zap when my white light hit him, but it wasn't worth arguing. The less involved in telekinetics I got, the better.

"Hold up," Alisha said. "Y'all need to see this." She had a ledger open on one of the upended crates, and she motioned us over. "This other book takes up where the last one ended— and they added something more to the setup."

I read over her shoulder and puzzled over a pair of lines, a plus or minus, and some numbers.

Jibben scanned the page, twitched, and said, "What they added was an electrical current."

I took back the thought about Camp Hell. Maybe I'd been locked in that room all night while they showed me the dead woman's wig over and over, but at least no one was shocking me while they did it.

Now the saline tank seemed less like a benign experiment and more like a torture device.

And as dread dawned and we all turned to look at it....

The propeller did a lazy rotation.

CHAPTER 32

Jibben attempted to be the voice of reason. "Keep in mind that electrical currents can be used for muscle stimulation and pain management. The levels in Hinman's experiment were completely safe."

As he prodded a figure on the page for emphasis, the plink of a ping pong ball hitting the floor across the room made everyone jump. We all watched in silent dread as it did a hollow plink-plink-plink bounce against the concrete, then came to a stop when it butted up against one of the random crates.

Actually, all of us were watching...except Jacob. He'd started paging forward in the ledger. "The charge is increased with every experiment. And it says here that Tertz was eventually able to make the Rotational Indicator rock in a three-degree arc."

That meant nothing to me, but it must have been significant. Jibben pulled the ledger towards him and scanned the page. "This voltage would be uncomfortable."

"Define uncomfortable," I said.

"Tingling. Burning. Involuntary muscle contractions. And since saline is more conductive than plain water, the effects would've been intensified."

My flashlight flickered. Papers fluttered. The ping pong ball made a hollow rolling sound. The propeller did another turn. The Telekometer in my pocket ticked.

Alisha flipped the page, then turned another, and another. "No more Tertz." We all cut our eyes to the ledger again.

Gordon Tertz had been on every page—until, one day, he wasn't. Alisha had said he'd disappeared—at least according to some amateur speculation on YouTube. But people don't just vanish. And while foul play was always possible, I'd also worked plenty of cases where my "victim" was fed up with their life and just wanted a radical do-over. Usually with someone they'd been having an affair with...but not always. Some just took off because they were sick and tired of being sick and tired.

The stuff Tertz had seen in the service might've finally gotten to him. He could have had a falling out with Hinman. Or maybe he just ran away with a braless hippie chick with daisies in her hair.

But my gut was telling me something more sinister had happened. Maybe it was just my own Camp Hell baggage talking—but Occam's most obvious conclusion, in this case, would be that Tertz had taken one shock too many.

Jibben paged back to the last mention of Tertz. "The current is far beyond the level I'd feel comfortable using—but there's nothing here that indicates an adverse reaction."

Alisha did a double-take. "What do you expect someone to write down? *Oh, and by the way, I killed him.*"

Jacob caught my eye and said, "I think you should do another exorcism."

"So the seance was a crazy idea," Alisha said, "but you got no problem with an *exorcism*."

I ignored the jab. Frankly, I'd always thought the term *exorcism* was a bit loaded, though I'd never come up with anything better.

Without a visual on the ghost, it was hard to know where, exactly, I should focus. I considered slapping down some candles around the fish tank, then decided we might as well do the whole shipment, just in case.

I found my kit and started pulling down white light, and something throbbed hard, deep behind my left eye. It was so late it was early, and between the lack of food, lack of sleep, and the two rituals I'd already done, my body was none too thrilled with me. But I knew how far I could push myself.

Though that was probably what Tertz had thought, too.

"At least tell me I get to watch," Alisha said.

Performance anxiety wasn't an issue for me—but if I needed an assist from Jacob, I didn't want him under the scrutiny of either a civilian or a psychic researcher. "A Psych and a Stiff, that's how I was trained. Everyone else clears the room."

Jibben wheeled his way toward the door. "If you need anything, we'll be just outside."

Once he was gone, my flickering flashlight beam evened out. "I'm not sure Tertz was even the problem at all," I told Jacob, "or if all the crazy breakage is Jibben's doing—conscious or not."

"You're sure he's a TK?"

"My light doesn't jump to just anyone. And I don't *see* any ghost."

"But you've encountered things before that you couldn't see, only hear. If Tertz's focus was tactile, maybe he *is* here—and maybe he's been communicating the only way he knows how."

My money was still on Jibben, but given what we'd read in the ledgers, I'd rather be safe than sorry.

The fish tank was too heavy to move now that it was full of saline, so I set my candles far enough apart to include the whole room, all the way to the edges. With only Jacob watching, I could do some basic yoga to refill my tank. As I flowed through Warrior I and into Warrior II, I had to ignore the alarming sounds my knees made and just focus on my mojo. I wouldn't say I was entirely rejuvenated, but I should be good enough to prevent a ghost from puppeteering my physical shell.

"Gordon Tertz—I'm not sure what happened to you, and if you feel like talking about it, I'll listen. But you're dead—heck, most of the folks you even knew are dead—and it's long past time for you to move on. You feel the pull of the other side? Don't fight it. It's where you're supposed to be."

Given that all the TK shenanigans had quit the moment Jibben left containment, I hadn't really expected anything to start moving. So I nearly jumped out of my own skin when a massive thud echoed through the room.

The white light I'd been so carefully coaxing hit my crown chakra like a psychic sledgehammer, and for a moment I thought I saw a faint webwork of red energy flicker across Jacob's forehead.

True fear. It's as good a psyactive—though nowhere near

as long-lasting.

But the energy dump was definitely big enough to prep my handful of salt. Whenever I activate my salt, it takes a lot of visualization and a bit of finesse to align it to my intentions, so I was surprised how fast it lit up to my inner eye...and kept on lighting.

Salting is no exact science—but there's usually a rhyme or reason as to where I've spilled it. Now, my third eye was bombarded by glints and glimmers from all over the place, and I couldn't figure out where the hell to look.

And then a huge bang sounded through the room.

My mojo spigot opened wider still and the floor flashed white—and I realized that everywhere we'd tracked around the saline, our footprints had dried to sodium. Sidewalk salt is a different beast—magnesium, potassium, whatever—so I'd never activated an entire freaking floor before. And instead of being helpful and adding to my oomph, it totally scattered my focus.

A third bang split the air, and Jacob called out, "Vic, by the ceiling!"

Scattered white light haloes were wreaking such havoc with my vision, I didn't make immediate sense of what was happening. But then it resolved into a beam of light shining down through an air vent. A few more thumps and the face-plate came crashing down—followed quickly by the boots of a rescue worker dangling from a cable. Jacob and I hurried to clear Hinman's old lab gear out of the way so the guy didn't end up waist-deep in questionable equipment. As physical concerns intruded and my focus shifted, my etheric confusion receded until the salt on the floor was nothing more to me than a subtle rasp of grit.

The guy on the rope had a powerful flashlight strapped to his forehead—and thankfully, the beam was solid.

He said, "Lucky thing you got trapped in this part of the building—" Clearly, we had very different definitions of the word *lucky*. "This is the only spot with vents big enough to navigate."

He asked if there were any injuries—cripes, where to begin?—and we grabbed Jibben and Alisha from the hall. Of the two of them, Jibben was by far the worst for wear. But Alisha was the civilian, and Jibben refused to evacuate until he knew she was safe.

"Don't worry," the rescue guy told her as he strapped her into the harness with him. "I've got you."

As he trussed her up against him in stiff velcro tabs, Alisha looked at Jibben and said, "You're a class act, Doc." And then she smirked at Jacob. "You too, Cargo Shorts—thanks for keeping your cool."

Finally, she settled on me, and gave her head a rueful little shake. "If you ever change your mind about that seance, I'd better get an invite."

"You'll be the first one I call."

As the two of them winched up and disappeared through the vent, a fragment of conversation reached my ears—Alisha asking the guy if he was single—and it sank in that we were actually getting out of there. No doubt the Kennedy was bumper to bumper and we should seriously consider taking surface streets back to the cannery. But getting out of this damn basement would be one giant step closer to getting home.

"I dread to think about the cleanup," Jibben said. He gestured at the train wreck of scattered crate contents in containment, but I suspected the gesture encompassed all of the lab. "But I take it that at least your ritual was successful?"

Well, no...we'd been interrupted partway through—

I turned to tell Jibben to get back out into the hall and saw the air all around him sparkling as if he was standing in a frozen snow globe, and every glint was candlelight refracting off a shard of broken lantern glass hanging in the air. "Close your eyes," I barked out, and thankfully he didn't ask why, just did it as the glass sucked towards him and pummeled him like a sandblaster.

The gadget in my pocket was ticking away like a time bomb and the air around us had gone frigid. My breath streamed out in the candlelight as bits of glass tinkled to the floor. The flashlight in Jibben's hand popped, while Jacob's wildly strobed. And as my irises flexed to let in more of the flickering light, the galvanic conductor lit up like a pinball machine, pulsing with a blinding purple light that made my eyes water. It flared once, twice...then shattered with a sound so delicate it was practically melodic. Light narrowed to that of Jacob's flashlight. Meanwhile, all around us, shards of glass rose, glittering, into the air.

"Tell me what to do," Jacob said urgently, shaking the last remaining light source in hopes of keeping it alive.

"Don't touch me—nobody touch me!" I felt fried and frazzled and my mojo was coming in rough. The last thing I needed was for it to hop into anyone else.

The caster of Jibben's chair was caught on some of Luther Hinman's crap, and he toppled over sideways trying to shield himself from another bombardment of glass.

"Gordon Tertz," my voice was getting ragged from the strain of yelling at ghosts, "this isn't your lab—this isn't your fight." I gestured at the twitchy guy on the floor, bleeding from dozens of tiny cuts. "This isn't Hinman."

Tiny ticks sounded all around us as more bits of glass rose from where they were scattered among the open crates and old manilla file folders. The fan blade stopped...then started spinning in the opposite direction. The remaining flashlight beam flickered harder—until, finally, its lightbulb popped and plunged us into utter darkness.

CHAPTER 33

Someone had to do something.

And that someone was clearly me.

"Answer me this," I yelled to Jibben as I flicked on the lighter from my kit. He was on the floor, shielding his face with hands covered in bloody nicks. "Have you ever forced a test subject to do something dangerous?"

Even cowering on the floor talking through his fingers, he managed to sound affronted. "Never!"

"You're sure? You never shot 'em up with psyactives, maybe deprived them of sleep? You never motivated 'em with a little zap?"

"What on earth are you talking about?" Jibben peeked out from between his hands. "That's barbaric!"

"Oh, come on. You never wanted to make a big splash— some big discovery that'd blow the lid off everything?"

"Why would I? Psych is proven. Beyond that shadow of a doubt. My only job is to help us understand. You know this yourself. We'd never put a subject in harm's way. Not just because it's unethical. But because they're our colleagues.

Our friends."

And all of Jibben's good pals called him Heebie Jeebie behind his back.

He definitely needed some better friends.

Clunking in the air ducts announced the rescue worker was nearly back, and I addressed the room at large. "Jibben—Howard—is going. He's served enough penance...for the damage he never did."

You don't realize just how much glass is all around you until you're waiting for it to randomly explode. Jacob had possessed the self-control not to leap in and grab my white light, but he was clearly relieved to now have a task to perform. He helped the rescue worker strap Jibben in, and the battered, bleeding scientist disappeared through the air ducts.

I stood beneath the opening and watched the two pairs of dangling feet winch away, listening intently for the sound of anything else falling on, breaking over, or exploding near poor Jibben. But as far as I could tell, the ascent was going off without a hitch.

"What happened?" Jacob whispered. "Did the spirit follow Dr. Jibben?"

Hard to say, what with there being no lightbulbs left for it to blow up. "If the interval between pulling out Alisha and Jibben is anything to go by, we only have a couple of minutes before the rescue guy is back."

I looked up into the shaft. One by one, starting all the way back with Big Boy Leonard, everyone in our group had been taken out, one way or another—just like in a cheesy horror flick—and now it was just Jacob and me.

And *both* of us had damn well better make it to the end.

"You're going next," Jacob informed me.

"The hell I am."

"Don't fight me on this. We both know I'm the one with all the defenses."

It's a bitch trying to argue with someone you know damn well is right. Plus, there's also only so long you can hold onto a flaming lighter—and with a belated curse, I had to let it go out. In the dark, the distant sound of the rescue workers, noises carrying through the air duct, seemed louder. So did my labored breathing—and the sound of my pulse thudding in my ears.

"So," Jacob said cautiously. "Are you okay?"

The atmosphere was edgy and tense, and the whole room felt like a pregnant pause. "I'll manage. What about you?"

He let out a shuddering sigh. "Exhausted. Relieved. Worried. I know if anyone should be able to handle this, it's us...but we still haven't figured out what *this* even is. What should we do while we're waiting for the fireman to come back?"

Awful big of him to take my opinion into account for a change. But I wasn't sure what the best course of action would be—just get the hell out and live to exorcize another day, or take care of the situation before it got away from us. Not that I'd ever had even the semblance of control, not since I marched blithely down here yesterday and handed over my gun. "We don't even know for sure that it's Tertz we're dealing with," I was so beat, it sounded like I'd been gargling with sand, "and I haven't had a visual on him. If only we could see what we were—"

With the clunk, whir and buzz of a bunch of machinery starting up...the lights came on. Even as I was filled with a giddy sort of relief, after so long in the dark, it felt like staring into the sun. But we could finally see again, really see, not just scattered glimpses by the strobe of a blinking flashlight. I've always maintained that you're better off seeing what you're up against than not-seeing. And I planned on scrutinizing every inch of the room, determined to uncover whatever secrets might've been lurking in the dark.

Once I blinked away the afterimages, it looked more like the tornado we'd been hearing about had touched down right here inside containment. Every crate was open, and the contents were tossed from one end of the room to the other. Each work table held an experiment, incriminating ledgers were everywhere—and, of course, broken glass and dried saline had the once-pristine cement floor sparkling.

I stripped out of my clean suit, eager to rid myself of the vestiges of containment. But as I was hopping out of the pant leg, I nearly keeled over when a phone on the wall started to ring. First thought? Haunted phone. But then, of course, I realized that with the power back on, if anyone needed to talk to us, it was the most logical way.

I picked up the receiver. "Hello?"

"Oh, thank God." Laura Kim was beyond relieved. "Vic, are you okay?"

I'd been better. "I'm fine. *We're* fine. So, were you planning on telling me about Jennifer Chance's body anytime soon?"

"What *about* the body? Is her spirit—?"

"No. But did you really want to risk it?"

Laura let out a sharp sigh of relief. "I wanted to tell you *in person*—and I'd been planning on doing it just as soon as I got back." Even though I'd avoided telling Jacob about it for as long as possible myself, I was hardly mollified. "Right now, I'm on my way to headquarters, but I'm still at least an hour out." A car horn bleated. "Maybe more—so we'll debrief tomorrow. I'm told it won't be long until the magnetic door locks are back online, but they can't give me an exact time-line. Do you want to be extracted through the vents or wait for the doors to open?"

Given how long we'd been stewing in that basement, it would seem like a no-brainer to go ahead with the extraction. But while rescue workers might go winching themselves around every day, I was none too keen to take a trip through the ventilation system. They might be wide enough to fit through, but they weren't spacious by any means. Add to that the potential of a poltergeist screwing with me while I was trapped inside the duct...and I knew what I had to do.

And, as a bonus, we could stop arguing about who would go first.

"We'll wait for the doors. And, Laura—I'll be holding you to that conversation."

"Of course you will."

We hung up, and I turned to Jacob and said, "I bought us one more shot at handling this thing for good. But my insides feel more battered than Jibben's outsides. Totally fried. I've got one more power-up left, and that's it. So whatever you do—"

"Don't let it jump to me. I know the drill." He held up his hands and backed away, crunching over broken glass. "Whatever happens, I'll stay clear."

My one-eyed headache was gone now...and a whole-head extravaganza had taken its place. No doubt I could use a granola bar, but I'd thrown my last one at Alisha. I took a steadying breath and tried to fill my tank, but it was like trying to cram twelve ounces of coffee into a ten-ounce travel mug. I trotted out every last trick I knew, from standing like a yoga warrior to visualizing my chakras to imagining the whub-whub-whub sound of my Mood Blaster app.

My mojo felt ragged and harsh. But eventually, I corralled it into something I could tap. I gathered my sorry self to banish our poltergeist for good. "Okay, Tertz," I announced to the room at large. "Let's do this."

The overhead lighting flickered briefly.

Jacob locked eyes with me from the other side of the room, across whatever remained of the Argus Institute, braced like he was ready for a tackle.

I opened up my crown chakra and urged it to take just a little bit more....

The room went white. Power surge—that was my first thought. Then I realized that the only circuits getting blown were mine. Etheric energy rushed out of me through my threadbare chakras. But it hadn't hopped into Jacob this time.

It was in the poltergeist.

My biggest fear about an angry ghost catching me with my energetic pants down is getting booted out of my own body. But Tertz wasn't interested in wearing my skin suit.

He was too busy pummeling it.

All the crap scattered around the place—all the paperwork, the office supplies, the vintage scientific detritus—everything rose up in the room as if gravity had suddenly failed. And it all started pelting us like we were stuck inside a giant blender.

"What the hell happened?" Jacob called.

"He grabbed it—he grabbed my light." Now I wished I hadn't been so damn insistent on Jacob keeping his distance. If that power had jumped into him, at least one of us would be full.

"Focus," Jacob said. "We'll do this together. I'll just...." he fended off a flying calculator with his forearm. "I can't find the veil."

Neither could I. The veil showing up when we needed it was something I just took for granted. Kind of like doing dishes. Turn the tap, and water appears.

Until it doesn't.

And even if we *could* get a plumber to call us back—which, in this day and age, they never do—I doubted he'd be much help.

I zeroed in on my crown chakra and pulled at the white light, and damn near blacked out. Fine. I couldn't use my light? I'd use my gear instead. Locating my exorcism kit was no mean feat, what with everything whirling around in a maelstrom, but eventually I spotted my Florida Water spritzer wedged at the back of a work table, and then my flip-top jar of salt rolling around on its side. I'd trained on the firing range until aiming my gun and squeezing the trigger was muscle memory. So, why not exorcism?

I'd certainly had enough experience.

"Gordon Tertz, go to the light," I said, pumping Florida water into the whirlwind of crap. "Fuck!" I blinked away a vicious, perfumey stinging sensation as it blew back in my eyes. I envisioned my salt activating—Christ, my head—and flung it with my eyes squeezed shut tight. I can normally feel the crystals scatter. But with everything flying all around me, the salt was just one more handful of whirling grit.

"I can't find the veil," Jacob repeated urgently.

Apparently, it wasn't fucking *there*.

"We've gotta get out of here," I called through the vortex. We had to regroup. I couldn't make Tertz go anywhere until I recharged.

Jacob turned to the door and pulled. And pulled again. "It's locked!"

Sonofabitch.

CHAPTER 34

If I thought I'd felt naked when I realized I couldn't get my sidearm back, it was nothing compared to being drained of white light and locked in a room with a freaking poltergeist. The smart thing to do would be to put Jacob between me and the threat. But this ghost was literally everywhere.

"Red energy," I hollered through the spinning morass. "Do your base chakra!"

But Jacob had been locked in this basement without food or sleep just as long as me. And he'd been flexing his telekinetic muscles the whole damn time.

Which meant we were both running on empty.

Was there anything else in my kit I could use? I couldn't light any candles—not unless I wanted all the flying crap to turn into flying *flaming* crap—but there must be something. I spied the little exorcism case flattened against the far wall, shielded my eyes with my forearm, and set off through the whirlwind...only to stagger sideways as a ping pong ball rolled directly under my foot.

I flailed and knocked into one of the crates, tipping the

whole thing over. More office junk spilled out: yellowed phone books, a box of adding machine tape, the cardboard banker's box labeled *Samples*—the lid of which flew off and smacked me in the head. I peeled it off and released it into the cyclone.

But the contents of the box stayed right where they were.

That couldn't be random.

Gingerly, I knelt. The box was musty and frayed, with one corner held together by a cockeyed strip of duct tape that likely came later, as things got moved around in storage. Inside was a jumble of stuff, all of it vacuum sealed in big squares of plastic. I pulled one out. A yellowed handkerchief. Innocuous enough. Then another—a lock of hair. I pulled out one more....

A tooth.

Well, shit.

I stuck my hand down to the bottom and the temperature in the room plummeted. Jacob dove toward the box, breath streaming out behind him. "Don't touch that!" he barked out, but it was already too late. A shock raced up my arm, and I thought I'd end up electrocuted like Darnell. But it wasn't a physical shock, and instead of being thrown back, I felt my crispy etheric channels blow open wide.

The room flashed white. It left me uselessly blinking away afterimages that weren't on my retinas. I was clutching a hefty vacuum-sealed packet, and when I tried to let go...

I couldn't.

Those bricks of ground coffee you get at the store, the ones that are hard as a rock, at least until you break the package seal? That's what it felt like.

Only, it wasn't coffee inside.

It was ash.

"Give me that!" Jacob demanded, and yanked it from my grasp. My arm went dead, dangling uselessly as I swayed on my knees, fighting a looming blackout. The Telekometer, still in my pocket, was ticking away as Jacob focused so hard on the brick that the veins in his temples pulsed.

And the cyclone of rage whirling around us kept right on spinning.

Desperate, I reached for white light and got nothing. Nothing at all.

Then, in the grayness of my imminent collapse, I knew exactly what we needed to do. "Open it," I called out into the gale. Jacob glanced up sharply as a pair of surgical scissors skittered across the floor and came to rest against his knee. "Open it," I repeated—and before he could second-guess himself, he grabbed the scissors and plunged the point through the plastic.

I covered my eyes, fully expecting to get a reprise of the Florida Water blowback. But this wasn't just any mindless wind surging around us. It had purpose.

Like a nest of angry hornets blasting out of a hive, the ashes formed a single coherent stream. They didn't spiral around the room like everything else....

They flowed into the shape of a man.

My vision doubled. My physical eyes saw a spinning cloud of chunky ash in a vaguely human shape, but my etheric eyes saw something else: a kid. Okay, a guy in his mid-twenties. But, still, the lank hair to his shoulders, the wispy beard, the tortured expression. This wasn't a vicious killer. It was just a damaged young man.

And he couldn't have reminded me more of the sleep deprived twenty-something who kept returning the dead woman's wig. Trade that long hair for a flopped over mohawk and we could've practically been twins.

As we sustained our eye contact, the cyclone ebbed, and bit by bit, all the various stuff that had been pelting me dropped to the floor. Only the dust devil—the cloud of ash—stayed in the air. "Gordon Tertz?" I ventured, and the ghost's anguished eyes locked onto mine. What could I tell him, that he was okay? That hardly seemed right.

"Are those *human remains*?" Jacob demanded.

I motioned for him to sit tight. "Listen to me, Gordon. You're dead—"

"And Luther Hinman needs to answer for what he's done." Tertz's voice had that spectral, faraway sound to it, but it broke just as if it had come from a flesh-and-blood throat.

At least he knew he was dead...I guess a half century in a banker's box will do that. But convincing him about Hinman might be tricky. "About that. Hinman's dead, too."

The air around me crackled and small bits of stuff—push-pins, shards of glass, a granola bar wrapper—hovered off the ground.

"He's dead," I added hastily, "but I do think he got what he deserved."

"What's that supposed to mean?"

"Well...he never really made a name for himself. His theories weren't proven. In fact, all his theories were chalked up to pseudoscience—"

"But I was a huge part of those studies! They were my theories, too!"

The whirlwind started up again. It sent a sheaf of old papers pinwheeling around the room.

"We can give him a proper burial," Jacob piped in, and the stream of office supplies eddied.

"We can absolutely do that," I assured the ghost. "And we'll set the record straight."

Tertz gave me a cautious look. "How?"

"I can hear you, can't I? Anything you need to say, say it. I'm listening."

And so, haltingly, he began to speak.

"It all started with an ad in the paper...."

I'd like to say I was surprised by Tertz's story, but it was way too much like mine. Where I'd gone through a stint in the mental health machine, he'd gone through Nam—and both of us came out without a shred of hope for a decent future. Since Tertz was way more book-smart than me, he should've had more options. But the country was flooded with vets looking for work, so many of them coping with addiction and PTSD with no social safety net to catch them.

At first glance, he'd thought the Argus Institute was a joke.

Just like I'd initially thought Heliotrope Station was a bunch of suckers for paying me to sit on my ass.

Hinman wasn't paying much, but it was better than nothing, and since he let Tertz set up a cot in a back room of the office, it was a better deal than he could expect anywhere else. (The fact that three squares a day and a bed were a big factor in me signing up for my own slice of hell was not lost on me.)

The experiments started off benign. Staring at stuff. Writing things down. But when the ping pong ball claw-drop showed readings way out of average range...things got intense.

"I should've left. I don't know why I didn't. I don't know why I *cared* so much. But Dr. Hinman would tell me I was amazing, and significant, and that together, him and me—we were gonna change the world. And the way he said it..." the ghost shrugged helplessly. "I believed him."

It was no surprise he got caught up in Hinman's pipe dreams. Father figure, Stockholm syndrome, who's to say? But when the rest of the world insists you're worthless, you lap up whatever scraps of praise come your way.

Tertz was just glad to matter to someone, even if that someone was encouraging him to electrocute himself. He let Hinman push him past any sane limit because it beat feeling like a nobody.

I said, "I don't know Hinman—but it's possible he wasn't just blowing smoke. Maybe he really did think you'd change the world."

The whole room went still....

And then a shockwave of telekinetic energy blew through it like a hand grenade. "He knew the charge was too high—and he dialed it in anyway!"

I shielded my eyes. "Hinman was wrong—he was so desperate to prove himself, he'd do anything it took!"

"But was it all Hinman's doing?" Jacob interjected.

Don't get me wrong. I'd known Jacob was opinionated from the moment he shoved his tongue in my mouth and challenged me for using Auracel—and for some screwed-up reason, I *liked* that about him. But he could only hear half the conversation.

"Jacob—"

"I get it," he called out to the man-shaped cloud of cremains over the rattle and whoosh of stuff swirling around us. "I get what it's like to have a talent that no one else knows about. Something that's so hard to measure that you wonder if it even exists at all. To wonder if you're deluding yourself into thinking you're something you're not. And then the chance comes along to unlock it—to really prove you're special—not just to the world, not even to the person whose opinion matters most...but to yourself."

I'd been so busy seeing myself in the poltergeist, it didn't occur to me that Jacob was doing the same damn thing.

"I would have done the same, Gordon," he told the ghost. "I would have done the same."

Despite the fact that my psychic channels felt scoured out and spent, they still pricked up when the ethers shifted, and the glimmers of the veil took shape. I hadn't called it forth, and I don't think Jacob had, either. It was Tertz, knowing that finally, after all these years, he was understood.

But the sensation of the veil's arrival wasn't just registering on my sixth sense. With all the telekinetic energy flying around, I felt it with my physical body, too. Namely, in the slide rule that fell on my head and the binder clips bouncing off my shoes—and the sound that it made as a whole roomful of crap started dropping, piece by piece, from the air. Anything landing on the stainless steel work tables made a showy clang, while whatever hit the concrete floor gave off either a muffled thud, or the distinct clatter of something breaking.

And punctuating the whole thing was the plink-plink-plink of a half dozen ping pong balls dropping in their final trajectories.

I could've told Gordon Tertz to go to the light...but I didn't need to. It had been calling to him for decades. And for a telekinetic, the sensation would be really hard to ignore. Time doesn't pass for ghosts the same way it does to us folks in the physical plane, but even so, being bricked all those years and stuffed in a box must've been a fresh level of hell.

"Thanks," he said—not to me, but to Jacob. "I can tell you really dig where I'm coming from."

"He says thanks," I translated, although I probably didn't need to. Jacob can't see ghosts. But with Tertz being a TK—with him whipping his own ashes into a semblance of a body—Jacob finally got the visual he'd been so desperately wanting. Now Jacob could definitively verify that, no, what he sensed wasn't all in his head. And when he thought he felt something, it was because there was something there to feel.

The etheric body of Gordon Tertz began to shimmer. As it faded, his temporary physical form broke down. Its edges lost their shape as bits of ash fell away, until finally, like an hourglass emptying its final seconds of sand, the physical construct sifted to the floor....

And the spirit was gone.

CHAPTER 35

If before the exorcism, containment was looking like a tornado had blown through, afterward it looked like it was hit by a bomb—made even worse by the fact that we now knew about the human remains.

Most folks think that when you're cremated, the fire is so hot that there's nothing left of you but ash. In actuality, what you leave behind is more like gravel. But the funeral home grinds it up before they pass it along to the grieving family, so no one with a morbid bent goes digging through it to discover what's really left of grandpa.

I'd wager that Gordon Tertz had not been cremated by a funeral home. Or if he had, it was done on the sly, after hours, by a tie-dye-wearing caretaker that reeked of pot. Don't get me wrong, there was plenty of gravelly ash, but there was also a lot of other stuff, *chunkier* stuff, in the mix. Thankfully, Tertz's remains were all in one spot, more or less—which would make it a lot easier for the agency to give him the proper burial we'd promised. Still....

"I can't shake the feeling that we breathed some of him in,"

I told Jacob.

Giddy with the elation of having chatted face-to-face with his first ghost—a fellow TK, at that—he simply shrugged and said, "I guess there's a little Gordon in all of us."

We were pondering one of the scattered photos where a young, unbroken Gordon Tertz was looking hopefully at the camera when the rescue team found us. If they found it odd that we were standing there in an unlocked room when we could have been making tracks toward our car, they were tactful enough not to say anything about it.

I didn't envy the folks who'd be tasked with cleaning up the mess we left behind. Most likely, they'd be supervised by Jibben—and he'd be in his OCD glory making sure that every last molecule was accounted for.

Between security, rescue, and investigators, the elevator bay was in high gear. One of Jacob's Internal Affairs colleagues was snapping pictures of Darnell's body. Thankfully, the two of them knew each other well enough that a two-minute rundown of events made for an acceptable statement—and security handed over our service weapons without a fight.

Though the rain outside had died down, traffic was about as appalling as we'd expected. We took the surface streets home, calling Clayton every two minutes all the way there. Every call went right to voicemail. You might think that after the first couple of times, we would've got the hint. But in the face of building anxiety, if that green call-button is your only recourse, you damn well keep smashing it.

It was early afternoon on Sunday by the time we finally pulled up in front of the cannery—which, thank God, was clearly still standing. Jacob parked with one wheel on the curb and left his door hanging open as he splashed his way up the walk. I caught up with him (even after closing the car door) trying desperately to shove the key in the lock upside down with one hand while laying on the doorbell with the other.

Wordlessly, I took the key from him and opened the front door. We thundered through the vestibule and spilled out into the living room....

Only to find Clayton sprawled on the couch with his sock-feet on the coffee table, flipping through channels on the TV. "Your doorbell is like, super loud."

He was fine.

Perfectly fine.

The relief I felt over seeing that sullen face—ignoring me, as usual—rocked me so hard, I thought I might throw up.

I'd say Jacob was staring at his nephew like he'd seen a ghost...but that would imply Jacob was happy. The look on his face was too raw to even call it relieved. "Why didn't you answer the door?"

In his most *duh* tone of voice, Clayton said, "You *told* me not to."

Well...he had us there.

"Clayton," Jacob said raggedly—then dove onto the couch and scooped him up in a massive hug.

"Whaaat?" the kid whined, though secretly, I'm sure he enjoyed it...even though Jacob was squeezing him hard enough to pop bones out of their sockets.

When Clayton finally squirmed out of the death grip, Jacob asked him, "Are you okay?"

"I guess."

"But we were gone all night."

"Yeah, but emergency stuff kept playing across the bottom of the TV, so I figured maybe you were just stuck somewhere. Plus, I got a text from Vic before my phone crapped out." He shrugged. "So, I knew you weren't dead or anything."

Good thing I'm not a hugger. Otherwise, I might've embarrassed us all.

"Once, at school, there was a tornado siren right when lunch was getting out, and they made us all sit in the lunchroom for three more hours, even after it was time to go home, and then they even gave everyone a brownie and a milk. For *free*."

I'd blow someone for a brownie and a milk, though I couldn't say as much in mixed company. Since no one was dead or anything, as Clayton had so eloquently put it, I headed toward the fridge to shove something in my maw and stave off imminent collapse—

And stopped dead in my tracks in the kitchen doorway.

The room looked like Gordon Tertz had just vacated the premises. Dirty dishes took up the entirety of the countertop. The garbage can was overflowing. The smoke detector casing was hanging by a wire. And the toaster was on its side, disgorging a scattering of crumbs that looked like they could've come out of one of those vacuum-sealed scientific sample bags.

Taking in the disaster that used to be my kitchen, I tensed all over...but only for half a second. I might not be a fan of messes. But at least we wouldn't have to catalog this one for scientific posterity.

The pot of spaghetti on the stove was still kind of warm, though the noodles were in a solid mass, held together by the entire contents of a jar of parmesan. When I carved out a forkful and shoved it in my mouth straight off the stove,

I realized the sauce was actually ketchup. And then I took another big bite.

The city's power outages had been patchy. Some neighborhoods were still down. Some never got dinged at all. The cannery had gone dark, but only for a few minutes—just long enough for all the clocks to start blinking 12. Clayton hadn't been particularly fazed by any of it. Mostly, he was just annoyed with himself for not packing a charging cable for his phone and having to resort to non-streaming TV, though he allowed that our channel selection was adequate.

By the time Barbara showed up a few hours later to collect her kid, the kitchen was in some semblance of order and most of the clocks were reset. Clayton swore up and down he wouldn't mention exactly how long we'd left him alone, but Barb's got a way of eroding people's defenses. If he wasn't careful, something would eventually slip.

When Barb came stomping up the stairs, I clenched everything it was possible to clench, positive I was gonna be reamed within an inch of my life. But instead of demanding a play-by-play, questioning our choices, and accusing us of serious neglect, she launched into a diatribe about the traffic. "What, people can't drive around here when it rains? Hello, it's just water."

Was it possible she didn't know about the funnel clouds and half the grid going down? Maybe it was just local news. Or maybe living in a town that tests its tornado sirens every Wednesday at 11 am sharp breeds a certain kind of acceptance. Either way, I wasn't about to volunteer the information.

She turned to her son. "And what have you got to say for yourself, young man? Your phone gave out pretty quick.

I'll bet you're wishing you did like I said and brought your charger."

Clayton shrugged.

"Well," she said, "one of these days he'll figure out that I do know what I'm talking about. But I'm not gonna hold my breath. So—what's the verdict? Is Clayton mature enough to handle this band trip or not?"

"Actually," Jacob began—

Only to be cut off by his sister. "I wasn't asking *you*. Clayton's got you wrapped around his little finger. You'll say whatever it takes to make him happy. There's more to parenting than fun and games." She looked at me. "So, what do *you* think?"

"Me? I know less about parenting than Jacob does."

"Maybe. But you're not worried about whether or not Clayton *likes* you, so I trust that if he's not ready for that trip, you'll tell me."

"So, what you're saying is...Jacob would be the fun parent, and I'm the strict one."

The gloating went over her head, but I'm sure Jacob heard it loud and clear.

I didn't mention that the simple weekend slumber party turned out to be a trial by fire—literally, at one point, with a toaster that might not have survived. But when I said I thought Clayton seemed pretty capable of handling himself, I truly did mean it.

Jacob hugged Clayton goodbye so hard, I thought for sure the jig was up. But the real surprise came when Clayton, on his way out the door, treated me to a quick, one-armed, half-hearted squeeze. I dunno who was more surprised by this, him or me. Probably for the best that Barb didn't see. We would've been totally busted, for sure.

As we waved goodbye from the stoop, Jacob said through clenched teeth, "I never want to go through that again."

"The sleepover?" I gave a final wave as they turned the corner and were gone. "Sure, there was room for improvement, but if your sister hadn't dropped in on us out of nowhere—"

"Not that. The worry. The helplessness. The thought of coming home and finding him dead on the floor. And it being all my fault."

"You can't control the weather," I pointed out as I drew him in out of the rain. "And try as you might, you can't control what other people do, either."

"But if I'd just canceled my plans right away, I would have been here. And Clayton wouldn't have gone through this whole thing alone."

Frankly, I suspected the most traumatic thing that had happened to Clayton this weekend was the death of his phone battery. I hooked a finger through the belt loop on Jacob's shorts and tugged him up against me, then took his face in both my hands and said, "If you hadn't done what you did, then I would've had to face the poltergeist on my own. And we both know, the only reason Tertz finally moved on was because of what *you* told him." I pressed my forehead into his and sighed. "Without you, I can't guarantee I would have made it out of there."

Even with my face right up against Jacob's, the kiss caught me off guard. He grabbed me by the shoulders, swung me around and flattened me to the wall. And when he pressed his lips to mine, I could taste the desperation.

I don't know how anyone can cope with having kids. Loving

someone makes you vulnerable. And the harder you love them, the scarier it is knowing that something might happen to them.

I'd never let myself get too attached to anyone, not until Jacob came along. As his tongue skimmed my lower lip, teasing my mouth open, I looped my arms around his neck and held him tight.

He broke the kiss with a huff, grinding me into the wall. "I love you so much it hurts," he said, gravelly and low—and I realized that vulnerability cut both ways. I always forget about the chinks in his armor. And the wounds that manage to sneak through them surprise me, every time.

"It's okay," I said softly. "We're okay." I guided him into a kiss that was deliberately tender, with my hands still cradling his face.

Jacob's got this muscle in his jaw that gets a workout whenever he's frustrated or upset. If the sight of it flexing is painful, that's nothing compared to the feel of it throbbing beneath my fingertips. I backed him away with a gentle push. "We're okay, Jacob," I repeated, in my normal tone of voice.

The pain in his eyes said, *But what if it had turned out different?*

"Look," I said, "neither one of us thought that working for the FPMP was just crunching numbers and throwing salt. We were both fully aware of what we were getting into—and that the threat could come from any and all sides, including our own people. We've never come across a telekinetic ghost before, and I doubt we ever will again—"

"That's not it," Jacob insisted. "We're always putting ourselves on the line—we've been doing it since we joined the force. The risk comes with the job. Different risks, maybe. But the idea is the same." He sighed against my cheek. "Vic, I was so close to leaving you there to handle it alone—"

"But that's not what you—"

"I almost did. I knew how mad you'd be if I second-guessed you, if I thought you couldn't handle things on your own." Now was probably not the time to point out that, yes, I *had* been pretty pissed about him turning around. "I really struggled. Because the clouds looming on the horizon could have blown over—"

"But they didn't. And you were right."

"I don't care about being right. I care about *you*. And if I'd been selfish enough to just take off while you were here dealing with—" he gestured to the world at large. "With everything. If something had happened to you—how could I ever live with myself?"

"Something did happen. And you *were* here." I gave him another shove, harder now. "Now, let's go to bed before we both keel over."

Our second wind had long since blown away, but our thoughts were racing fast enough to keep us going. I'd shed my suit and stripped down to my boxers, but Jacob had the underwear around my ankles before I could even peel back the comforter. He shoved me down on the bed and I rolled over to face him, momentarily confused by all the dark smudges scattered over his arms and chest...until I realized he was covered in bruises from our ordeal with the poltergeist's tornado. And if he looked that bad with his sturdy olive complexion, my white pallor must look ten times worse.

I risked a glance down...and winced.

But Jacob, standing between my knees, was visually mapping

the bruises without flinching away. Maybe they were proving whatever elusive point he was trying to make. Or maybe he was just thinking about a different set of bruises—the love bites and fingermarks he'd left on me, back when our relationship was still fresh out of the box.

Things could have gone so much worse.

"C'mere," I told him. "Give me something else to think about." I might have been hoping to distract Jacob, but when it came right down to it, I needed the distraction just as much as he did. And when he lowered himself over me and began kissing his way across the black-and-blue souvenirs of our poltergeist run-in, pretty soon, all I could think about was where he'd trail that hot mouth next.

But when he moved across my chest and started working his way down my belly, I realized I needed so much more than just a thrill. I caught him by the hair and urged him to meet my eyes. "Up here," I said. "I want you face to face."

Wordlessly, Jacob climbed back across the bed until we were level again. His mouth found mine, but this kiss was different from the last one. It was needier now, yet totally sure.

His hand trailed down my side, tracing the path of one particularly nasty bruise–probably a whack I took from the tape dispenser. I gasped against his lips, but he didn't stop. Instead, he dragged his fingers lower still, to graze my hipbone and cup the curve of my ass.

I was getting hard already. While Jacob reached for the lube, I shifted to let my dick reposition to my belly. It twitched hard when he pressed in a slippery finger. We'd done this so many times before, it already knew exactly how this was gonna play out. Except this wasn't all those other times. This was now.

And we needed each other in a way that was raw and new.

Jacob was just as ready as I was, already angling my hips so he could pound me just the way I liked it. But there was an intensity on his face that made me suspect that for him, this wasn't just a replay of our greatest hits, either.

When he sank into me, we both moaned. But neither of us dropped the other's gaze. I figured the horror of the last couple of days would disappear. But somehow it was still there, imprinted on us like the bruises that covered us both.

I looped my legs around his, arching my back so his belly rubbed the underside of my dick. It's easier when one of us reaches between us to take care of business, but sometimes the intimacy of jizzing hands-free is worth the effort. Jacob knew the score. He caught my wrists in either hand and shoved my arms up over my head so that neither of us was tempted to make a grab for it.

In bed, I surrender to him quicker than a meth dealer with a K-9 clamped to his leg. He's always in control—and that's how I like it. But as we started to move, finding our rhythm, I realized that whenever a ghost showed up, I refused to hand over the reins.

Even when I claimed that's exactly what I was doing.

Could Jacob rip habit demons in half and shove ghosts through the veil? Sure. But deep down, some part of me always thought of those things as just finishing a task that I'd started.

Necessary...but hardly groundbreaking.

Glorified cleanup work.

But back in the lab, I'd been so spent, I was literally at Tertz's mercy. And ultimately, Jacob was the one who'd taken care of it.

Because he was every bit as capable as me.

Something shifted—something so big, I wondered if he felt it too.

He started fucking me, really fucking me, and I let everything go—the anguish, the guilt, the quiet realization that I'd finally come up against a ghost that was way too strong to handle. And once I'd released all that mental baggage, somehow I found myself in a profound center...the eye of the storm. Where everything simply *was*.

Jacob. And me. Moving as one.

He shoved into me over and over, never letting up on my wrists—and I never wanted him to stop. This was us, coming together in the wake of something that had almost taken us apart.

And finally I understood what this connection we had was really about. Not who could see the ghost or who could find the veil. It was about trust. And the knowledge that no matter what kind of ghostly shitstorm we found ourselves in, we'd always have each other's back.

The rapid-fire thud of Jacob's hips made a solid counterpoint to his fists holding me in place. The point of no return beckoned, and I welcomed it—a release that felt infinitely greater than the mere rush of pleasure.

I must've made some kind of sound as I came, because Jacob grunted and shifted, and now he was chasing his own peak instead of watching for mine. He came, hard. And when he let go of my arms, I immediately cradled his face with both hands, drawing him down into a tender kiss we shared as he rode out his final few thrusts.

When Jacob finally rolled off of me, we stayed that way for

a moment, staring up at the ceiling as we caught our breath. I let my head loll to one side to look at him, and he did the same, with exhaustion etched on his brow, but a soft smile in his eyes.

Of course Jacob was my equal. He was a man of steel.

And there I was, claiming to have figured something out, when all I'd really done was remember what I'd known all along.

CHAPTER 36

I'm not much of a funeral person. While I've learned that funeral homes are nowhere near as haunted as you might expect them to be, the fact that I'm a high-level medium means I'm better off staying home. The bereaved flock to me, hoping to send their dearly departed one final message. And for whatever reason, when I tell people it doesn't work that way, they think I'm just being a jerk.

But even though I'm more uncomfortable at funerals than most, it wasn't like I could ditch Darnell's service. Not only were we co-workers, and not only did we go to the same grammar school, but I'd watched the guy take his last breath. Maybe if just one or two of those things had been true, I could get away with skipping his wake. But with the trifecta in place, if I sat this one out, I really would be a jerk.

At least I didn't have to worry about what to wear.

The crowd who'd come to see off Darnell Thompson was pretty much what you'd expect. A bunch of black-suited federal agents looking quietly grim, and an equal amount of exuberantly grieving family.

Accidents are hard on families. No time to prepare, and it leaves everyone confused and reeling. I'm not sure if Darnell himself was religious, but his family sure was—and they were keen on trotting out every last Bible verse they knew. It was during the fourth or fifth passage that someone slid into the chair beside me—and not because it was the only available seat.

Alisha looked really different in her Sunday best than she had in a white clean room suit. The fancy church hat was an especially nice touch.

The gangly teenage boy at her side could only be Kelvin. Holy smokes, he was just a few years older than Clayton and he was practically as tall as me. He was exactingly polite, though no doubt he'd rather be doing whatever it is kids these days got up to.

As the current reading concluded and yet another cousin took the stand, Alisha leaned toward me and said, "Look at you and Cargo Shorts in your matching suits. Now I'd finally take him seriously."

I nodded. "He does clean up pretty good."

The cousin stumbled his way through a particularly dry passage, and while he did, Alisha whispered, "I wasn't sure I would get to thank you for everything you did. I tried looking you up. Spelled your name every way I could think of, but no Facebook, no Instagram—not even a LinkedIn page."

"Guess I'm not very social."

I don't think she bought it. Alisha wasn't born yesterday. "You're a hard man to pin down—but I'm glad you were there when things got real. Even if you think my poltergeist was all in my head."

Eventually, the marathon of inspirational readings drew to a close, and Laura Kim took the stand. She'd been working around the clock since lightning took the FPMP offline with 80% of the staff out of town. But she was The Fixer, and getting the place up and running again was right in her wheelhouse. Plus, I had the sneaking suspicion that Laura preferred picking up the pieces after a natural disaster to a silly scavenger hunt.

If you didn't know Laura, you'd never suspect that she'd been up the last three days straight putting out administrative fires. Immaculately pressed in a charcoal gray suit, she tamped a couple of note cards on the podium, flipped through them, then set them face-down with a sigh and spoke from the heart.

"In this life, it's rare to meet someone who truly understands the difference between right and wrong and chooses to stand firmly on the side of right—no matter the personal cost. Agent Thompson was that kind of man. He epitomized the type of bravery that makes you check your own moral compass and aspire to be better. Darnell leaves us with a legacy that extends far beyond the walls of our workplace...he leaves us with an example of what it means to be a true hero."

People filtered up to kneel by the casket and pay their respects. I almost bailed—after all, I'd seen my share of his lifeless body by the flickering light of my flashlight. Amid the milling sea of black-suited coworkers, I probably could've gotten away with ditching, too. But I decided I might prefer to remember the cleaned-up, sanitized version of Darnell, and not the image I was currently carrying around, with him sprawled on the elevator bay floor with his eyes half-open while his repeater attacked the security door.

Darnell's body looked good, I supposed. (That's what everyone was saying about him, anyhow.) And planting myself on the kneeler in front of it with Jacob wasn't too weird—even if I didn't exactly pray. The casket, the flowers, everything was the best money could buy, since he'd died on active duty and Big Brother's pockets were deep. But the poster propped up on the easel beside the coffin was distinctly homemade.

Photos—so many snapshots. There was Grillmaster Darnell at the barbecue. And Winter Darnell with a snowboard. And Son Darnell with some graying parents. Tons of candid shots, all of them filled with family and friends and evidence of a guy who did so much more than show up at his post, scan you with the naked machine, and hold your gun hostage. But the photo that drew me in the most was Preteen Darnell... standing there in a tracksuit the height of fashion a few decades ago, showing off a pair of red and white Air Jordans that must've been the envy of every kid on the block. He stood with his arms crossed, challenging the camera to find him anything less than cool. Even though he was wearing coke-bottle glasses.

"Darnell wore glasses?" I blurted out.

A few people turned to look, and one of the cousins made her way over. "Were the two of you close?" she asked.

"We had a lot in common," I said. At least, I'd thought we had. Every photo of Darnell where he was any younger than Kelvin, he had on a huge pair of glasses.

His cousin saw where I was looking. "Darnell got contacts. And, once he was old enough, LASIK. Funny, isn't it, how people change?"

"Ain't that the truth?" I said, considering how Jacob used to think he was "just a Stiff."

I stared at that poster for a while longer, scrutinizing all the childhood photos, trying hard to figure out why my memories of Darnell no longer fit. Because Memory Darnell hadn't worn glasses. And maybe it was just my shoddy, swiss-cheese recollections. But something just wasn't adding up.

"Vic," Jacob said, low in my ear. "We need to go now. It's time."

Right. I didn't have the luxury to stick around and piece my thoughts together. Laura had paused in the doorway, just long enough to turn back and give us a meaningful look, so I grabbed a prayer card and headed out to the car to meet her at HQ.

Still, on my way back uptown, I couldn't shake the feeling that something was just "off." I turned around the prayer card in my hands, puzzling over what it might be, and then my gaze fell to his name: Darnell Isaiah Thompson.

Wait a sec...the kid I'd gone to school with was Darnell *Tompkins*. No wonder Grownup Darnell hadn't recognized me.

With a sigh, I briefly considered looking up the original Darnell to see what had become of him. But he was probably better off without me bringing the scrutiny of the whole FPMP down on his shoulders, all for the sake of indulging my own random curiosity.

"Alisha's son seemed like a good kid," Jacob ventured.

"I have a feeling she puts up with zero crap from anyone, least of all him." Judging by the silence that followed, I also had the feeling this conversation wasn't really about Kelvin. Eventually, I said, "I'm sure we would *both* be plenty strict."

"Maybe. But I think we need to admit that what we have—what we do—isn't cut out for family life. We're part of something bigger. And we can't provide the stability, the *safety*, that a kid deserves."

Or a dog, for that matter, though I figured I shouldn't bring it up, just to be safe. "You've got no argument from me." Heck, I never thought I'd have a normal life. So it's not like I was disappointed.

Jacob reached across the console and grabbed my hand. "And, to be honest, I don't want to share you. Not with anyone."

I truly hoped he wasn't buttering me up to get a dog.

We pulled into HQ and made our way down to the lab. It looked really different with the staff there and the lights on—though containment, I noted, was now sectioned off with orange traffic cones and a stern *Authorized Personnel Only* sign.

In the hall, Dr. K greeted us with his typical jovial Russian veneer. I supposed it was as good a professional mask as any. "I heard you had quite the adventure while I was gone. My lab may never be the same."

Speaking of cleanup on Aisle 7... "What about Gordon Tertz? Is whatever's left of him destined for a file cabinet in the bowels of the FPMP, or will he get a proper burial?"

"The situation is delicate—which I'm sure you understand. Mr. Tertz has a niece, and under other circumstances, we would offer to release the ashes to her—though they've never met, he has no estate, and no doubt she would just tell us to dispose of them anyway."

But these weren't other circumstances. And the FPMP couldn't risk the chance of the niece starting to ask questions.

Not in the age of the social media they so assiduously keep me away from.

Dr. K went on. "While research is, of course, the entire purpose of this laboratory—we must also consider the safety of our people…which recent events have made quite clear. Director Kim and I have decided that the risk of retaining the ashes outweighs the benefits."

Jacob said, "So what did happen to his remains?"

"A minister who has performed certain discreet tasks for the Program has given the poor soul a proper goodbye. The final resting place is anonymous. But I'm told it is quite peaceful. If your report is anything to go by, I think Mr. Tertz would be pleased that his contribution eventually furthered the science of telekinesis."

"How so?" I asked.

"This energy transference between light workers and TKs you theorized holds promise—"

Images of Camp Hell flooded my brain. It must have registered on my face.

"Don't worry, Agent, we won't call on you for more than just the occasional test. Between Bethany Roberts and Dr. Jibben, we have what we need."

Hopefully, Bethany would still have time for the yoga. Not only was my white light more stable nowadays, but my sciatica hardly bugged me at all anymore.

By now, we'd made it to the incinerator room. On my normal rounds, I'd been there plenty of times before. I'd even seen the stuff slated to be burned. Used PPE. Retired test tubes. Dead plants. The FPMP goes through lots of consumables in its quest for knowledge, so there's always a steady stream of stuff that needs disposing.

But somehow, it never occurred to me that I might've been personally acquainted with whatever was slated to be burned.

Laura was already waiting for us by the incinerator...along with a sheet-draped form shaped conspicuously like a body. Over the past few days, I'd thought of a million and one things I wanted to say to my boss, but what came out of my mouth was, "Seriously, Laura? You were gonna let me do my rounds without a word while *she* was just on the other side of the vault?"

If anyone had a worse track record with Jennifer Chance, it was Laura—whose finger, thanks to that psycho, had squeezed the trigger of the gun that killed Roger Burke.

It's no small thing to take a life. Even one as despicable as Burke's.

Laura looked particularly resigned. "When you reported two years ago that Dr. Chance's spirit had been dealt with, I deemed that her body posed no threat. Was this not correct?"

"You know I'd never blow smoke about something like that. But a heads-up still would've been appreciated. In person, or not."

The incinerator itself was as high tech as the rest of the lab (aside from the copier graveyard.) The hulking metal apparatus was set inside a shell of protective thermal bricks, and powerful ventilation hummed in the background.

Dr. K keyed an access code into a control panel on the wall and scanned his ID. "Everything is strictly cataloged for National," he said. "I doubt anyone actually looks at the logs, but no doubt an algorithm would alert them if anything unusual had been disposed of." He winked. "Lucky for us, the cleanup after the storm generated so much waste."

He looked at me expectantly. So did Laura. And Jacob. And I realized I wasn't just there for my own sense of closure.

I called on white light with a wince, fully expecting to have come through the poltergeist encounter as bruised on the inside as I was on the outside—but the mojo flowed clean and sure. I had my salt and my Florida Water spritzer in my pocket, but I didn't need them. Two years ago, I hadn't just nudged Chance through the veil—I'd escorted her there myself. And when Jacob peeled back the sheet to triple-check that she was gone, we found nothing more than a very mottled cadaver.

All the freezing and thawing had not been kind. The cranial incision was particularly ragged, and the corner of her mouth had sagged in a disgruntled frown. Unfortunately, it was quite possible that some techs in the staging department had constructed this corpse out of gelatin and 3D printing for the sake of making me think the body was well and truly gone.

As I pondered whether or not the cadaver was even real, Dr. K asked Laura, "Would you like to say a few parting words?"

She spared a disdainful glance at the body. "Burn in Hell."

I couldn't have put it better myself.

CHAPTER 37

At twice the temperature of a normal crematory, the incinerator had done its job well—but there was still a handful of ash left over. Laura didn't want so much as a speck left behind in her building, so the four of us trooped out to the overpass and tipped the bag into the train yard below.

As what was left of Jennifer Chance drifted away on the wind, I realized I'd just covertly disposed of a body. Me, a former homicide investigator. I wasn't sure how to feel. Hypocritical? Complicit? Guilty? Weirdly enough, no.

Mainly, I was relieved. And I strongly suspected Jacob was, too.

Once we were back in the car, he said, "I was thinking we might stop and see Dr. Jibben on the way home. Let him know how things turned out."

We'd heard it had taken an entire team nearly five hours to pick out all the glass, but that wasn't what kept Jibben in the hospital. A torn ligament in his leg had required surgical intervention, and they'd been monitoring him heavily in case he threw a blood clot.

Normally, I don't go out of my way to make buddy-buddy with anyone from work. But we'd been through a hell of a lot with Jibben, so it only seemed right to pop in and do a bit of awkward smalltalk.

As we made our way up to the hospital, Jacob said, "I've also been thinking that it might be time for me to break the cone of silence."

Cautiously, I said, "Which one?"

"Mine. What I can do. What I am."

I thought he'd been awfully even-keel these past few days. Turned out he'd just been gearing up to capsize everything we've been working so hard to keep afloat. "Jacob—"

"You heard Dr. K. Research is turning the corner on tele-kinesis—thanks to something *we* did. Doesn't that mean anything to you?"

Frankly, no. Just relief that another medium was better at flowing light than I was, so I wouldn't be conscripted into a bunch of experiments. But Jacob had never developed the healthy sense of self-preservation that I'd had to cultivate over the years.

He said, "What if there's a reason we're not meant to be parents? Maybe we were meant to leave a different legacy? Maybe we were meant for something more."

Sometimes, the best way to disagree with Jacob is to keep your mouth shut. That way, he doesn't have anything to argue with. But as we headed up to Jibben's room, I really had to bite my tongue. We passed a few more hospital visitors in the hall. One was carrying a potted plant, another was lug-ging around a big stuffed get-well-soon bear. I wondered if we should've stopped to pick something up for Jibben. But given his OCD tendencies, I suspected that the best gift we could give him would be *not* showing up with a goofy ceramic angel in our hands.

Although maybe he'd like a book of crossword puzzles. Something that would both help pass the time and make him feel smart. He did have a thing for puzzles and games. I supposed I could run down to the gift shop and grab one—

"I'm just gonna go, uh.... Jacob?"

While I'd lagged behind a couple of steps, Jacob had gone stock still in Jibben's doorway. As he frowned and double-checked his phone, I caught up with him and peeked in.

The bed was empty. Not *I'm-in-the-can* empty. *Empty*-empty. Bed stripped. Personal effects gone.

"It's the right room number. Maybe they moved him to a different ward," Jacob said—a bit too quickly, so obviously his first thought was the same as mine. That Jibben was dead. "Or maybe he was released."

Dr. K would've said something if he'd been released, so I highly doubted it.

We spotted a nurse in cheerful purple scrubs walking by and flagged her down. "We're here to see Dr. Jibben," Jacob said.

The nurse looked confused. "I don't think there's a Dr. Jibben on this shift. Unless he's new—"

"Howard," I supplied. "Howard Jibben. He's a patient."

Jacob said, "The patient who's in this room...or at least, he was."

The nurse glanced in. "There's no one in this room."

Jacob gave her the slow-blink he reserves for folks who seem deliberately obtuse. "Could you look him up and see where he is?"

When she hesitated, he flipped open his wallet and flashed his federal ID, and suddenly she became a lot more willing to help us. "Let me check." She keyed open the tablet she'd been carrying and scrolled around. "Nope, there's no one in this room. How do you spell the name?"

While Jacob put the thumbscrews to the nurse, I opened up my crown chakra and headed into the vacant room, scanning for an outline, a shadow, anything that shouldn't be there.

No ghost.

"Jibben?" I said softly. "You here?"

I paused beside the bed, tilted my head, and listened.

Nothing.

But Jibben was a TK. And if he died and left something behind, it might not be visual or auditory. It might be tactile. I go through life so much in my own head, I really don't stop to think about how the rest of me actually feels. Closing my eyes, I tuned into the sensation of my own skin. The air on my face. The slight pinch of one shoe. The little throb where I'd been slacking on my yoga. And—

"Holy—"

I jerked my hand back where something distinctly fuzzy had brushed up against it, only to discover a young kid in a hospital gown holding the stuffed animal I'd just seen trooping down the hall.

"I got a bear," she said matter-of-factly.

"That, you do." Now if my heart could just stop pounding in my throat. "So, why're you here?"

"My dad is giving me a new kidney."

Mediums are piss-poor candidates for transplants. My expression must've said as much.

"Most people got two," the kid informed me. "But you only need one."

"I've never really thought about it."

Pleased to have told me something useful, she looked over her giant bear at the empty bed. "What happened to the man?"

Good question. "What do *you* think happened to him?"

"Don't you know? Some guys dressed like you took him away."

A sick feeling settled in the pit of my gut. "He must've been feeling better, so they came to take him home." If, by *home*, you meant some dank cell in Washington DC where scientists from National could wire him up with electrodes and pump him full of drugs.

Maybe I was imagining things...and maybe Laura really had just sent over someone from HQ to give him a ride. But when I found Jacob had gotten nowhere over at the nurse's station—when they claimed that no one named Jibben had *ever been their patient*—I knew the scenario I'd envisioned wasn't farfetched at all.

Jacob said nothing as we climbed back into the car, though the grim set of his mouth spoke volumes. Instead of heading home, he swung by Montrose Beach, where there was plenty of sunbathing, jogging, and rollerblading action, but only a few intrepid swimmers braving the early-summer cold of Lake Michigan. We found a bench by a rocky stretch to sit and watch the waves lap the shore. Eventually, beneath the camouflaging sound of the surf, Jacob said, "I can't believe I was willing to offer myself up like a sacrificial lamb."

I pried his hand off his knee and threaded my fingers through his, toying with the hard edge of his wedding band.

"I would've stopped you. And, look, you came to your senses without any help from me."

Jacob leaned into my arm. "I just thought we were finally beyond all the secrecy. Think about how much psych research has changed since the Argus Institute's time. Just a few decades later, all the supposed pseudoscience became legitimate research. But telekinesis was still the big holdout. I just thought that if I helped normalize TK, then maybe we could finally stop looking over our shoulders. Maybe we could finally be happy."

"We are happy." And I knew Jacob. Now that he finally saw himself as a legitimate psych, no way would he ever go back to being "normal."

I spotted a flat stone nearby. With a quick squeeze, I let go of Jacob's hand and stood, picked up the stone, found a good lull in the waves, and slung the stone at just the right angle. It skipped four times before the lake claimed it. Not bad, but maybe I could do better. I picked up another stone... skip, skip, plop.

Soon enough, Jacob came over to try and outdo me—just like I'd hoped he would. If there's anything more certain than death and taxes, it's Jacob's need to compete. As he sent a stone dancing across the water's surface, he said, "It's all in the wrist."

The clicker in my pocket said otherwise, ticking as the stone hopscotched away. And though the etheric push probably hadn't given Jacob any extra skips, it confirmed what I already knew.

Jacob might be a fantastic liar. But his control on his talent needed work.

It was tempting to hold on to the Telekometer, since it would come in handy if Jacob's old self-doubts ever started to resurface. It had taken some real sleight of hand on my part to replace Hinman's device with the compass from my exorcism kit. I'd known the lab would match every last shard of glass to the manifest, so I couldn't just pocket the thing and hope to get away with it.

But nobody monkeyed around in my kit but me, and once I replaced my original compass, no one would be the wiser.

Jacob skipped another stone, and I pulled the device out and watched the needle click. If I could spot a TK with it, so could the goons from National. It just wasn't worth the risk.

Besides, I could tell when Jacob was trying to move things by the look on his face.

I wound up and pitched...and the gizmo skipped even farther than Jacob's last stone, before it was sunk by a wave.

Jacob squinted. "Was that...?"

"Never mind. We didn't need it."

After all, we had each other.

And that was how I intended it to stay.

ABOUT THE AUTHOR

Jordan Castillo Price has lived through several power outages in various cities. The longest one, nearly a week, was in Chicago—and the temperature was well over 100 degrees. Frustratingly, the people across the street still had power, and flaunted it by playing an electric guitar (very badly) on the porch.

She has no quarrel with microwave lasagna, though she does wish the portions were bigger.

ABOUT THIS STORY

I recently inherited my mother's house and moved back to Buffalo, the city where I grew up. At the grocery store, someone said hello to me—and I kind of think he said my name, though maybe I misheard and it was just a random friendly hello because we happened to lock eyes.

But if it was my name, and this guy did know me...how?

Back when I worked at a public library, I used to get spotted all the time. People would say, "I know you from somewhere..." with that particular squint that indicates that they can't quite place where that somewhere happened to be.

It's been more than thirty years since I've lived in New York, though, and I can't imagine anyone who knew me then would recognize me now. Not unless they had context—like they were driving by my old house and saw me taking out the garbage. (Which did happen with my childhood next door neighbor, and funnily enough, she looked exactly the same to me.)

There's a guy on the street my mother always claimed I knew, and his name rang zero bells. Recently, my neighbor cousin also mentioned him to me, and added, "You guys used to wait for the bus together."

Still, no bells.

Maybe it was him at the store?

I suppose I'll need to dig out the yearbook and try to jog my memory before I embarrass myself.

All this to say, I can really relate to Darnell Thompson—but thankfully, it's the part where Vic attempts to remind him of second grade, not the part where he electrocutes himself trying to be a hero.

www.ingramcontent.com/pod-product-compliance
Lightning Source LLC
Chambersburg PA
CBHW020405260626
47156CB00007B/2246